SUMMIT BOOKS
Simon & Schuster Building
Rockefeller Center
1230 Avenue of the Americas
New York, New York 10020

Originally published in Great Britain by Faber & Faber UK

Manufactured in the United States of America

1 3 5 7 9 10 8 6 4 2

Library of Congress Cataloging in Publication Data
Dibdin, Michael.
Dirty tricks/by Michael Dibdin.
p. cm.
I. Title.
PR6054.I26D57 1991
823'.914—dc20 91-21300
CIP
ISBN: 0-671-69545-2

Dirty Tricks

MICHAEL DIBDIN

SUMMIT BOOKS

New York London Toronto Sydney Tokyo Singapore

by the same author

THE LAST SHERLOCK HOLMES STORY

A RICH FULL DEATH

RATKING

THE TRYST

VENDETTA

For Syb, ***sine qua non***

Comedy is the public version of a private darkness. The funnier it is, the more one must speculate on how much terror lies hidden.

Paul Theroux, *My Secret History*

24 February

Dear Charles,

Albeit with an ill grace, H.E. has now accepted the two-tier arrangement 'de facto and pro tem'. He made various disgruntled remarks about being in the same position as Soviet diplomats *vis-à-vis* the KGB, but took the point about the need to avoid attributable documentation. An old-school FO wallah, he would be happier reporting solely to Whitehall, but at the end of the day he's one of us, and sufficiently vain to be flattered at having a 'hot line to Downing Street' as he put it. I'm sure you will be as relieved as I am that he's taking this attitude. A new appointment at this stage could do nothing but harm.

Having established my bona fides, I then explained that our real reason for 'rocking the gunboat' (to quote H.E.) was not so much to bring this fellow to justice as to divert media attention from the recent allegations concerning clandestine links between the two countries. I quoted, to some effect I think, Bernard's remark that the man in the street has only so much time for a banana republic like this, so if the lead story is SEX FIEND SHIPPED HOME IN CAGE, no one will have any further interest in the place.

H.E. accepted this readily enough, but getting it across to the other side has been considerably more difficult. Although his views are perfectly sound, the Generalissimo is an unsophisticated man who finds it as difficult to imagine that the British press can make a *cause célèbre* out of a sordid sex murder as he does to understand our embarrassment should the secret protocols come to light. His view is simple: Downing Street is as anti-Communist as he is, so what's the harm if it comes out that the SAS has been training his death squads, or that the PM's personal economic adviser helped him manage an economy in which eight families own 94 per cent of the GNP? To make matters worse, the junta is extremely touchy about any reference to its human rights record, and this makes it very difficult to communicate the key issue, that while we are quite prepared to co-operate with our ideological allies anywhere in the world, we cannot always afford to be seen to be doing so.

In the course of a gruelling two-hour audience at the Presidential Palace, I laboured hard to get this point across, and specifically to point out the destabilizing effect of any unwelcome revelations in the present UK political climate. I even went so far as to drop a heavy hint that a negative result might contribute to the very real possibility of a socialist government in Westminster and an abrupt end to the mutually advantageous exchanges between our two countries. This drew a raised eyebrow from H.E. but no perceptible reaction from the other side.

To be perfectly honest, I think the initiative's going to have to come from that end. We've by no means wasted our time here. The ground has been prepared, and all that's needed now is a touch of His Mistress's Voice. But time is of the essence. The hearing begins next week, and the Justice Ministry need to be informed as soon as possible so that they can make the necessary arrangements to ensure that a favourable verdict is brought in. In fact extradition might well be granted without any intervention – the evidence sounds pretty conclusive – but with so much at stake it would be unwise to take any unnecessary chances. A brief telephone call should be quite sufficient. The Generalissimo may be tiresome in some ways, but at the end of the day he too is one of us.

Yours,
Tim

I

First of all, let me just say that everything I am going to tell you is the complete and absolute truth. Well yes, I *would* say that, wouldn't I? And since I've just sworn an oath to this effect, it might seem pointless to offer further assurances, particularly since I can't back them up. I can't call witnesses, I can't produce evidence. All I can do is tell you my story. You're either going to believe me or you're not.

Nevertheless, I *am* going to tell you the truth. Not because I'm incapable of lying. On the contrary, my story is riddled with deceptions, evasions, slanders and falsifications of every kind, as you will see. Nor do I expect you to believe me because my bearing is sincere and my words plausible. Such things might influence the judges of my own country, where people still pretend to believe in the essential niceness of the human race – or at least pretend to pretend. But this country, in its short and violent history, has had no time to develop a taste for such decadent indulgences. Yours is the clear-sighted, undeceived vision of the ancients, who knew life for what it is and men for what they are, and did not flinch from that knowledge.

So I do not say, 'Believe me, for I cannot tell a lie.' I wouldn't hesitate for a moment to lie my teeth off if it was either useful or necessary. Only it isn't. As it so happens, I am actually innocent of the murders detailed in the extradition request before you. It is therefore quite simply in my own best interests to tell you the truth.

It began, inevitably, at a dinner party. That's where the social action is in my country, among people of my class. Half the English feed fast and early and then go down the pub to drink beer, the other half eat a slow meal late and drink wine before, during and after. (I am anxious that you should understand the customs and manners of the country where the events in question took place, so different from your own. Otherwise it may be difficult to appreciate how very *natural* it is that things should have turned out as they did.) When I say dinner parties, I mean drinking parties with a cooked meal thrown in. And with Karen Parsons in the state she was that evening, there seemed a very real possibility that it would be. Both she and Dennis were chain-drinking. This was perfectly normal. But even then, before I knew her at all, I sensed that normality was not really Karen's thing. She could fake it, up to a point. She could put it on, like a posh accent, but it didn't come naturally to her.

I'd met the Parsons a week earlier, at an end-of-term social at the language school where I was teaching. We rolled up at the same time, I on my bike, the Parsons in their BMW. I thought at first they must be students. No one else I knew could afford a car like that. But as soon as they got out I realized I was wrong. What is it that sets us Brits apart so unmistakably? The clothes? The posture? Whatever it was, the moment I saw the Parsons I knew them for British as surely as though they'd had the word stamped on their hides like bacon. The man was thickset and heavy, like a rugby player, the woman thin and bony. I didn't give them a second glance.

Parties at the Oxford International Language College, like everything else, were designed with cost-effectiveness in mind. Clive had to have them, because the competition did, but since the benefits were at best indirect he had to come up with the idea of asking the students from each country to get together and prepare a 'typical national dish'. These were then combined as a buffet and served back to the students together with one free soft drink of their choice. Subsequent or alternative drinks had to be paid for at saloon-bar prices, so Clive managed to turn a profit on the evening.

In previous years he had forbidden staff to bring their own booze 'so as to avoid making an invidious distinction'. This had caused a ripple of protest. No more than that, for we were all on renewable annual contracts and Clive never tired of reminding us just how many eager applicants there had been the last time he'd had to 'let someone go'. Nevertheless, he had relented to the extent of allowing the teachers to bring a bottle as long as it was kept out of sight of the paying customers. The result was that we all kept making surreptitious trips to the staff room to refill our plastic beakers. I was lingering near the assembled bottles, wondering who on earth could have brought the Bourgueil, when I was joined by the man I had seen stepping out of the BMW. He walked over, holding out his hand.

'Dennis Parsons. I do Clive's accounts.'

Close up, he looked softer and less fit than I had thought, not so much rugby as darts. Spotting my empty beaker, he grasped the bottle I had been admiring, carefully covering the label with his hand.

'Have some of this.'

His voice was filled with self-congratulatory emphasis. I stuck my nose in the beaker and hoovered up the aroma in the approved fashion.

'Like it?'

'Very much.'

I got busy with my nose again, then took a sip and gargled it about my mouth for some time.

'What do you make of it?'

I frowned like someone who has just been put on the spot and is afraid of making a fool of himself.

'Cabernet?' I suggested tentatively.

Dennis grinned impishly. He was enjoying this.

'Well, yes and no. Yes, and then again no.'

I nodded.

'I see what you mean. Cabernet franc, not sauvignon.'

That shook him.

'But is it Bergerac or Saumur?' I mused as though to myself. 'I think I'd go for the Loire, on the whole. But something with a bit of class. There's breeding there. Chinon?'

Dennis Parsons breathed a sigh of relief.

'Not bad,' he nodded patronizingly. 'Not bad at all.'

He showed me the label.

'Ah, Bourgueil! I can never tell them apart.'

'Very few people can,' Dennis remarked in a tone which suggested that he was one of them.

After that I couldn't get rid of him. The man turned out to be a wine bore of stupendous proportions. I must have kept my end up successfully, though, for just before he left Dennis sought me out and invited me to dinner the following Friday.

'Can't speak for the food, that's Kay's department, but I think I can promise that the tipple will be up to par.'

As for Karen, she left not the slightest impression on me. Apart from that initial glimpse of them both getting out of the car, I literally have no image of her at all. I emphasize this to make clear that what happened the following weekend was as unforeseeable as a plane falling on your house.

Dennis told me that he lived in North Oxford, but that was geographical hyperbole. True, the street he lived in was north of the city centre, but that didn't mean it was in North Oxford. My country is full of distinctions of this kind, and in the congenial climate of Oxford they flourish to form a semantic jungle through which only the natives can make their way. Thus it's the Isis not the Thames, the Charwell not the Cherwell, the Parks not the park, and Carfax is not the latest executive toy but a crossroads. There's a street called South Parade and, half a mile *south* of it, one called North Parade. The area where the Parsons lived lay not in the desirable temperate zone called North Oxford but further north, too far by half, in the boreal tundra of pre-war suburbia out towards the ring road, beyond which lie the arctic wastes of Kidlington, where first-time buyers huddle in their brick igloos and watch the mortgage rate rising.

Nevertheless, even though it wasn't quite the real thing, Dennis had done all right for himself. When I was young, accountants used to be figures of fun. Not the least of the many surprises I got on returning home was to find that all that had changed. For the kids today, the people we used to snigger at are role models, swashbuckling marauders sailing the seas of high finance, corporate raiders whose motto is 'Get in, get out, get rich'. Dennis Parsons was an accountant of the new 'creative' variety, for whom the firm's actual turnover represents only the original idea on which the completed tax return is based. When it came to cooking the books, Dennis was in the Raymond Blanc class. Socially, though, he and Karen, who taught part-time at a girls' school in Headington, were both from a lower-middle-class, comp/tech background, and it may not have been only the fearsome price of property in the North Oxford heartlands which had put them off moving there. Even after five years they were finding it a bit difficult in Oxford, you see, a bit *sticky*.

Still, it wasn't these fine distinctions that were uppermost in my mind that Friday evening in April when I turned off the Banbury Road into the quiet, tree-lined avenue where the Parsons lived, but the rather more obvious contrast, the gaping *abyss* between these genteel surroundings and the ones in which I myself was then living. For if property values and social status north of St Giles shaded imperceptibly from one microclimate to another, the other side of the Cherwell they just dropped out of sight. We didn't have much time for subtle distinctions down in East Oxford. They weren't our style. We went in for agitprop caricature and grotesque exaggeration. Derelict vagrants hacking their lungs up while a group of students in evening dress pass by waving bottles of champagne, that sort of thing. I was always surprised that you could cross Magdalen Bridge without having to show your papers, that you could just *walk* across. It felt like Checkpoint Charlie, but in fact no one tried to stop you except the alkies lurching up off their piss-stained benches with some story about needing the bus fare back home to Sheffield.

As I wheeled my tenth-hand push-bike through the gates of the Parsons' large detached house and made my way across the gravel forecourt past the guests' Volvos and Audis, I began to feel uncomfortably out of my depth. These people were armed and dangerous. They had houses, wives, cars, careers, pensions. They bought and sold, consumed and produced, hired and fired. They ski'd and sailed and rode and shot. Once I could have seen them off by asserting that I had no interest in such things, preferring to live from one day to the next, unfettered by possessions and responsibilities. But that wouldn't wash any more, not at my age. It would be like the denizens of Magdalen Bridge claiming they drank VP sherry rather than Tio Pepe because they preferred the taste.

Once I got inside the house I began to cheer up. The Parsons had tried, you could see that. They had tried and they had failed. The furnishings were an indiscriminate mess: a bit of Habitat here, a dash of Laura Ashley there, a few near-antiques, some Scandinavian minimalism, an MFI recliner-rocker, and let's bung a tank of Japanese fighting-fish in the corner. They knew their own taste wouldn't do, poor dears, but they weren't quite sure what *would*. Well not those fish, for a start-off. Or the block-mounted Manet print in the down-stairs loo. There there was the collection of Demi Roussos and Richard Clayderbuck albums, and the Skivertex-clad set of 'Great Classics of World Literature' ranging from *Ulysses* at one end to *HMS Ulysses* at the other. None of those would do. To say nothing of Karen's Merseyside vowels and over-eager laugh. To say nothing of *Karen*.

As I said earlier, the drink was flowing freely. Dennis was an assiduous host, constantly on the move, opening bottles, disposing of empties, topping up everyone's glasses and handing round salty snacks in case anyone's thirst began to flag. But one look at Karen was enough to confirm that her present state wasn't simply the result of fast-lane drinking since the guests arrived. She'd been at it since tea-time, since lunch, since she got up. In fact the prospect of hosting a dinner party was so fraught with terrors that she'd probably started to get drunk for it the night before. The initial elation the rest of us were experiencing was as far away as her childhood. She'd been there and come back, and been again. It's not quite so good the second time around, never mind the fourth or fifth. By now she had the look of a refugee, a displaced person. She was *elsewhere*.

The people who had put her in such a tizzy were a solicitor, a computer analyst and someone in advertising. The Parsons wanted to know people like that. They didn't know why. They didn't know what they were going to do with them. They were on heat socially. They needed to couple with the big dogs.

When Dennis summoned us to table, I ended up with Karen on one side of me and the computer analyst's wife on the other. Marisa? Marika? The British authorities will no doubt have the name, if you're interested. As far as that sort of thing goes they can't be faulted.

'What do you do?' she fluted.

I told her I taught English to foreign students.

'Oh, that must be interesting,' she said. Meaning, that must be boring *and* badly paid.

'And you?' I inquired politely.

She made a little throw-away gesture.

'Oh, I'm just a housewife!'

Meaning, my husband's weekly lunch bills exceed your monthly income.

I took very little part in the conversation. There are certain topics about which I have nothing to say, and they covered almost every one of them that night. The guests' children, recent ailments, accomplishments, acquisitions and priceless sayings of. Preparatory schools in Oxford, their relative value for money. The public education system, its declining educational and social standards. A good start in life, the importance of providing one's children with, particularly these days. You would never have guessed from the way the Parsons talked that they were childless. The subject was *de rigueur* and they knew it. We then moved on to the spiralling property prices in Oxford, the purchase price of the Parsons' house compared to its current estimated value, the solicitor's recent attic conversion, and so on and so forth.

It was towards the end of the main course, some sort of *en croûte* affair which Karen must have bought oven-ready at Marks and Spencer's, that the muscles in the arch of my right foot suddenly seized up. The Parsons' slimline dining table was too low for me to get a proper purchase to relieve the cramp. The pain was agonizing. I groped around with my foot for the table-leg and pressed down hard until the spasm gradually subsided. A moment later, to my astonishment, I felt an answering pressure on my own foot.

It took me a moment to work out what was going on. There are fashions in these things. When I grew up, young people had various ways of intimating to each other a desire to become better acquainted, but playing footsie-footsie was not generally one of them. That was what was happening though, and the foot in question belonged to none other than mine hostess.

I was terrifically embarrassed, but Karen did not once so much as glance in my direction, and after a while I began to suspect that she had made a mistake too. The ad-man opposite had been casting meaningful glances at her all evening, and the likeliest explanation seemed to be that she and Roger were doing a number together and I'd inadvertently got caught in the crossfire. The state Karen was in, it was a wonder she knew who her own feet belonged to, never mind anyone else's. I threw myself with apparent enthusiasm into a conversation Marietta and the solicitor were having about the difficulty of finding and keeping reliable cleaning ladies.

Some time later I got up to go to the loo. Karen also rose, muttering something about checking to see how the meringue was coming along. I stopped to hold the door open for her. As it swung shut behind her, she jumped me.

I mean that quite literally. Karen taught physical education, so she was in good shape. As I turned, she sprang forward like a cat, leaping up to straddle my hips with her thighs. Instinctively, to prevent her falling, I grabbed her buttocks. By then her mouth was all over mine, her tongue darting in and out. I just stood there like a punch-drunk boxer, taking the punishment she was handing out. I had no idea who she was or who I was or where we were. What was happening clearly had no connection with what had been happening before or would, presumably, happen afterwards.

It wasn't until I heard Dennis say, 'I'll just fetch up another bottle of the Hunter Valley' that it was borne in on me that the woman who was frenching me and bringing herself off on my belt buckle was none other than Karen Parsons, the wife of Dennis Parsons, who was currently six feet away on the other side of the dining-room door and closing rapidly.

Karen reacted before I did. Obeying some primitive burrowing instinct, she pulled me into the loo and locked the door behind us. We held hands in the dark while someone tried the handle.

'Won't be a mo,' I said.

'Oh, are you still in there?'

It was Dennis, stopping off for a pee on his way to replenish the supply of social oxygen, already anxious about what the others were saying about him behind his back. Meanwhile, on the other side of the door he was impatiently eyeing, Karen and I were locked in a windowless room about five feet by three, with no possibility of escape short of flushing ourselves down the lavatory.

I've often speculated since on what would have happened if we'd just given ourselves up at this point. There would, I imagine, have been an ugly scene. I certainly wouldn't have been invited back to the Parsons', but I could have lived with that. At the very worst, their marriage might not have survived. They would have, on the other hand.

Instead, I flushed the toilet and opened the door just wide enough to slip through the gap. Dennis gave me the vague smile of complicity that men exchange in lavatorial situations. I grasped his arm firmly and led him away.

'Could I have a word with you?'

He frowned.

'In private,' I added, leading him into the kitchen. I

slammed the door behind us to let Karen know the coast was clear.

'That bloke across the table from me, is he gay, do you happen to know?'

Dennis's brow puckered more intensely.

'Roger? You must be joking.'

'In that case I think he just made a pass at your wife.'

You could tell right away he didn't want to know. Things were going all right, the evening was a success. Dennis didn't want anything to change that.

'How do you mean?'

'Well, he started playing footsie-footsie with me,' I explained. 'But if he's not that way inclined, he must have mistaken my foot for Karen's.'

I glanced down at the limb I was illustratively wiggling, only to find an involuntary erection making my trousers stick out like an accusing finger.

'Not Roger,' Dennis replied dismissively. 'Too busy giving it to his secretary, by all accounts.'

I shrugged.

'I suppose he might have had cramp or something. Still, I thought I ought to let you know.'

'Oh yes, right, fair enough. Seen Kay, by the way?'

'She went upstairs, I think.'

I'd heard the door spring open and the stairs groan as she made good her escape. She'd be sluicing her face down with cold water, I assumed, vowing never again to drink so much that she lost control of herself in such an embarrassing, such an appallingly dangerous and potentially disastrous way.

Ah Karen, how I misjudged you! But I'd never met anyone quite like her before, you see. Even little Manuela, of whom more anon, wasn't in the Karen Parsons league. Knowing what I know now, I imagined she was stretched out on the marital bed finishing the job. She would have left the door open and the landing light on so that she was clearly visible from the stairs. If Dennis came looking for her, she might hear him in time, or she might not. That would have done it for her, the uncertainty.

Something had, at any rate, when she returned to the dining room a few minutes later. The frantic animation, the barely-suppressed hysteria, had been replaced by a languid, dopey calm. At the time I thought that the drink had finally taken its toll. The stuff circulating in her veins by then must have been a cocktail in which blood was a fairly minor ingredient. It didn't seem at all surprising that she'd slowed down a little. It was a wonder she wasn't in a coma. She paid me no particular attention. For my part, I had other preoccupations. Thanks to Karen's attack I hadn't been able to pee, and when my organ switched from reproductive to urinary mode I realized that my bladder was bursting. In the end I pretended to be worried that I had left my bicycle lamp on and dashed outside to relieve myself in a flower-bed.

Through the dining-room window I heard someone inside say, '. . . on a *bicycle*!'

'The eternal student,' Dennis remarked. They all laughed.

I stood there trembling with humiliation and anger. For a moment I thought of getting on my joke transport and heading back to the East Oxford slums where I belonged. Only I didn't belong there, that was the whole trouble. If I belonged anywhere, it was with these people, the *lumpenbourgeoisie*, in whose eyes I'd lost caste, fatally and irrevocably. Besides, it had come on to rain, and the prospect of arriving home soaking wet to find my housemates Trisha and Brian curled up in a post-coital stupor in front of the TV was more than I could bear, so I swallowed my pride and went back inside.

Nevertheless, Dennis's comment still rankled, and looking back on what had happened earlier I pondered the possibility of evening the score by seducing his wife. She fancied me, that was clear. The problem was my end. To drag Karen's personality into it would be an unfair handicap, but even from a purely physical point of view she wasn't my type. I like my women big and round and female. Karen Parsons wasn't like that at all. She was anorexically skinny, her bosom almost imperceptible, her rump flat and hard. As for her face, it was one I had seen countless times in buses and supermarkets, dole queues and pubs, waiting outside schools or factories, at all ages from fifteen to fifty. Its only striking feature was a large, predatory mouth, like the front-end grille on a cheap flash motor. Definitely not my type, I decided, even if it did mean getting even with Dennis. I just didn't fancy her and that was all there was to it.

How simple life would be, if it was as simple as we think!

The rain was falling harder than ever as I cycled home down the Banbury Road, through the science ghetto on Parks Road and into a time-warp. It was 1964, and I was on my way back from seeing Jenny, a very lovely, very sweet and gentle first-year history major at Somerville. I had rooms in college that year, so instead of turning east along the High I carried on down Magpie Lane and round the corner into Merton Street, taking care over the cobbles, treacherous when wet. The half-hour was just ringing from the massive bell tower, there was a muffled sound of organ practice from the chapel, the light was burning in the porter's lodge and the gate lay open – but not to me.

I pedalled back to the High Street, past Magdalen and across the bridge to the Plain. It was now a year later. Jenny had digs on the Iffley Road and I was going there to see her, to tell her, to break it to her, to break her fragile, trusting heart. I had conceived a passion for another, you see. Liza wasn't at university. That was one of her main attractions, quite frankly. Universities weren't where it was happening, and particularly not Oxford. It was happening in Liverpool, where giggly Karen had just started at the local secondary mod, and in London, where Dennis Parsons was fast learning that the prime number is number one, and where Liza was studying art at the Slade. The things that were going down were urban things, street things, classless things. Oxford felt like a trans-atlantic liner in the age of bucket shops and cut-price charters.

I almost didn't bother to take a degree, it seemed so pointless. Liza agreed. Francis Bacon never went to art college, she pointed out. In the end I went along and scraped a pass, largely to avoid the horrendous scenes with my parents that would ensue if I came away from the temple of learning empty-handed. They'd been considerably bucked when I got a place at Merton, you see. We were respectable Home Counties middle class, but nothing special, nothing to brag about. Not that our sort is given to bragging in any case, but it had given my dad – a branch manager for one of the High Street banks – a certain quiet satisfaction to be able to let his staff know that his son was 'going up' to Oxford. In fact he got more out of it than I did, I think. He'd missed out on all that because of the war, and he never tired of dropping references to 'noughth week' and 'encaenia' and 'schools' and May Balls. But it wasn't those balls that were important to me, and timid undemanding Jenny couldn't compete with Liza's inspired experimentation, nor a damp drab flop on the Iffley Road with the joss-stick-scented nest lined with Liza's fauvist daubs where she and I lay after our bouts of dirty love, toking and talking, turning the world inside out.

That was where I had made my bed, back in the mid-sixties. Now, a quarter of a century later, I was still lying in it. I'd chosen London over Oxford, and that's what I'd got. The Cowley Road isn't Oxford, it's South London without the glamour. But even that was too chic for me, so I turned off into Winston Street. Winston Street made the Cowley Road seem pacey and sharp. Winston Street was where I lived. I chained my bicycle to the railings and climbed the north-facing steps, slimy with moss, where the puddles never dried. Trish and Brian had gone to bed. I made a mug of decaf and sat looking round at the crumbling plaster ceiling, the curdled paintwork, the tatty carpet and the flophouse furnishings.

The place belonged to Clive Phillips, who also owned the school where the three of us taught. Indeed for all practical purposes he owned *us*. Our rent was £120 a month each, exclusive of gas, electricity and water. Clive had bought the house five years earlier, before prices soared. Even if he was still paying off a mortgage, he had to be making at least £2,500 a year out of us, not counting the fact that the property had quadrupled in value. He was rumoured to own upwards of a dozen such houses in various parts of East Oxford, all let on short leases to students or teachers, in addition to his own home in Divinity Road. What with all those houses, plus the school, he must have been worth close to a million pounds, give or take the odd thousand.

Clive was twenty-nine years old.

Still, money's not important, is it? That's what I was brought up to believe. Niceness was what counted in life, not money. I was brought up to believe in niceness the way other people believe in God. I lost my faith when my parents died. They'd taken pride in planning for every eventuality, but there was nothing much they could do when an oncoming driver had a heart attack at the wheel and steered straight into the path of their Rover saloon. The estate turned out to be worth considerably less than I had hoped. My principal inheritance was a justification for any irresponsibility I cared to indulge in thereafter. I wasn't going to make the same mistake as my parents, forever denying themselves what they wanted now so that they could look forward to their retirement with complete peace of mind. Since every day could evidently be my last, I was going to make it count. Experience was all, and I set out to grab it with both hands, drifting from country to country, from one relationship to another, a heedless, hedonistic round with never a thought for tomorrow. But though I refused to age, the students and the other teachers grew younger year by year. Eventually I decided that I'd had enough. It was time to retire, to return to England-land, to the genteel sheltered accommodation I'd fled more than a decade earlier.

The moment I got back I realized that things had changed. The demolition crew had been in, the wreckers and blasters, the strippers and refitters. The attitudes and assumptions I'd grown up with had been razed to the ground, and a bold new society had risen in their place, a free-enterprise, demand-driven, flaunt-it-and-fuck-you society, dedicated to excellence and achievement. Something new, unheard-of! Created by this one woman! She had spurned the hypocritical cant beloved of politicians and addressed herself directly to the people, showing how well she knew them, telling them what they whispered in their hearts but dared not speak, calling their bluff! 'You don't want a caring society,' she had told them, in effect. 'You *say* you do, but you don't, not really. You couldn't care less about education and health and all the rest of it. And don't for Christ's sake talk to me about culture. You don't give a toss about culture. All you want to do is sit at home and watch TV. No, it's no use protesting! I *know* you. You're selfish, greedy, ignorant and complacent. So vote for me.'

And they had, over and over again, so many times that no one except me seemed to remember that things had ever been different. I felt like Rip Van Winkle, an anachronistic laughing-stock, a freak. Failure was no longer acceptable, particularly in someone with my advantages. I had thrown away my chances in life, pawned them off for a few cheap thrills. And it was too late to do anything about it. In the new Britain you were over the hill at twenty-five, never mind forty. The key to success, an article in the local paper informed me, was to sell yourself hard, but I had nothing to offer that anyone wanted.

Except, perhaps, for Karen Parsons.

So my phone call to the Parsons' household the next day was in the best traditions of the society in which I found myself living. Indeed without any wish to evade my responsibility for subsequent events, I think I may fairly claim that in everything I did *in re* Karen and her husband I was market-led. There was a hole waiting to be plugged. I had identified a need and was aiming to satisfy it.

Dennis answered the phone. I thanked him for dinner and said how much I'd enjoyed myself.

'The reason I'm calling, actually, is that my wallet seems to have disappeared and I wondered whether I could possibly have left it there.'

'Hang on, I'll ask Kay.'

I stood looking down at the pavement below the payphone while Dennis padded across the wall-to-wall carpeting and called distantly to his wife. Half-eaten turds of Spud U Like nestled on a bed of throw-up curry. I looked up at the concrete-grey sky, still surprisingly free of graffiti. I tried not to look at anything in between.

'It's OK, we've got it,' Dennis said in my ear.

'Sorry?'

'When do you want to come and pick it up?'

I got my wallet out of my pocket and held it up in front of my eyes.

'You've got it?'

'Kay found it when she was clearing up. She was going to ring you but we don't have your number. Look, we're going shopping this morning, we could drop it off if you like. Where do you live?'

This brought me to my senses. I would rather have died than let the Parsons see where I lived.

'No, I don't want to put you to any bother.'

'It's no bother.'

'Well actually I'm going out this morning too.'

But I was talking to myself. There was another muffled exchange at the other end.

'Why don't you pop in this afternoon and get it? I'll be going out briefly at some stage, but Kay'll be here.'

Fair enough, I thought as I walked home. I was beginning to appreciate Karen Parsons. I've always been good at thinking on my feet. It's the other kind of thinking I've never been able to muster, the long-term stuff. 'Never confuse strategy with tactics,' one of my tutors advised me, but I can't even remember what the words mean. Over the short distance, though, I'm pretty impressive, and I admire the same quality in others. I liked the way Karen had picked up that my story about the wallet was in fact a message, and I liked the message she was sending back even more. It was risky. If I marched round there and demanded my wallet in front of Dennis, she would be in deep doo-doo. She was trusting me not to do that, putting that power in my hands. I liked that, too. It's good to go dutch on power. I've always made a point of borrowing money from women early in the relationship so as to give them a hold over me. It also helps when the time comes to break off the affair, because you can talk about the money instead of feelings and love and messy, painful stuff like that.

At a quarter to three I was in position behind the grime-sprayed glass of a bus shelter on the Banbury Road. The entrance to Ramillies Drive was about thirty yards away on the other side of the road. There I stood, waiting for Dennis's car to emerge. It was mizzling steadily, so I had lashed out on a minibus ticket, which cost more than a taxi would here. The afternoon was cold and raw, and I soon regretted my choice of clothing, a light linen suit dating from my time in this country. But I wanted to present an exotic image, a man of the world blown in from foreign parts to bring some much-needed glamour to Karen's drab suburban existence.

I had hoped she would be able to get rid of Dennis quickly, but it was almost 4 o'clock before the red BMW finally appeared and roared away in the direction of the ring road. By that time I was chilled to the bone, exhausted from the relentless battering of the traffic, sullen and depressed. This had better be good, I thought grimly as I crossed the road and walked up the cul-de-sac to the Parsonage. This had better be *bloody* good.

I had to ring the bell several times before Karen finally appeared. I knew at once that something was wrong.

'Oh, it's you.' She sounded surprised and displeased. 'Dennis isn't here.'

She was wearing clingy jeans and a ribbed woollen sweater which emphasized the lines of her body. It still wasn't my kind of body, but dressed like that it looked quite different, a gym teacher's body, supple, firm and fit.

'I know that,' I said. 'I've just spent an hour and a quarter waiting for him not to be here.'

'Why did you do that?'

Ah, I thought. Right. Fine, if that's the way you want to play it.

'Sorry if I misunderstood. Just give me my wallet and I'll be off.'

'I haven't got your wallet.'

'I know you haven't.'

We measured each other with our eyes.

'Then what are you doing here?' she asked.

This was not the first time I had dabbled in adultery. I've always had a yen for married women – it's something to do with being an only son, I suspect, some sort of Oedipal urge to play Daddy's part with Mummy – and I knew by experience how much care and tact is needed. However tenuous it may have become, once a marriage is under threat it can suddenly turn into a territory which has to be defended at all costs, like the Falklands. Neither partner has given it a thought for years, but let some outsider come barging in as though he owned the place and it's war. Perhaps I had been too forward, I thought, taken too much for granted. After what had happened the previous evening exquisite delicacy had seemed uncalled for.

'I assumed you wanted me to come. Why did you say you had my wallet otherwise?'

She shrugged pettishly.

'You're late. I thought Dennis would still be here.'

I tried this on from various directions, but it still didn't make sense.

'Speak of the devil,' said Karen.

There was a swish of gravel as the BMW drew in. Dennis clambered out looking disgruntled.

'Bloody thing's on the blink. There's another up your end of town somewhere, but I can't be bothered.'

Registering my look of bewilderment, but mistaking the cause, he added, 'Car wash. I go every Saturday. Prevents grime build-up.'

He grasped my elbow and led me through the hallway and into a long room knocked through the whole length of the house. A three-piece suite and coffee table occupied the front half, a fitted kitchen and dinette the rear. These were the real living quarters, as opposed to the receiving rooms on the other side of the house, where guests were entertained. Dennis apparently saw me as 'family', or at any rate as someone he didn't have to impress. What I still couldn't understand was why he wanted to see me at all.

Almost the biggest shock of the many I had sustained on my return home was the loss of the social cachet I had enjoyed for so many years. In Spain, in Italy, in Saudi – well, no, forget Saudi – and above all here, among your warm-hearted and hospitable people, I had been sought-after, even lionized. As a foreigner and a teacher, I was the object of general interest and respect. At the end of the EFL training course I did in London, a British Council type gave us all a pep talk before we were packed off to Ankara or Kuala Lumpur. 'Never forget, you're not just teachers,' he told us, 'you're cultural ambassadors.'

The funny thing was that in a way the old fart was right. Socially, we benefited from a sort of diplomatic immunity. We were extraterritorial. The rules of the local game didn't apply to us. I didn't appreciate this freedom until I lost it. I took it for granted that I could associate with people from all walks of life, from every background. It seemed perfectly natural that I should spend one evening being waited on by uniformed retainers at the home of an important industrialist whose son I taught, and the next in a seedy bar drinking beer with a group of workers from the factory where I gave private courses in technical English. Someone rightly said that language exists to prevent us communicating, and of no country is that more true than my own. I never made more friends as easily as when I was among people whose language I spoke badly and who barely spoke mine at all. In a land where trendy cafés display neon signs reading SMACK BAR and SNATCH BAR, no one's going to pick up the linguistic and social markers that pin the native Brit down like so many Lilliputian bonds. Subtle but damning variations of idiolect are unlikely to count for much in a country where people go around wearing tee-shirts inscribed with things like 'The essence of brave's aerial adventure: the flight's academy of the American east club with the traditional gallery of Great Britain diesel'. Do you know what that means? I don't. But it must have meant something to someone. You couldn't just *invent* something like that.

But things were very different back in the land of dinge and drab, of sleaze and drear and grot. Teachers are not figures of respect in my country. They're the bottom of the professional heap, somewhere between nurses and prison warders. And I wasn't even a real teacher. The only remarkable thing about me was the fact that I was still doing a holiday job at the age of forty. I was just damaged goods, another misfit, another over-educated, under-motivated loser who had missed his chance and drifted into the Sargasso Sea of EFL work.

Yet here I was, in sedate and semi-exclusive Ramillies Drive, being urged to spend the rest of the afternoon with a successful chartered accountant and his wife, being plied with expensive wine and prawn-flavoured corn snacks, being *courted*. What was going on? Were the Parsons into troilism? 'Suburban couple seek uninhibited partner, m or f, for three-way sex fun.' That was the sort of thing I could imagine Denny and Kay going in for, at least in theory. It would go with the decor. But in practice Dennis was too repressed to actually go through with it. Even his drinking had to be packaged as an aesthetic experience.

'Good green fruit on the nose. Young and vibrant. Soft round buttery fruit in the mouth, trailing off a little on the finish. *Very* chardonnay. Lovely concentrated body. Surprisingly firm grip.'

He bought his wine from a mail-order firm, I later discovered. Each case came with tasting notes, from which Dennis was given to quoting extensively. The point of the whole performance was only partly the usual snobbery and one-upmanship. The essential purpose was to disguise the fact that Dennis was an alcoholic. He wasn't out to get drunk – perish the thought! – but to savour the unique individuality of each wine to the full. Dennis didn't drink, he degusted. Well fair enough, whatever it takes. But if he couldn't even get pissed in his own living room without all this blather it was hard to imagine him asking casually if I'd care to step upstairs for some kinky sex.

Still, I wasn't complaining. I didn't know what was going

on, but I was happy to be there, sipping Dennis's eight-quid-a-bottle plonk, trading glances with his vibrant young – well, youngish – wife and openly admiring the charms of her lovely concentrated body. Since I wasn't in a position to return the Parsons' hospitality, I felt an obligation to provide conversational value for money, so I embarked on a series of anecdotes about my time abroad, some true, all exaggerated, a few plain invention. You may have the house and the car and the job and the security, I was saying, but I've *lived*. That's what I was saying to Dennis, at any rate. The messages passing between Karen and I were more complex. As the wine took hold I glanced in her direction with increasing frequency, often to find her already looking at me. Or else she would turn round, as though sensing my gaze on her skin, and for a moment as brief and yet momentous as a pause in music our eyes talked dirty. Then she slumped back in her chair, mouthing the nicotine-dosed chewing gum she used instead of cigarettes, and I thought I must have imagined an intensity of which she was surely incapable.

That evening the Parsons were meeting friends for an early meal before going on to the opera. How times had changed, to be sure! When I grew up, opera had all the allure of a *thé dansant* on Bournemouth pier. Now it was like Wimbledon. People who couldn't tell Weber from Webern went along to cheer their favourite tenor and be seen with their bums on a fifty-quid seat. Dennis thoughtfully offered to drop me off in town.

'Save you 30p, it all adds up,' he said, reducing my glamorous cosmopolitan personality to its due place in the Oxford scheme of things.

He paid for that, though. Just before we left, while Dennis was in the loo, I grabbed his wife and kissed her on the mouth. Karen made no attempt to break away or to respond. She just stood there, trembling all over. Then the toilet flushed and we wrenched violently apart, as though each of us had been struggling to get free all along.

Dennis appeared in the doorway, grinning cheerfully.

'All set?'

When I worked abroad, I lived like a gentleman of leisure. Unless I was awakened by the departure of a bed-fellow who had to work or study, poor girl, my day began at about nine or thereabouts, with a leisurely shower and a small black coffee. The rest of the morning I might spend at the beach, in season, or in the park or a café, reading or catching up on my correspondence, or chatting to friends and acquaintances, as the whim took me. Then came the delicious moment of the *aperitivo*, that sense of the whole city beginning to wind down towards lunch, which I took at any one of a dozen excellent and welcoming restaurants where I was sure to be hailed and called over to one table or another. After a leisurely meal it was out into the sun-drenched streets again, replete and relaxed, in boisterous good-natured company, for an excellent coffee and a cigar.

Sated with a whole morning of freedom and indulgence, work seemed almost a pleasure, the more so in that my students were in the same post-prandial daze as myself. All serious business was dispatched in the morning. No one expected to achieve anything much after lunch, so the mood was languid and light-hearted, as though we were just pretending. The hours slipped past almost unnoticed. Outside the window dusk had fallen, the sky glowed in exuberant shades of green and pink. Soon my working day was over, but the night had only just begun, the streets and piazzas just beginning to hum with life. Where would I spend those precious, unforgettable hours tonight, and with whom?

Since his return home, the prodigal's life had been rather different. Classes were no longer in the afternoon and evening, after work. They *were* work, and the students, who were paying through the nose for them, were grim, resentful and bloody-minded. My day began at seven with unwanted glimpses of Trish and Brian's intimacies, followed by slurped tea and munched toast in the communal kitchen. Then it was on to my bike and off to spend the rest of my day banged up with a bunch of sullen, spoilt brats in order to make Clive Phillips even richer than he already was. 'The eternal student,' Dennis had joked. The joke, of course, was that the real students were currently being head-hunted for posts with starting salaries in excess of 20K.

That term, the second half of each morning consisted of a two-hour mental sauna with my 'Fake' Early Intermediates. There were seven of them, and it was a source of perpetual wonder to me that they'd ever learned to speak their own languages, never mind anyone else's. The exception was Helga, a Euro-slut from Cologne who should have been several grades higher but kept deliberately failing the aptitude tests so as to be with Massimo. A Latin looker whose stock response to any correction was an impatient 'Izza same!', Massimo combined staggering conceit, total ineptitude and a winsome, self-ingratiating charm which would have been hard to take in a toddler, never mind a beefy twenty-year-old. He and Helga sat at the back of the class, groping each other up in a flurry of smirks and giggles. In front of them sat Tweedledum and Tweedledee, a pair of Turkish twins whose soft, pale, shapeless, perfumed flesh irresistibly suggested the cloying sweetmeats of their native land. Then there was Kayoko, the Girl Who Couldn't Say No. Asked, for example, if she was from New York, the Tokyo-born lass would blushingly reply, 'Yes, I'm not.' Yolanda and Garcia rounded out this select group. Yolanda was a spotty, bespectacled girl from Barcelona who spent her time translating every word I said into Spanish for the benefit of Garcia, a missing-link anthropoid from one of your immediate neighbours. For reasons which will become clear in due course, I prefer not to specify which one. Nor is Garcia his real name. In fact, given his track record, even his real name probably wasn't his real name.

It wasn't like working here, where I could slip into Spanish when things got ropey, and afterwards we'd all go to the bar and tone up the group dynamics over a few drinks. The only *lingua franca* this lot shared was English, and they didn't speak English. Not only that, but they were never *going* to speak it. I knew it and they knew it, but we couldn't admit that we knew it. We wouldn't have understood each other, for one thing. So all I could do was to prance about waving flashcards and realia like a second-rate conjuror at a children's party, and try not to glance at my watch more than once a minute.

The main item on the agenda the following Monday was a listening comprehension exercise based around a tape-recorded 'authentic' conversation. In fact I'd carefully scripted the whole thing, grading the language to keep it within the students' capabilities. 'Fake' Intermediates were students who had done the Beginners' course but learned nothing from it. Indeed most of them had made a kind of negative progress. Not only were they still ignorant of the language, but they now had a sense of personal inadequacy – totally justified, I might add – which manifested itself in a stubborn refusal to learn anything. The aim of the gist-listening session was to try and break down this hostility by showing the group that they could understand two native speakers talking 'naturally', in this case about a shopping expedition. Ideally they were supposed to pick up that the woman (Trish) was asking the man (me) for money – an all-too-authentic situation, this. The first run-through was a complete failure. Even my most basic pre-set question ('How many people are talking?') proved to be over their heads, so I rewound the tape and tried again. If all else failed I could usually rely on Massimo getting an ego-boosting tip from Helga, who wasn't allowed to take part herself. We were about half-way through the second audition when the door opened and Karen Parsons walked in.

I wasn't best pleased to see her. It was bad enough to have to spend my days acting as occupational therapist to a bunch of linguistic basket-cases without having my social acquaintances dropping in to witness my degradation. Moreover one of Clive's many draconian rules was an absolute ban on personal visitors during school hours. There was even a story, not necessarily apocryphal, that when a message arrived to tell one of the teachers that his father had died, Clive had insisted on waiting until the lunch break before passing it on. I already had reason to suspect that I was by no means flavour-of-the-month at the Oxford International Language College. If Clive caught me entertaining a lady friend in the classroom, I would be out on my ear in no time at all.

So when I asked Karen what she thought she was up to, I was merely expressing my irritation and anxiety at this interruption. As usual, we were at cross-purposes from the start.

'I won't go behind his back,' she said. 'It may seem stupid, but that's the way it is. What happened the other day was wrong. I was drunk and I . . .'

She fell silent, looking uncertainly at the students.

'Don't worry,' I told her. 'They won't understand as long as you speak quickly.'

I was being tactful. Given Karen's broken-nosed vowels and head-banger intonation, they wouldn't have understood if she'd spelt it for them.

'You mean I could say anything at all?' she asked with a mischievous smile.

I glanced at Helga, but she was busy sticking her tongue in Massimo's ear. Karen took something from her handbag and slipped it into her mouth like a communicant self-administering the host.

'Just my knickers,' she murmured, catching my eye.

'Sorry?'

'Nicorette. Denny won't let me smoke. Kills the taste of the wine, he says.'

She fell silent. Then an internal bulkhead gave way somewhere and she blurted out, 'We don't do it any more, not really. Not enough. And I need it, and sometimes . . .'

She broke off.

'Ooh, this *is* fun, isn't it?'

As she eagerly scanned the blank faces turned like sunflowers towards us, I felt almost faint for a moment, overwhelmed by her excitement and my own desire. I no longer cared about Clive finding us together. I no longer cared about anything but the sexual charge passing between us.

'I want you, Karen,' I murmured. 'I want you properly.'

She squirrelled away at the nicotine-laden gum.

'I know. But I can't. At the end of the day, he's still my husband.'

'What, so you'd be sick as a parrot if we went over the moon together?'

This was the tone to take with Karen, I decided. Coming on all awed and respectful would just put the wind up her. Most women don't really have a very high opinion of themselves, so if you start treating them as something special they think, 'Oh God, sooner or later he'll find out the truth, and then he'll despise me.' Much better to make it clear from the start that you've seen through them, and you *still* fancy them rotten.

She shrugged stubbornly.

'That's the way it is.'

'You interrupted my class just to tell me this?'

'What? No, I just dropped by to invite you to dinner on Saturday. We haven't got your number, you see. I was going to leave a note, but there was no one at Reception and then I heard your voice in here. Thomas and Lynn will be there. He's Denny's partner, you'll like him. Half past seven for eight.'

I nodded curtly.

'Fair enough.'

At the door she looked back.

'And I am sorry. About the other. I just can't. I do like you, but I can't.'

The door closed behind her. I looked round at the class, my finger hovering above the tape-recorder.

'All right, let's try again. How many people are there and what are they talking about?'

Helga put her hand up.

'There is a man and a woman,' she enunciated fastidiously. 'He wants to – how do you say? – "fuck" her? And she, I think, also wants to fuck him. Yes, I'm sure she does. But her husband is a problem.'

I nodded coolly.

'I see. And why is her husband a problem?'

To my astonishment a forest of hands shot up around the class.

'Izza money,' said Massimo. 'Always same ting widda womans.'

'She is want more,' ventured Yolanda.

'Yes,' Kayoko chimed in. 'Can't get enough.'

Like the kraken stirring in its primaeval sleep, one of the Turkish twins rumbled into speech.

'Chopping,' it said.

I stood staring at them in utter bewilderment. I was the only one who hadn't understood.

You know those days when you've *got it*? When everyone looks at you expectantly and everything you do is significant, when men defer and women give you cool, appraising glances? What *is* that stuff? Maybe the clothes, you think, but the next time you wear that outfit you're The Invisible Man. No, it wasn't the clothes. So what *was* it? Certainly not the radiant glow of confidence and success, or it sure as hell wouldn't have worked for me that Saturday round at Ramillies Drive. Which it did.

I was irresistible. I could have levitated, spoken in tongues and changed the Perrier into Dom Perignon. I disdained such vulgar exhibitionism, however. I made no attempt to impress or ingratiate. When Thomas Carter asked me how I liked Oxford, I made a wry face and said, 'Mmmm . . .' Normally I would have sounded like a tongue-tied half-wit, but that evening my response appeared to hint at the inexpressible depths and nuances of my infinitely complex relationship with the city, together with a gentle rebuke to a question which was either fatuous or unanswerable. The Oxford manner, in short, the knack of which consists wholly in getting away with it.

I could have got away with murder that Saturday night, although under the present circumstances I had better add that I made no attempt to do so. What I *did* get away with was arguably worse than murder, and revealed for the first time something of what I was letting myself in for by getting involved with Karen Parsons. One might even argue that if that elusive mantle of desirability hadn't happened to fall on my shoulders on that of all evenings . . .

But the past conditional is a notoriously tricky area, even for mother-tongue speakers, and there's no point in speculating on which way the final result might have gone if we wouldn't've scored that first goal, Ron. The fact is that before the evening was over I had not only penetrated Karen sexually, but perhaps even more important we had shared a good laugh together at Dennis's expense. If you can make her laugh, they say, you're half-way there. If you can make her laugh while you're coming in her mouth, then you might be said to have arrived. And if you can do all that with her husband just a few feet away, blissfully unaware that he's the butt of the joke, then yours is his house and everything that's in it, old son.

The other guests that night were Dennis's partner in Osiris Management Services, Thomas Carter, his Welsh wife Lynn, and a menopausal colleague of Karen's called Vicky. Compared with the Parsons' previous dinner party, this was a relaxed affair. As an American, Carter was a non-combatant in the class warfare which terrified the Parsons. This was just as well, because as a native he would have been a bit hard to take. Thomas Carter came right out and told you that he thought England was the only truly civilized country in the world and that as the most English of English cities, Oxford was its heart and soul, the core of everything that had formed us, the repository of our values and the guarantor of our standards, an expression in stone of our whole Western civilization, a cultural Stonehenge which, etc, etc.

In England, that kind of patriotism is something you do with other consenting adults under the covers with the lights out, and usually comes with various unpleasant side-effects such as xenophobia, anti-Semitism, Anglo-Catholicism and so on. But Thomas Carter was from Philadelphia, and his love for Oxford and for England was a pure boyish enthusiasm as innocent as a passion for preserved railways or real ale. He was also very charming, an easy smiler, witty, relaxed and vivacious. With the British, any relationship begins heavily in debt. You have to spend years and years working off the initial residue of suspicion and diffidence before you're even out of the red, let alone seeing any positive return for your efforts. Meeting Thomas reminded me that human relations don't have to be like this, that in other countries you open your account in credit, and unless you squander that goodwill by behaving like a complete arsehole, the mutual warmth continues to grow with every subsequent encounter, as though it were *natural* for human beings to get on together.

Lynn Carter presented a striking contrast to her extrovert mate. Her personality was drab, earnest and humourless and her appearance calculatedly unattractive. To be honest, it looked as though she had given up on being a woman. Not that I'd blame anyone for that. Let's face it, would *you* want the job? Lynn Carter had put in her time down there on the sexual shop floor – there were two teenage sons to prove it – but now she'd taken early retirement. Fair enough, but where did that leave her husband, so full of vim and vigour? Where did Thomas go to get retooled these days? Who was mucking him out and hosing him down? It had to be Karen, I reckoned. I wasn't vain enough to think that the way she had come on to me that first night was solely down to my resistless charms. Like the Carters', the Parsons' marriage was in turn-around, only there it was Dennis who was the sleeping partner. Karen had admitted as much the day she came to the school. Which left her as Thomas's *vis-à-vis*.

On another occasion, this suspicion might have been calculated to cripple me with a sense of my own worthlessness. Who was I to be taking on a contender like Thomas Carter, a management consultant and the owner-occupier of a £500,000 property set in the accessible Arcadia of Boars Hill? My Early Intermediates had unwittingly pointed out the parallels between Karen's refusal to 'go behind Dennis's back' and the recorded conversation about money and shopping I had played them. In other words, the reason for my coy mistress's quaint sense of honour was nothing more nor less than financial prudence. Whatever Dennis's other shortcomings, he footed the bill. My salary was barely enough to keep me in sliced white and undies, never mind maintain Mrs Dennis Parsons in the style to which she had become accustomed.

As if to make this quite clear, the other charity guest that night was Vicky, a career spinster with beefy-jerky skin and a mouth as tensely muscled as an anus. During one of her absences from the room everyone shook their heads and agreed that Vicky was 'a very sad case'. The implied judgement on me, Vicky's notional partner, should have been enough to send me into a screaming spiral of paranoid depression. But that evening nothing could touch me. The only effect of these humiliations and challenges was to make me even more determined to overcome Karen's scruples.

Dinner itself was a relatively painless affair. Karen wasn't trying to impress anyone, so we ate promptly and quite well. She seated me on her right, and I made my first direct pass as soon as we sat down. The first course was avocado with prawn cocktail dressing. No problem there. While my right hand spooned up the sweet pulp and hefted my glass of Alsace riesling, my left explored the contours of my neighbour's inner calf and the hollow behind her knee. I'd expected some token reluctance, a bit of chair-shuffling and so on. There wasn't much else she could do without attracting attention, but I definitely expected a bit of the old argy-bargy before she let me get down to business. I mean, it's traditional, isn't it?

But Karen didn't have much use for tradition. She stiffened when I touched her, just for an instant, the way you do when you feel something on your leg and aren't sure what it is. After that the only clue was her heightened responses to everything *else* that happened, a too-eager agreement, an over-emphatic laugh. Like she was high, not on booze or pills but some of that good mellow shit that used to go the rounds at the first dinner parties I ever went to, at Liza's place, when the world was young and lovable.

I'd like to comment briefly on two aspects of Karen's response to my attentions, both of which are fundamental to a correct understanding of later events. The first was what I might call her physical candour. To an amazing – even an alarming – extent, Karen Parsons was totally straightforward about what she wanted to do with her body and what she liked having done to it. The quality I'm referring to was something common enough here in Latin America, but very rare in the land of booze and animal fats, where the women seem to have taken to heart mad Hamlet's advice to let their honesty admit no discourse to their beauty. Even in bed, they're hypocrites. Karen wasn't. If you put your finger up her bum while she was coming, she didn't pretend to object just to stop you running away with the idea that she was the kind of woman who wouldn't object if you put your finger up her bum while she was coming. On the other hand, she wasn't a Manuela either. There were limits to what Karen would let you do. It was just that she didn't lie, to herself or others, about what they were.

My second observation demonstrates the absurdity of the idea that our relationship was, to borrow the elegant formula adopted by one news comic, 'the perverted passion of two sex junkies who would do anything – even kill – for their fix'. In fact what the same tabloid, in a characteristic retreat into prudery, terms 'the sexual act' was never more than a *terminus ad quem* for us. This is evident from Karen's ecstatic reaction to my attentions that evening. It may be mildly titillating to feel a hand on your knee during dinner, but in itself it's not going to bring you off, is it? 'The hurricane of their all-consuming lust for each other,' continues our over-titillated hack, 'swept away every obstacle that stood in its path.' The author of these words clearly had his pen in one hand and his dick in the other, and had forgotten which was which.

The truth is exactly the opposite. Karen and I went out of our way to place obstacles in our path. We became connoisseurs of obstacles. We collected them like rare orchids, gleefully sharing our latest acquisitions and discoveries. That was the secret of Karen's *empressement*. It wasn't what I was doing that was turning her on but the fact that I was doing it there, doing it then, in front of her husband and her husband's partner and her husband's partner's wife and one of her own colleagues. Karen wouldn't commit adultery behind Dennis's back, but there was nothing that excited her more than doing it under his nose. Feeling my hand on her leg, the fingers fanning out, stroking to give pleasure, squeezing to show need, a little dumbshow of love being played out on her skin. And meanwhile, above-board . . .

'Jane Grigson says to sweat them lightly in butter.'

'Perspire, surely?'

'I still swear by Delia.'

'Did you know you can *chambrer* wine in the microwave?'

While Lynn and Thomas and Vicky and Dennis chattered, I sat back and let my fingers do the talking. Nevertheless, after ten minutes or so my hand on Karen's knee was starting to feel like one lump of meat resting on another. It was time to sign off before familiarity bred contempt, and just in case it already had I decided to hurt her.

A gentleman may be defined as someone who never inflicts pain unintentionally, and where women are concerned I've always prided myself on being a perfect gent. Apart from Manuela – we really must find time for a word or two about Manuela soon – I've never got any mileage out of hurting women. This is a cultural difference, I think. Here in Latin America there's traditionally been a lot of pain involved in relations of all kinds, from the family to the state that is modelled on it. There are complex historical reasons for this, just as there are for differences in the amount of seasoning used in cooking. People here are used to a fairly high level of pain, just as they're used to a lot of chilli in their food. Life would be bland without it. I was astonished by the amount of pain that Manuela seemed to thrive on. It was only when I stopped hurting her that she got worried. She thought I was cheating on her, you see, hurting another woman behind her back.

Anyway, before taking my hand away I reached over and pinched the tender flesh on the inside of Karen's leg until she moaned. Conversation stopped and everyone became frightfully solicitous. Karen brushed them off with talk of a 'little twinge' that she got from time to time and rose briskly to clear the table. I muttered something about helping and followed her out. I found her standing by the sink, which she was filling with hot water.

'Have you seen the furry liquid?' she asked without looking round.

The last thing I had expected from Karen was an imaginative feel for language, but this was almost poetic: the soap foam as fur on the skin of the water. With a sudden rush of tender emotion I hugged her.

'Oh, it's you,' she said, and kneed me in the groin.

'Anything I can do?' ventured Vicky, appearing in the doorway. 'What are you doing down there?'

I smiled at her over gritted teeth.

'Banged my funny bone.'

'Ah, there it is!' cried Karen, seizing a plastic bottle with green lettering. 'Furry liquid', I realized belatedly, was simply her Merseyside pronunciation of the well-known brand of washing-up liquid which the Parsons favoured.

'God it's big.'
'Enormous.'
'Impressive feel in the mouth. Tremendous length.'
Dennis glanced at his tasting notes.
' "The aroma leaps out of the glass and assaults you while your senses wallow in big good fruit and a long, long finish." '
He inhaled deeply.
'Big, hard, hot, juicy, fruit attack on the nose.'
'Generous but well-structured body.'
'Soft but beautifully tight. Very firm.'
'Relaxed tannic grip.'
'Lingering finish.'
'Long final note.'
The scene was the Parsons' living room. Not the sitting room across the hall, to which we'd retired after dinner. That was for guests, and the guests had gone, Vicky by half past ten, the Carters an hour later. By now it was almost one, but Dennis still wanted to party. Karen was lying stretched out on the sofa facing me, staring up at the ceiling. Since the departure of Thomas and Lynn she had drunk much and said little. Dennis lay sprawled in the armchair between us, his feet propped on the glass-topped coffee table amid an array of empty bottles. In the course of the evening we had sampled a wide variety of wines, and were now experiencing a woozy sense of disassociation that was like being drunk and hungover at the same time. It was nevertheless quite a shock, when I next glanced in Karen's direction, to realize that she was masturbating.

I instinctively looked away, the way children do when they see something naughty, as though witnessing it might incriminate them. Then I looked back. There was no doubt about it. Her left hand was curled down under the hem of her skirt, which she'd pulled up on that side. She was wearing a short-sleeved blouse that left her arms bare to the elbow. The muscles rippled lightly as she worked. Her right knee was raised to form a screen that prevented Dennis from seeing what was going on, but she made no attempt to conceal it from me. On the contrary, she was staring at me with an almost manic intensity.

I thought I had just about run the gamut of sexual experiences, but nothing like this had ever happened to me before. I found it incredibly erotic, and the more Dennis maundered on about boiled sweets on the nose, the more erotic it became. His wife's head gradually fell back, her mouth open and her eyes still pinned to my face, the whites showing like a frightened horse. Her legs were slightly parted and her toes curled convulsively, as though trying to find some support to relieve her vertiginous predicament.

'Your glass is empty,' yawned Dennis. 'Kay asleep?'

'I don't think so.'

She was staring at me imploringly, unable to move the way she wanted, the way she needed to. She couldn't quite get there on her own, not with having to lie so still and make no noise. Neither, of course, could she stop. I raised my hand to my mouth, as though politely concealing a yawn. My eyes clamped to Karen's, I extended my tongue and flicked the tip rapidly up and down, flutter-tonguing the air. She came almost at once, in a series of tense repressed tremors that forced a dulled gasp from her.

'Oh, you still with us?' Dennis murmured.

'Till death do us part.'

Her husband squinted at her blearily.

'Thought you were going to start doing your imitation of a sleeping sow any moment.'

The tone of voice revealed the intensity of his disgust, not just with his wife's snores, but with her physicality as such. 'We don't do it any more,' Karen had said. I could believe it.

She rose unsteadily to her feet.

'Good night,' she said.

'Don't bother waiting up,' Dennis told her. 'It'll only be me, I'm afraid.'

He fetched a bottle from the sideboard.

'Now then, this'll see us right. Thirty-year-old armagnac. Landed and bottled. Over a grand's worth you're looking at here, and you know how much it cost me? Not one penny. Friend of a friend. You scratch mine and vice versa. Payment in kind. Lot of it goes on.'

Bloody typical, I thought. It's not enough for the rich to be rich, they have to boast about their perks and fiddles and scams as well. That way they screw you twice over. They're rich enough to pay for it and smart enough to get it for free. As for you, you're not only poor, you're stupid. Which is why you're poor, stupid.

'What was that about not waiting up?'

'What?'

'You told Karen not to wait up, it would only be you. I mean who else would it be?'

I thought he'd sussed what was going on, of course.

'Didn't you notice?' he smiled archly. 'As soon as he left, all the air went out of her.'

At the far end of the room, Karen appeared in the kitchen doorway, a glass in her hand.

'You mean there's something going on between her and Thomas?' I asked.

Dennis shook his head, then tapped it with two fingers.

'All up here. Takes some of them that way. It would all have been different if we'd been able to have children.'

I frowned.

'You mean Karen . . .?'

Dennis nodded.

'Poor kid. Tough on her.'

I glanced down at the kitchen. Karen had disappeared again.

'Shame to dump this on the dregs,' said Dennis, surveying his glass moodily.

'I'll get fresh ones.'

As soon as I rounded the line of fitted units screening off the kitchen I saw her slumped on the floor in the corner, huddled up as though against the cold. For a moment I thought she had passed out. Then her eyes registered my presence, and started to water. She looked so utterly pathetic that I bent down and comforted her silently, stroking her hair, kissing her face. She kissed me back, and then she wasn't pathetic any more.

'To the left of the sink,' Dennis called loudly.

I straightened up, opened a cupboard at random and took out two tumblers. As I did so, Karen unzipped my fly.

My first reaction was of embarrassment. I hadn't even had a chance to *wash* it! My mother always told me to put on clean underwear in case I got knocked over and taken to hospital, but the possibility that someone's drunken wife might decide to revenge herself on her husband by going down on me was not a scenario we had ever discussed. The other source of embarrassment was the very real possibility that Dennis would stroll over at any moment and catch us at it. Already I could see myself standing there, tongue-tied and grinning sheepishly, the star of a bedroom farce which had gone badly off the rails. So while it would clearly be an exaggeration to say that I didn't enjoy the experience at all, my main preoccupation was to get it over. Only I couldn't. And while there are situations in which it is possible for the male to simulate orgasm, fellatio is not one of them.

'No, no!' Dennis shouted. 'The *snifters*, man! The *snifters*.'

He had swivelled round in the armchair and was staring at me irritably. Dennis hated being kept waiting for his drink. Feeling like a character in a split-screen movie, I opened another cupboard and took out two brandy glasses. But I still couldn't come, and to withdraw without doing so would, I felt, be the height of bad manners. I pretended to find a smudge on the glasses, rinsed them, dried them and held them up to the light.

'You going to be there all night?' Dennis demanded.

'Just coming.'

It wasn't much of a joke, but then it didn't take much to make Karen laugh. Laugh she did, at any rate, and those convulsive movements succeeded where her more calculated efforts had failed. I grasped her hair with both hands, binding her head against my loins while I came in her mouth, loudly and at some length.

'What on earth's the matter?'

He was on his feet now, and walking towards us. I waved him away as Karen thoughtfully tucked me in and zipped me up.

'Cramp. It's OK, it's passed.'

A few moments later, balloon of armagnac in hand, I was listening to Dennis recount with great self-satisfaction how he'd come by the priceless spirit, when our attention was drawn by the sound of running water from the kitchen. Karen stood there filling a glass of water.

'I thought you were in bed,' said her husband.

Karen rinsed her mouth out and spat in the sink.

'Just been clearing up a bit.'

'You mean eating up! Never happy unless she has something in her mouth,' he confided to me. 'You wouldn't think it to look at her, would you?'

'Oh, I don't know.'

Karen giggled hysterically, spluttering water all over the counter.

I knew then that we were bound to go all the way, wherever it might lead, whether we wanted to or not. As for Dennis, well, after that killing him would have been a kindness, wouldn't it?

There are times, frankly, when one longs for a video camera. All these words! It's absurd, these days, like submitting a portrait in oils with your passport application. Oh yes, very tasteful, sir, a very speaking likeness I'm sure, and such tactility in the brushwork, but what we really wanted was a while-you-wait snapshot, a quid the strip of four down the machine. The kids these days don't bother with language. Even life doesn't do much for them. It's just not state-of-the-art any more, life. How can you be sure what really happened unless you can rerun it in slo-mo? To say nothing of mashing the boring bits down to a slurry of images, hosing them away with a touch of your finger.

Which is what I'd like to do now, ideally. What would you see? Karen and I on the sofa, Karen and I in the back seat of the BMW, Karen and I at the river, up the alley, down the garden, round the corner, in the pub. Our movements are furtive, frantic and compulsive. Our pleasures are brief and incomplete. Our frustrations are enormous. Because if you look closely at the background of every scene, you'll see Dennis.

Do you believe this? I didn't, and I was there. Even while it was happening to me, I couldn't believe it. Here was a woman who would go down on me in her husband's presence, but wouldn't touch me, wouldn't speak to me, wouldn't see me, unless he was there. And when I asked her why . . .

'He's my husband, isn't he?'

'Karen, you blew me. Remember? You stroked yourself off in front of me. It's a bit late to be coming on like the Angel in the House now.'

'I won't cheat on him, I don't care what you say. I just won't. I like you ever such a lot, I really do, but the bottom line is I'm still married to Denny.'

The wonder of it is I didn't kill her *then*, never mind later. It was bad enough being mercilessly teased and tantalized, without having to listen to this sort of humbug. Because what all the fine talk came down to was hard cash. If Dennis dumped her, Karen and I would be another Trish and Brian. I could quite appreciate that she didn't want that. *I* didn't want it either. I just wished she'd cut out the bullshit about cheating on Dennis. We could have saved ourselves so much time and grief.

My relationship with Karen may have been stormy, but her husband and I got on perfectly. I had finally worked out why Dennis was so keen on me. Although a barrow boy at heart, he had a yen for the finer things in life. The condition was that the transaction be conducted in whorehouse terms: he paid the trick, he called the shots. There was nothing very remarkable about him in this respect. You only have to walk into any art gallery these days to see that the real action is in the shop. Most people want to like art – they know it's good for you, or at any rate looks good on you – but face to face with a great painting they feel like gate-crashers at a Mayfair reception. Back in the gallery supermarket they can happily check out the product like so many pin-ups, wallet in hand, the big spender, in control again.

That's how Dennis felt about me. I was everything he would never be: Oxford educated, widely travelled, still more widely read, a man of the world at ease in several languages. My saving grace was poverty. With the cash to match my pretensions I'd have been a menace for our Dennis. As it was, I was cheap at the price. An extra bottle of wine and some spare grub and he had himself a harmless court jester whose sallies were guaranteed to shock or amuse. Roll up, roll up! See the Eternal Student! Watch him go through his repertoire of quotes and quips. Listen to him sing for his supper. Didn't he do well? Now watch him cycle home in the rain. He's nearly forty-two, you know, and still living in digs!

I couldn't have cared less what Dennis Parsons thought of me, of course. If his judgement rankled, it was only because it accorded perfectly with my own. It was that inner voice that made me cringe as I lay sleepless on my lumpy mattress listening to the pogoing of the bedstead against the wall next door, where my co-tenants were pursuing their nightly quest for the elusive grail of Trish's orgasm. I was merciless with myself, but the only thing I envied Dennis was his money. We thus had a perfect relationship: each of us felt that he could patronize the other.

OK, let's roll it. The hands of the clock spin round, the pages drop off the calendar, shots of punting and cricket replace those of rowing and rugby. It's summer, and the English middle class prepare for their annual pilgrimage to the land of their putative forebears. Actually Dennis and Karen's ancestors most likely dwelt among the cattle and kine in a wattle-and-daub *barrio* beneath the castle jakes, but their descendants cultivated a taste for wine and continental cooking, went riding and spent the obligatory two weeks a year in a rented villa in the Dordogne. They and the Carters were to have shared it that year with the computer analyst and his wife, but one of this couple's children was involved in an accident and they had to cancel at the last minute. Very much to my surprise, Dennis asked me if I wanted to go instead.

'It won't cost you anything except for booze and eats. Their holiday insurance will cover the rent, and since Thomas and I are both taking cars there'll be plenty of room. It's just to make up the numbers, really. It gets a bit dull with just the four of you, and of course everyone else has already made plans.'

The only problem was my work. June to September is open season for EFL students. During the winter Clive scraped by as best he could, bagging a rich brat here, a group of businessmen there, but come summer he cleaned up, netting the poor startled witless kids in droves. To pack and process them he needed staff, so our terms stipulated a minimum of two months' summer work, the understanding being that when contracts came up for renewal, priority would be given to those who had put in most time on the slime-line.

But I was no longer in awe of Clive. Had we not dined together? And had I not wiped the floor with the little squirt, conversationally speaking? Judging by his expression, Clive had not been best pleased to find me ensconced in the Parsons' sitting room that night. He didn't mind socializing with his staff as long as it was on his terms and at their expense, but to meet them as equals on neutral ground was another matter. None are so ruthlessly exclusive as those who have worked their way up from the ranks. That evening Clive could only grin and bear it, but when I told him I wouldn't be able to do the second summer course he was distinctly cool. I explained that I'd found someone to substitute for me – one of the Carter boys was looking for holiday work – but he kept making objections about unqualified staff, mentioning a notorious case a few years earlier when one malcontent teacher wreaked his revenge by teaching a group of teenage Italians that the English greet each other in the street with the phrase 'Piss off, wanker.' Half the class had to be invalided home, and Clive's name was still mud in Emilia-Romagna. I assured him that Nigel Carter wouldn't dream of playing tricks like that, but the discovery that my replacement was the son of the friend of a friend, one of his own kind, was a further blow. Nor was he at all happy with the idea of me swanning off to France with the Parsons.

'Do I detect a wick-dipping situation?'

'I *beg* your pardon?'

Contrary to what the course books say, we do distinguish between familiar and formal modes of address in English, between *tu* and *usted*. It's just that we don't do it grammatically.

'SAS training, isn't it? Who dares wins. Faint fart never won hairy lady.'

'What *are* you talking about?'

Clive ran a hand through his hair and gave me his wide-boy grin.

'Our K.P. Sauce. Nice lips, shame about the teeth. Abandon hope all ye who enter here. Asbestos sheath time.'

He kept up this sort of thing a while longer, but I refused to be provoked and in the end he had to let me go. I rushed out to a payphone to break the good news to Karen. Her reaction was less than ecstatic.

'Aren't you glad?'

'I suppose so. It's just . . .'

'What?'

She sighed.

'It isn't going to be easy, that's all.'

By contrast, her husband sounded genuinely pleased that I was coming. But of course he didn't have anything to lose, as far as he knew. Karen did, and I could quite understand her apprehension at the prospect of trying to maintain her rigid code of etiquette beneath the hot southern sun, in a festive holiday atmosphere, with both of us under the same roof twenty-four hours a day.

Personally, I didn't think she had a chance.

In anticipation and retrospect, holidays come into their own. We're all salesmen then, armed with brochures, videos and amusing anecdotes. Real time is more problematic. Looking back, that holiday in France formed a point of no return in my relationship with Karen. On the ground it felt very different: confusing, stressful, messy, tiring, incomplete, frustrating.

The villa had turned out to be a converted barn featuring renovated stone walls, distressed oak furniture, and a large resident population of rats, bats, wasps, flies, spiders and cockroaches, all of which strongly resented our intrusion into their habitat. A farm on the other side of the lane provided fresh eggs, the stench of cow shit, and a rabid mongrel roped to a tree who barked for twenty minutes whenever a car went by. The main selling point was a heavily-chlorinated pool in which we swam (except for Dennis, who didn't know how) and a variety of insects drowned. The tiled terrace, complete with metal table, coloured parasol and Ricard ashtray, commanded an extensive view of a valley studded with similar villas, similar holidays.

Thomas Carter had found the property 'through a friend', and there were some mutterings of discontent about his choice. From my point of view, though, it wasn't the house that was the problem but the people. In Oxford, Karen's insistence that our affair be conducted in public was just about feasible. At the villa it was out of the question. There were seven of us sharing the place, the Carters' eldest son and his girlfriend having invited themselves along at the last moment, and their movements were completely unpredictable. I would have needed an air traffic control centre to keep track of where everyone was at any given moment. Moreover, as the joker in the pack, the only person without a partner, I was a subject of general interest, and to make matters still worse, Lynn Carter had conceived a pallid intellectual crush on me and was always hanging around trying to engage me in conversation. 'It isn't going to be easy,' Karen had remarked when she heard I was coming. Not easy for her to deny me, I'd assumed she meant, not easy to continue denying herself. But Karen had been on these holidays before. She knew the score. Not easy for *us*, was what she'd been warning me, being so near and yet so far, so tantalizingly inaccessible to each other.

Meanwhile I saw her breasts for the first time. So did everybody else, for that matter. The rest of her was also naked to all intents and purposes. Karen didn't dress well, trying unsuccessfully to disguise her wolfish sexuality with lambs-wool pullovers and flowery skirts. But once stripped of sheep's clothing, her body made stunning sense. As I watched her turn and bend and lie back, oiled and tanned, her supple contours powered by a madness only I knew about, the idea that Karen 'wasn't my type' seemed a quaint irrelevance. I felt like a kid again, skewered by desire, every passing girl a kick in the balls, humiliated and tormented by lust. Women never understand the way it *hurts*. They've never felt the pain that lies behind all the hatred we can feel for women, our need to hurt them in return.

It soon became clear that I was not the only moth cruising Karen's flame. The Carter boy, Jonathan, known for some reason as Floss, took to spending long hours by the pool in a barely concealed state of voyeuristic arousal. He and his girlfriend Tibbs were supposedly en route to a camping holiday in Italy, but the lure of Karen's nudity proved too powerful and this project was indefinitely postponed. The shameless bitch openly encouraged her young admirer's attentions, summoning him to fetch her a drink, move the parasol, even to rub sun cream on her topless back. All quite harmless fun, no doubt – even Karen wasn't going to seduce her husband's partner's teenage son – but I was not best pleased, especially since Tibbs showed no reciprocal interest in me. An energetic girl, she spent the day swimming, jogging, cycling and hiking before retiring to their tent, blissfully ignorant that the thrust of Floss's nightly attentions was directed not at her but the succuba who also haunted my dreams.

The fact that I had an admirer in Thomas's wife just made matters worse. Not only can't you always get what you want, half the time you get what you don't need either. I certainly neither wanted nor needed Lynn Carter, a woman of uninspiring appearance and a dreadful bore to boot. Since Karen Parsons was denied me, I resorted to polishing up my French with *Thérèse Racquin*, but the moment I settled down to read Lynn would flop down near me and solicit my views on waste recycling or food additives. The only interesting thing about our colloquia was that they excited Karen's jealousy.

'You two spend a lot of time talking,' she remarked one day, materializing beside my chair as Lynn shambled off into the house in search of tea to counter the Dionysiac influence of the southern sun.

'Lynn does a lot of talking. I do a lot of listening.'

'You talk too! I saw you.'

Karen had been in the pool. Her breasts were covered now, but I could see the shape of the aureoles through the wet fabric. Water dripped from her crotch and streamed down her legs. I dared not touch her. Lynn might reappear at any moment, Thomas was rambling in the woods somewhere near by, Floss and Tibbs were playing badminton just round the corner. Ironically enough, only Dennis, sleeping off a heavy lunch, posed no threat to my desires.

'What you talk about then?' my tormentor demanded.

My eyes caressed her body languidly.

'Mrs Carter's taste runs to topics of fashionable concern. Her position is essentially uncontroversial, eschewing any extreme ideas which might conceivably add a flicker of interest to her otherwise predictable views. I sit there going "Mmm" and "Mmm?" at appropriate moments and greedily noting your every twitch and shudder down by the pool. In my mind's eye, your body is liberally smeared with a mixture of walnut oil and Nutella spread. I am slowly removing it with my tongue.'

Karen looked sullenly down at the crazy paving, where a small ant was wending its way homeward with part of a dead butterfly on its back.

'You never talk to me.'

'I understood that it was forbidden unless Dennis was within earshot.'

'You never talk like that to me!' she repeated shrilly.

I have never liked shrillness, particularly when allied to Liverpudlian vowels and a cock-teaser's soul.

'Karen,' I replied coldly, 'you and I have absolutely nothing to talk about.'

But I mustn't let you run away with the impression that I spent all my time lounging around the pool. In fact such moments of leisure were relatively rare. Although the subject was never directly mentioned, it was subtly intimated in various ways that I was beholden to the Parsons for what was after all a free holiday, and was therefore expected to do rather more than my bit when it came to chauffeuring, chaperoning, shopping and suchlike chores. What made this all the more piquant was that so far from being free, the holiday was in fact bankrupting me. 'It won't cost you anything except for booze and eats,' Dennis had told me. What he hadn't mentioned was that we would be dining out in restaurants which had attracted a nod from Michelin, a faint damn from Gault-Millau or a paragraph of wet-dream prose in a British Sunday. My share of the bill rarely came to less than £30. What with contributions to the housekeeping, the holiday was going to end up costing me the best part of £500.

There was no point in protesting, of course. The Parsons and the Carters were incapable of conceiving that anyone could be financially embarrassed by a lunch bill, particularly one which, as Dennis kept pointing out, was 'bloody reasonable'. At least I had the money, painfully scraped together with a view to eventually taking a PGCE-TEFL course to upgrade my qualifications and enable me to escape from Clive's power. Every penny of that meagre capital represented a pleasure foregone, a temptation denied, yet now I found myself wasting it on meals I didn't want with people who regarded me as a poor relative. I was thus in the interesting position of paying to be patronized, asset-stripping my future and still cutting a despicable figure. Dennis would never let me forget what he had done for me, and come September I had nothing to look forward to except another year of slavery on Clive's treadmill.

One day towards the middle of our second week there Thomas Carter returned from a trip to the local market town with the news that he had bumped into a friend of his who was staying not far away. She had invited us all to lunch the following day, he said. It cannot be simply the distortions of hindsight that cast Alison Kraemer in the role of spoiler, for the effect was to throw us all into a foul temper, heightening the existing tensions until they exploded a few days later with devastating results. The very first view of the house put a dampener on our mood. Set a short distance off a minor road, approached by a winding drive flanked by poplars, it was everyone's image of the 'little place in France', rustic but well-proportioned, manageably spacious, restrained but not austere, a Cotswold farmhouse with a French accent. That much was real estate, available to anyone with the right money, although it didn't help to discover that Alison and her late husband, a philosophy don at Balliol, had bought it back in the early sixties for less than £2,000. What no one could have bought, what wasn't for sale at any price, was Alison's way with the place. Every geranium, every chicken, every snoozing cat was in its place, like so many movie extras. But that gives the wrong impression, for there was nothing whatever contrived about the effect. If only! What a relief it would have been to be able to dismiss it all as a *Homes and Gardens* photo-call, carefully stage-managed to make visitors drop dead.

If I am to do better than merely throw up my hands and assert that Alison Kraemer was in some indefinable way 'the real, right thing', then I would suggest that the distinguishing characteristic of her ascendancy was the way she denied you any possibility of mitigating it. Most people go just that little bit too far, opening up a blessed margin of excess along which our wounded egos can scuttle to safety. With the upstart Parsons that margin was as wide as a motorway, of course, but even Thomas Carter, Nature's gentleman, couldn't help getting it ever so slightly wrong, in his case by bending over backwards to minimize his achievements and rubbish his accomplishments in order to spare you the painful comparison with your own lacklustre status. Both, in their different ways, were measuring the distance between themselves and others. Alison Kraemer simply didn't seem conscious of it.

Lunch was an omelette and a salad and cheese and bread, and it was the best meal we'd eaten all holiday. The eggs were from Alison's hens, the leaves from her garden and hedgerow, the cheese from a neighbour's goats, the bread chewy and wood-scented. Alison presided in a relaxed way, finding things for people to do, drawing them out, drawing them in. She did not offer us a tour of the house. She did not put on a tape of Vivaldi. She did not press drink on us. It was all most agreeable.

I can imagine what's going through your minds at this point. This answer is no, I didn't fancy her. Not remotely. Not then, not later, not at any time. Alison was resolutely unerotic. This had nothing to do with her looks, which were traditional English upper-middle class, soft and rounded, sweet yet sturdy. If the daemon that fired Karen had invaded Alison's body, locking its carapace to her face and swarming down her throat like some nifty parasitic alien, it would have had her coming on like Mae West in no time at all. The material was there, but Alison simply didn't project, physically. Nevertheless, she had a strong effect on me, and an odd one. In her presence, after almost a year, and in a foreign country at that, I felt I had finally come home.

When we returned to our gentrified cow-flop that afternoon everything seemed tawdry, vulgar and second-rate. More significantly, so did every*body*. All the nagging discontents that had accumulated after ten days together burst out in a series of rows that increased in intensity and duration as the evening wore on. Broken corks and ineffective tin-openers sparked off major incidents. Unforgiveable things were said, and then repeated with morbid satisfaction by the aggrieved party in the manner of beggars displaying their sores. As darkness fell and the booze took its toll, people began to drop out. First Floss and Tibbs retired to their tent to dispel this foretaste of the middle-aged grossness that awaited them in the exercise of their healthy young bodies. Lynn sat slumped for a while in catatonic gloom, scratching bubo-like mosquito bites and reading about foreign horrors in an Amnesty International magazine, and then she too turned in. Only the Parsons stuck gamely to their gory sport, circling each other like bull terriers in a pit, with Thomas and I as spectators and referees.

The nominal subject of such quarrels is of course secondary to the couple's need to hurt each other, but in this case it appeared to centre on the Parsons' childlessness. From Dennis's drunken hints that memorable evening in Ramillies Drive

I had gathered that the reason for this was Karen's sterility, so I was somewhat surprised to find her going on the offensive.

'God knows why you ever married me! It certainly wasn't for sex.'

Dennis grinned.

'You reminded me of my mother, darling.'

'Too bad you couldn't make *me* a mother.'

I held my breath, waiting for the knock-out punch. If what Dennis had told me was true, Karen was wide open. But he said nothing.

'Time we got some sleep,' said Thomas.

Dennis drained his glass.

'Right.'

'Not with me you bloody don't,' Karen told him, striding into the house. The bedroom door slammed shut behind her.

'You can have my room, if you like,' I said.

I made it easier for him by saying I wasn't tired, I wanted to stay up and star-gaze, and anyway the sofa in the living area was very comfortable. All of these were lies. What I was really counting on was finding my way to the bed which Dennis had been denied. I needn't have worried about him being too delicate to accept my offer. In fact he didn't even seem to feel that it required any show of gratitude. Why shouldn't he take my bed? I wasn't paying for it, after all.

I sat outside beneath the upturned colander of the night sky until Dennis's snores had settled into a consistent rhythm, then made my way inside the house and across the living area to the door behind which Karen lay naked. I was sure she would be waiting for me, but the door was locked. I tried calling softly, but there was no reply, and I did not dare make more noise for fear of disturbing the others. In the end I retreated to the sofa, where I spent a cold, uncomfortable and furiously sleepless night.

I was awakened shortly after dawn by Floss and Tibbs. They

were finally off to Italy and wanted to make an early start. When Dennis emerged I reclaimed my room, flopped out on the sheets impregnated with his distinctive odour and slept fitfully until just after ten, when a hot slice of sunlight which had been working its way across the bed reached my face.

The house was silent. The surface of the swimming pool was quite still, except for a set of small rings around a drowning fly. I jumped in and frothed about a bit, then went back inside and made some coffee. The silence, like the sunlight, was palpable, sensuous. I lay back on the hot canvas of a recliner and closed my eyes, soaking it in. I may have dozed off for a while.

Some time later I heard a chink of glass and looked up to find Dennis sitting at a nearby table with a half-empty bottle of chilled rosé. Lynn and Thomas had gone walking with Alison, he said. He didn't say where Karen was. We sat drinking wine and nibbling olives. Dennis was knocking the stuff back like lager, not even bothering with his usual patter. After a lunch of Roquefort sandwiches and the remains of last night's salad, he went inside to lie down. I curled up in the shade of the parasol and tuned in to the natural static.

I was aroused by a metallic clatter. To my unadapted eyes the scene looked as bleached-out as an over-exposed snap-shot. I could just make out a figure wheeling a bicycle up the drive. It disappeared round the corner of the house. I sat up, rubbing a patch of raw skin where the sun had found out my shoulder. Inside the house doors opened and closed. Pipes hummed, drains slushed, the gas geyser whomped into action. I skipped across the baking flagstones, eyes clenched against the brutal light. In the living room, Dennis lay across the sofa on his stomach, face flabbed up at an angle on a cushion, mouth gaping. I padded past him, towards the bathroom. The door was ajar. In the shower cubicle, water hissed on ceramic tile or clattered on the green plastic curtain, according to the gyrations of the nude body within.

No one of the post-*Psycho* generation likes being surprised in the shower, so I closed the bathroom door loudly behind me. The curtain twitched aside and Karen's face appeared.

'Be finished in a mo.'

I stepped out of my swimming trunks. Her expression hardened.

'I'll scream!' she warned.

I pulled back the shower curtain, exposing her fully. We stood inches apart, divided by the spray of lukewarm water, not touching, our eyes locked together with almost coital intensity. Then, without the slightest warning, just like that first time so many months before, Karen jumped me. Her legs hooked around mine, her arms clasped my neck. I'd had a soft erection before, but as our mouths collided – we hadn't even been able to *kiss* all week! – it hardened up painfully. Even now I half-suspected that she was just teasing, but in the end it was she who wriggled and twisted until we docked.

After that I don't remember very much, except that in our ecstasy the fatal word 'love' passed our lips for the first time. I don't recall which of us spoke it first, but as the end approached we were both mouthing it imploringly, like a prayer, like a spell. By then our approaching orgasms had synchronized to form a freak wave of emotion which threatened to wipe our personalities clean. Then it peaked, and we were riding it, and now the words were exultant, incantatory. Whether it was that in that heightened state I had a premonition of what was to follow, or was simply recalling Dennis's corpse-like stupor in the next room, I felt a perverted thrill, as though I were desecrating the most holy altar of all. For what we had just created was not a life but a death, and one that was to take far less than nine months to gestate.

II

'Love's dart, being barbed,' to quote a couplet familiar to every schoolchild here, 'cannot retract, only plunge more deeply i' the panting breast.' Or as they put it in the locker-room, once you're in, you're in. What happened that afternoon was the product of countless details, all of which had to be just right. If it hadn't been so hot, if there had been no row the night before, if Dennis hadn't passed out, if I'd fallen asleep, if any of the others had been there, if Karen had come back later, if she'd gone straight to the pool rather than taken a shower, if any or all of these had been the case, then intercourse would not have occurred.

Once it had, though, it was relatively simple to convince Karen that the whole thing had been inevitable. No one likes to be made to look like a mere creature of chance. It was simply too demeaning to believe that the experience we had shared had been dependent on such things as the amount of booze Dennis put away that lunchtime. We had to repossess what fate had handed us on a plate, and the only way to do this was to claim that we had willed it all along. When I broke the matter to Karen on the deck of the ferry going home, however, I sugared the locker-room logic in language more akin to the elegant formulas of your illustrious bard.

'We can't put the clock back, Karen. What's happened has happened. Now we know how it feels to be together fully, how can we be content with anything less?'

Thick Britannic cloud massed overhead. The Channel swill chopped and slapped all around. Dennis and the others were propping up the bar, Karen was supposedly selecting duty-free perfume. No one cared what I was doing.

'I know,' she sighed.

Karen Parsons never ceased to astonish me. I'd been expecting her to put up a stiff rearguard action, protesting that holidays were one thing and everyday life another, that she had only surrendered to me in a moment of weakness which she would regret for the rest of her life, and so on and so forth. I was confident I could wear her down eventually, but I certainly never expected her to come across at the first time of asking. But instead of prevaricating and procrastinating she came over all gooey, stroking my hand and squeezing my arm and saying she didn't want to lose me but she was frightened, frightened and confused, she didn't know what to do.

This was a Karen I hadn't seen before, and one I didn't have much time for, to be frank. After my belated conversion from the outworn pieties of my youth what I wanted from Karen was a crash course in greed, voracity, cheap thrills and superficial emotion. What attracted me to her was her animality. The last thing I needed was her going all human on me. Karen was a magnificent bitch, but when she tried to be human she turned into a Disney puppy: trashy, vulgar and sentimental.

When I kissed her, she twisted against me urgently, and then I understood. Actions, not words, were the way to Karen's heart. On the level of language she was frightened, confused and unsure what to do, but her body spoke loud and clear. I looked round. There was no one about apart from a couple of youths stoning the seagulls with empty beer bottles. I led Karen up a narrow companion-way marked 'Crew Only' to a constricted quarterdeck partially screened by the lifeboats hanging from their cradles. We did it on the sloping lid of a locker, our jeans and knickers round our ankles. It was what you might call a duty fuck. A pallid sun appeared like a nosy neighbour spying from behind lace curtains. The wind ricochetted about the deck, raising goose-bumps on our bare flesh. A seagull on one of the lifeboats regarded us with a voyeur's eye. It wasn't much fun, but we did it, and that was the main thing. Until we had made love again, that first occasion at the villa was in danger of becoming the exception which proved the rule. As a unique event, Karen could file it away in her snapshot album as one of the interesting things that had happened during her holiday in France. But as soon as it was repeated, its individuality merged into a series extending indefinitely into the future. By the time we returned to the bar Karen's extramarital virginity had been lost beyond recall.

Back in Oxford, I discovered that I was not only broke but unemployed. Clive Phillips, the council estate dodger who had got on his bike and into the fast lane, had fired me. Well he didn't *need* to fire me. Like all the teachers, I had a one-year contract renewable at Clive's discretion, which in my case he found himself unable to exercise.

'I don't think I can do it,' is how he put it when I phoned him. 'I just don't think it's on, quite frankly, at this particular point in time.'

The technical term for the speech-like noise that babies produce before they learn to talk is 'jargoning'. That's what I did now.

'The fact of the matter is, several of the teachers on the course you missed because of skiving off on holiday, a number of them have asked me if they can stay on for the autumn term. Comparisons are insidious, I know, but I have to say they're good. Sharp, hungry, keen as mustard. Thatcher's kids. Make me feel my age, tell you the truth! Anyway, what with you not being around and that, I felt constricted to give them a crack of the whip. Only fair, really.'

You knew this was going to happen, didn't you? 'Watch out!' you yelled as I set off on holiday. 'Look behind you!' You saw it coming a mile off. I didn't. I really didn't. When I put that phone down, I was in tears. I couldn't believe the universe could do this to me. Deep down inside, you see, I still believed that life was basically *benevolent*. I wasn't naive enough to expect the goodies to win every time, but over the long-haul, and certainly in the last reel, I sort of weakly, vaguely, wetly assumed that things would come right. I should have realized that Clive would dump me at the first opportunity, that he had in fact been looking for an excuse to do so. Clive didn't want quality or experience in his teachers. Quality expects rewards, experience makes comparisons. What Clive wanted was callow youth.

At such moments of crisis, some people resort to drink. I couldn't afford drink, so I resorted to Karen instead. The only advantage of being dumped by Clive was that it made this a lot simpler. Dennis's mornings were fully taken up meeting clients, delegating responsibilities, processing figures and accessing data. His afternoons were much less predictable, and that was also when the bulk of Karen's contact hours were timetabled. So if I'd still been giving Clive the best part of my days, occasions for dalliance would have been rare and risky. As a gentleman of leisure it was a breeze. Dennis Parsons was blessed with behavioural patterns which were etched into his brain like circuits in a microchip. When it comes to the detail of everyday life most of us just muddle through somehow, but Dennis was a Platonist. When he went to the toilet, for example, his aim wasn't just any old crap but the closest possible approximation in this imperfect world to the Eternal Idea of Dennis-Going-to-the-Toilet. This had been of something more than philosophical interest to Karen and I in our pre-coital phase, since it meant that we could count on at least a minute thirty seconds before he reappeared, or as much as three minutes forty-five seconds if we heard the seat go down for a big jobby.

Now we had moved on to bigger and better things, this predictability still stood us in good stead. At 8.57 every weekday, Dennis went out to fetch the BMW from the garage. Exactly one minute later, he backed it out on to the drive and turned round. Leaving the engine running, he then returned to the house to collect his executive briefcase and other relevant impedimenta. At 9 o'clock precisely, just as the pips ended and the news began, he got back into the car and drove off. I observed this routine the day after I learned that my services were no longer required at the Oxford International

Language College, and I knew that barring an Act of God I could set my watch by it thereafter. As soon as Dennis had roared off towards the offices of Osiris Management Services I strolled down Ramillies Drive to the Parsonage and rang the bell.

Karen came to the door in her dressing-gown. I pushed past her into the hall and closed the door behind us.

'What are you doing?'

I untied the belt of her dressing-gown and got my hands inside.

'Don't!'

To my surprise, she was wearing panties underneath her nightdress.

'Stop it! Don't! I can't!'

'You already have.'

'No, I mean I *really* can't.'

I stared at her.

'I've got my period,' she said.

'So what?'

She frowned.

'Don't you mind?'

'Not if you don't.'

To prove it, I gave her head. The effect was electric. Overwhelmed by this proof of my devotion, Karen abandoned herself as never before. The fact that we were making love in the Parsons' matrimonial bed, the sheets still warm and smelly from their previous occupant, may have had something to do with it as well. Unavoidably detained in a traffic snarl-up in Park End Street, Dennis couldn't be with us in person, but he was present in spirit, and the result was quite literally indescribable.

That morning set the pattern for our love-making. Outwardly, my habits hardly changed at all. I still left Winston Street every morning for the long cycle ride through town and up the Banbury Road. At about ten to nine I tethered the bike to a lamp-post and proceeded at a leisurely pace on foot to the Parsons'. I had to wait at most a couple of minutes before Dennis opened the back door, walked across to the garage, unlocked it, swung the door up and stepped inside. While he was out of sight of the gate I walked up the drive, opened the front door with the key Karen had given me, and ran upstairs. After that it was a race. I reduced the odds by wearing a pullover, slip-off shoes and no underwear, but it was still touch and go. The idea was to be in Karen's bed, in Karen's arms and, ideally, in Karen, by the time Dennis paused to call 'Goodbye, darling' from the foot of the stairs.

Dennis's unwitting participation in our mating was so exciting that we soon overcame any lingering doubts about the risks involved. So far from abandoning our folly, we started pushing it as far as it would go. This was made perfectly clear by our spontaneous reaction one morning when it seemed that the game was finally up. Dennis had shouted goodbye and gone out as usual, closing the front door loudly behind him. In the bedroom upstairs his wife and I were making love slowly. But instead of the genteel growl as the BMW drove off, Dennis's footsteps crunched back across the gravel to the house and the front door opened.

'Kay!'

He started to climb the stairs. Karen thrust her pelvis against me and raked my buttocks with her fingernails.

'Did you call Roger about Saturday?'

'Forgot.'

'Oh for God's sake, Karen. Have you got any idea of the number of things I have to keep track of every day? Calls to make, people to see, papers to consign? All I ask of you is to make one phone call to firm up a social event, and you can't even get that together!'

While Dennis maundered on, Karen filled her mouth with

my shoulder and neck, then broke away to shout her brief replies in as normal a voice as possible. I was working her hard by now, trying to make her lose control. With Dennis just a few feet away on the stairs, it was the sexual equivalent of Russian roulette.

'Sorry.'

'It's no use being bloody sorry, just get it done. Today, all right? This morning. Phone him at work. Have you got the number?'

'Nah!'

'Well it's in the book. Acme Media Consultants. Just don't forget again, understand?'

'Wanna!'

'What?'

There was a pause. Dennis squeaked up another couple of steps.

'Are you all right?'

'Flubbadub.'

'You sound a bit funny.'

'Gawn,' Karen squawked. 'Slate!'

This was an appeal Dennis couldn't ignore. After a moment we heard his footsteps descending the stairs again.

'Just don't forget to make that call!' he shouted from the hallway.

By now Karen's neck was a tree trunk of muscles that branched out across her face, slitting her eyes, tauting her lips, draw-stringing her throat. As the BMW finally drove away they all let go at once, releasing an answering roar that seemed to come all the way from her sex and anus, rippling up her spine and out of her gaping mouth.

'That was the best ever,' she gasped as we lay side by side, our arms and hips touching lightly. 'Whatever would we do without him?'

I had my ideas about that.

Like the brick she was, Trish had kindly offered to subsidize my share of the rent until I found another job. Thanks to her I still had a roof over my head, but this economic patronage subtly altered relations between us in a way that did nothing to improve my self-respect. I had finally hit rock-bottom, down there with the bums and dossers, unable even to pay my own way in Winston Street. The only work I could find was with Clive's main sharp-end competitor, a school offering short courses to businessmen on company accounts. They paid through the nose for 'one-to-one intensive tuition from qualified experts supported by sophisticated resources incorporating the latest technology'. The fees worked out at £25 an hour. I got £6.50, or rather less than a fiver after deductions. The director of studies, an obnoxious little shit who knew exactly where we both stood, received me in audience after I had waited for three-quarters of an hour. With an air of great condescension he told me that he was 'prepared to give me a try-out' for a few hours a week. If this was satisfactory, he might 'exploit me more extensively' in the new year.

This wasn't quite what I told Dennis when he brought the matter up.

'Clive tells me he's had to let you go.'

I assumed a sphinx-like smile, as though my present situation were part of a long-term career strategy which would yield staggering results when it finally matured.

'Let's say we agreed to go our separate ways.'

'So what are you up to now?'

'On a day-to-day basis? I've gone freelance. A little angle I've worked out. Can't say more at the moment. You know how it is.'

Dennis laughed knowingly.

'Too right. Half my clients don't even want to let me know what they're up to. Think of me as your psychiatrist, I say. If you don't tell me your dirty little secrets, how can I help you?'

He topped up our glasses.

'Got a pension plan, have you?'

I admitted that I hadn't quite got around to organizing that aspect of my life yet.

'When you're ready, just let me know. I know someone, doesn't work for us, quite independent, nothing in it for me, don't worry about that. Absolutely brilliant though. Put together a beauty for me, tailored exactly to my needs. Most plans are like off-the-peg suits, they fit everyone more or less and no one perfectly. With this bloke, it's all bespoke. Costs a shade more now, but when it's time to cash in you'll be glad you did, believe you me.'

His fingers jabbed and sketched as he explained the details. Dennis was a genuine enthusiast for financial matters. A well-made pension plan inspired in him the same emotions as an estate-bottled single-vineyard wine of a good year, and about the same amount of waffle. I had to listen for a good hour while he burbled on about variably apertured annuity options and the like. But in his eagerness to demonstrate how wonderful the scheme was, he let drop the fact that in the event of his death Karen would inherit not only the house, fully paid-off under the terms of their endowment mortgage, but also a lump sum amounting to almost half a million pounds. He was unwilling to disclose the still more impressive amount accruing on his retirement at age fifty-five, but this was of purely theoretical interest to me. I didn't really rate his chances of living that long. The fact is that I had already begun to give serious consideration to the possibility of doing away with Dennis Parsons.

I foresee that this statement will excite a certain amount of comment. Indeed, my legal representative has strongly advised me against making it. All I can say to that is that I have a higher opinion of your judgement than he has. A hundred years ago, most people would have violently and indignantly denied that they ever felt the desire to make love with anyone other than their marital partner. To do otherwise would have been tantamount to branding yourself an obscene, inhuman monster, an outcast from civilized society. Yet we now know that everyone has promiscuous sexual fantasies all the time. The people we worry about these days – the monsters, the ogres, the threats to society – are the ones who refuse to admit it.

The same applies, I believe, to the question under discussion, except that while our sexual desires are now the subject of free and frank discussion, our homicidal ones still dare not speak their name. It is striking that at a time when just about every other human value has been called in question, the value of life is still universally accepted as an absolute. Despite this, I have no qualms about admitting to men of your culture and experience that the demise of Dennis Parsons seemed to me to be jolly desirable. I just couldn't work out how to bring it about. What it comes down to is that most people, myself included, are just not up to murder. We make a big show of our moral objections, but what really puts us off are the technical ones. Most of us couldn't stick a pig either, but that doesn't stop us eating pork. If we didn't have butchers to do the necessary, we'd be vegetarians out of sheer ineptitude.

Perhaps it helps if you hate the intended victim, but I had no reason to hate Dennis. I rather liked him, in fact. My objections to his existence were purely utilitarian. I wanted to make large-scale improvements and extensions to my life, and to do so Dennis would have to be demolished. But how? It would have been easier if I could have discussed it with Karen. After all, it was in her interests as much as mine. If Dennis discovered that we were committing adultery, as he was bound to eventually, we would both end up in poverty. If he died before finding out, on the other hand, Karen got everything and I got Karen. So when she asked me where we'd be without him, my urge was to reply, 'Rich.' But despite her impeccable bed-cred, Karen was in most respects a very conventional person compared to someone like Manuela.

It's really about time we tackled Manuela, who seems to have become a recurring reference point in this story. I met her on a *colectivo* here in the capital, standing face to face in the rush-hour crowds. What sort of face did she have? She must have had one. I'm sure of that. I'd have noticed if it had been missing. No question about it, she had a face, but I'm buggered if I can remember what it looked like. I recall her bum, though, in vivid detail. It was one of those long drawn-out Latin bums, the ones that start just above the knees and peter out somewhere round about the coccyx. Apart from that she was unremarkable, short and stocky, solid-breasted, round-shouldered, with sturdy hips and ankles, not yet fat but genetically programmed for early obesity. The foreknowledge of that fate gave her flesh a deliciously transient ripeness, a brief doomed perfection on which I loved to gorge myself. Her lips were satisfyingly full, tensed to one side as though expecting a blow at any moment. I expected her to limp slightly. She didn't, but something about the way she moved confirmed my suspicion that she saw herself as damaged goods.

Even before we'd exchanged a word, I knew that she would let me do anything I wanted to her. Not that she would like it. She would hate it, and me, and herself most of all. But she wouldn't say no. Manuela was the product of a relationship between the sexes firmly grounded in the realities of the marketplace. In the last resort, anything is preferable to spinsterhood. If you can't get loved, get laid. If even that fails, get raped. That's the bottom line. There were no doubt tribes whose females thought differently, but they died out. We're the survivors. We may not be very nice, but we're here.

Manuela no doubt had her personal preferences and tastes, like everyone else, but she didn't make the mistake of thinking that they were of any importance in the matter. She knew that men were total shits, that there were no limits to their depravity, selfishness or filthy desires. But she wanted a man, so she knew she'd have to pay a price, any price. That was why I had to break off our relationship in the end. I had to live with myself for the rest of my life. I didn't want to know what I was capable of, given the opportunity she was offering me.

But while Manuela was a mirror in which I glimpsed troubling facets of my own personality, hers presented no problems. Her licentiousness was entirely passive, reflecting not her own desires but those of the man she was with. What did she want? I never asked her, but I don't imagine oral penetration figured as high on her list of priorities as it did on mine, and she could probably have done without the anal variety altogether. In fact at the risk of sounding patronizingly sexist, I would be prepared to bet that what Manuela really wanted was to get married, settle down and have lots of children. But she knew that no man was going to suggest that, not to her. The best she could hope for was that someone would come along and abuse her in various disgusting and incomprehensible ways. Then just possibly – there were no guarantees with this sort of investment – he might let her have a child in return, if only to give him someone to abuse when they both got older.

A wish for children was about the only thing Karen and Manuela had in common, apart from their interest in me. Even where the sexual acts were identical, there was an essential difference. I did them *to* Manuela, but *with* Karen. Objectively, Karen was prepared to go almost as far as her predecessor, and her eager greed more than made up for the thrill I used to get from subjecting dogged, cow-like Manuela to the same routines. But Karen's sexual behaviour was in marked contrast to her rigid conventionality in all else. For people of my generation, children of the sixties, sex and freedom are so inextricably connected that it is difficult for us to accept that someone can be totally uninhibited in bed and still have a *Reader's Digest* mentality. For Karen, though, good sex was just one of the amenities to which everyone aspired. Like videos, satellite TV, whirlpool baths and microwaved paella, it was a form of in-home entertainment, an affordable luxury to enhance your lifestyle. Karen kept *The Joy of Sex* by the bed and *The Joy of Cooking* by the stove, and approached both activities with the same brash, cheerful, unsubtle gusto. If I'd suggested to Manuela that we murder someone, she would no doubt have gone along with it as she went along with everything else I suggested. She might have drawn the line if I'd suggested murdering *her*, but even then I wouldn't have counted on her being able to break the habit of a lifetime. But with Karen such frankness was out of the question, and without her co-operation, getting rid of Dennis looked like just another of the many pipe-dreams I had indulged in over the years. But this one was to come true almost immediately, without my even lifting a finger.

The first thing to say about what happened is that it was Dennis's idea from the start. So much for the jerk-off theories put forward by the police, in which I figure as an adulterous version of George Joseph Smith – not the brides in the bath but the wittol in the water. I would be tempted to suggest that the Thames Valley CID read too many detective stories, except that I doubt whether they read at all. Late-night TV is more their speed. Wee-hours brain-numbers, junk videos from the 8-till-late take-out, that's what's formed their model of reality. The trouble with that stuff is not that it's bad, but that it's not *bad enough*. Life makes the worst video you've ever seen look like a masterpiece, and the episode I'm about to relate was well down to par in this respect.

One of the many alienating features of unemployment is that weekends lose their magic. On the contrary, I was coming to dread them. Not only was there no chance of seeing Karen, but Trish and Brian took over the house with heavy hints about housework that needed doing or how if only the back garden was cleared we could plant organic vegetables. To avoid this aggravation, I used to spend my weekends going for long walks by the river. I joined it at Donnington Bridge and walked downstream, past Iffley Lock and under the by-pass to Radley, or up to Folly Bridge and through the back-streets of Osney to Port Meadow and Godstow. In summer the water is home to huge plastic bathtubs in which unhappy families sit self-consciously picking at their dog's dinners, or pudgy louts grow raucous on tinned beer. By October, though, these wally wagons had given way to splinter-thin rowing shells in which muscular lads sweated and gasped over their oars while a weedy wimp goaded them on to still greater suffering. I always relished this sight, which closely resembled the fantasies I had harboured at school, a gang of jocks and bullies tormented by a puny swot. A different pleasure was afforded when the cox was female. Not seldom were my solitary walks enlivened by the spectacle of some plain Jane on her back in the stern of the boat, imploring the team of half-naked, sweat-drenched males to keep it coming, watch their finishing, keep it firm, keep it hard.

On exceptionally fine days I used to prefer Oxford's other river. The Cherwell is quite different from the Thames, a toy stream winding through stately parks and bucolic meadows miraculously unencroached upon by the dreary outskirts of the city. Shy and secretive, not quite real and very safe, it is an apt setting for the young enthusiasts who flock thither on summer afternoons to recreate scenes from *Brideshead Revisited*. Striking is the contrast between their artfully-poled craft, laden with wind-up gramophones, teddy bears and pints of Pimms, and the aquatic dodgems of your average punter, bearing ghetto-blasters, squealing skirt and six-packs of Australian lager. Numerous collisions result, yet – such is the nature of class conflict in Britain – no damage is done, and the respective crews pass on their way as though oblivious of each other, hiding in silence and averted eyes the embarrassment of foreigners with no common language.

Despite the sunshine, there were more ducks than punts on the river that Saturday. It was brilliantly sunny, but with an autumnal edge, perfect walking weather. I strolled along the narrow path with the anticipatory exhilaration a fine morning bestows, that quids-in glow of youth, confident that there is more and better to come. But the wisdom of age told me that this parabola of promise would not be maintained indefinitely, but would peak and then decline. A psychological astronomer, I calculated its apogee at approximately 2 to 3 o'clock, unless of course I stopped for a drink. In that case I would peak earlier and higher and then feel like hell for the rest of the day. If I wanted to be happy I should have avoided the pub altogether, or at least had nothing stronger than mineral water. I knew that. So I ordered a pint of bitter, and then another. What it comes down to is that I can't handle happiness. I don't know what to do with it.

As I walked back from the bar with my second pint I caught sight of Karen and Dennis at a table in the corner. We all made much of the coincidence, though not as much as the police, for whom it amounts to damning evidence of collusion, malice aforethought, cold-blooded premeditation and goodness knows what else. Is it likely, they argue, that both the Parsons and I should have decided, quite independently, to visit that particular pub on that particular day at that particular time? If they had bothered to get off their bums and ask some questions, they would have discovered that the pub in question was a regular haunt of the Parsons, who went there for lunch every Saturday on their way back from the supermarket. As it also happens to be the only drinker on the Cherwell until you get to Islip, the murderous conspiracies and dark plots which so excite the Kidlington Kops amount to nothing more than the fact that when I opened my curtains that morning I saw the sun shining in a cloudless blue sky and decided to go for the longest and most pleasant of the river walks open to me.

The same fact was responsible for Dennis's insistence that we should take to the water. Here the police's version of events is not merely contentious but downright absurd. To believe them, Karen and I shanghaied the shrinking Dennis on to a punt by some underhand ruse worthy of a 'once-aboard-the-lugger-and-the-maid-is-mine' melodrama. It seems almost a pity to subject these lively fancies to the stern test of verisimilitude, but I feel constrained to point out three facts. The first is that the £20 deposit required on hiring the punt was secured by means of a personal cheque drawn on Dennis's account and duly signed by him. The second is that from the

Cherwell boathouse to the point where the tragedy occurred is a distance of over two and a half miles, including a strenuous portage, and took us nearly an hour. And lastly, when we reached Magdalen Bridge, Dennis insisted on coming alongside so that he could visit an off-licence at the Plain and buy a bottle of champagne, the sale being recorded in his credit card records. If you combine these three facts with another, namely that Dennis's fortieth birthday had fallen on the previous Thursday, an alternative explanation presents itself.

As soon as I joined the Parsons, I sensed something odd about Dennis. There was a manic air to the way he ate his steak and kidney pie. He stabbed his chips like a killer and poured beer down his throat as though his guts were on fire. Christ, he's sussed, I thought. Had I left some clue behind, a stray sock not his, an unfamiliar scent on the pillow? Or had Karen fessed up? She avoided my eye. Yes, that must be it. How much had she told him? Did he know that she'd revealed his habit of farting as he came, or that I had once worn his pyjamas while she blew me? The knife in Dennis's paw was sharp and serrated, with a sturdy wooden handle. I calculated angles and distances and located the nearest exit.

My fears were groundless. Dennis wasn't jealous, he was desperate. Time's wingéd chariot was sitting on his rear bumper, flashing its headlights. Where was the fun? Where was the glitter? What had happened to his youth? His mood was an explosive mixture of maudlin self-pity and forced gaiety, the latter predominating as he got drunker. He was out to reveal a spunky, sparky, spontaneous self which had in fact never existed. No idea was too off-the-wall, no scheme too madcap. He was going to have fun if it killed him, to coin a phrase. It was a shame to waste such a lovely day sitting indoors, he announced. Nothing would do but we must go out on the river. Our attempts to talk him out of this merely provoked his scorn. What was the matter with us? Had we forgotten what it was like to be young? Did everything need to be planned months ahead? Couldn't we just throw away our Filofaxes for one afternoon and *live* a little? There were plenty of people in the pub, and some of them must have overheard Dennis's vicious mockery of our suggested alternatives, a walk on Shotover or Otmoor, for example. But the police made no attempt to contact any of them, for the obvious reason that such evidence would have been a severe embarrassment to their preconceived ideas. After all, what sort of conspiracy is it when the victim has to browbeat his supposed aggressors into taking part?

In the end we gave in. The only thing on our minds was getting it over with. Dennis had an early-evening business appointment at a client's house. He wouldn't be gone long, he assured us, but the look Karen and I exchanged confirmed that it would be long enough. First, however, we had to let the birthday boy have his fling. There had been heavy rain the previous week, and the river was high and running quite swiftly. As soon as we cast off from the boathouse Dennis started poling downstream like a maniac. We nipped along past college grounds, through glades of poplars, to the point where the river divides in two. Instead of turning back or taking the upper channel, a long cul-de-sac ending at a floodgate, Dennis beached the punt on the rollers forming a portage over the weir.

'All hands to the ropes!' he shouted merrily. 'Look lively, ye lubbers!'

He started to haul the punt up the rollers.

'What are you doing?' I called.

He glowered at me.

'Have you seen *Fitzcarraldo*?'

'What's this, the TV remake?'

He single-handedly dragged the punt to the top of the portage, where it balanced precariously.

'To the Thames!'

'Oh Denny!' Karen unwisely interjected.

Her husband swung round on her.

'Don't you "Oh Denny" me! We're going to the Thames. At least, *I* am.'

The punt tipped over and started to clatter down the rollers the other side. Dennis ran down the concrete slope and leapt in as the craft relaunched itself with a loud splash, taking on quite a lot of water. He started poling furiously away. Karen and I looked at each other, half-amused, half-disturbed. We both knew he couldn't swim.

'How much has he had?' I asked.

'Lots. Champagne for breakfast, and he's been at it ever since. He says today's the first day of the rest of his life.'

'It could be the last, the rate he's going.'

Pausing only for a brief tongue-twister – she did that very well, Karen, where your tongues circle each other tantalizingly, barely touching – we gave chase along the footpath which runs through the meadows bordering the river. We hadn't gone far before we spied the punt entangled in the branches of a willow which had collapsed into the stream. By the time we worked it loose and got aboard again, Dennis's initial fit had passed, but he was still adamant that he wanted to get as far as the Thames.

'We'll just poke our nose out into the river and then turn back. I just want to be able to say I've done it, that's all.'

I took over the poling. We drifted down past Magdalen Fellows' Garden, borne along on the current with just the odd stroke to correct our course. I was saving my energies for the return journey. At Magdalen Bridge, Dennis went ashore for more champagne, which passed from hand to hand as we negotiated the lower reaches of the river. This stretch is attractive at first, with Christ Church Meadow on one side and a cricket pitch on the other, but as it approaches the larger river the Cherwell divides into two channels separated by a flat overgrown island, deserted except for a row of college boathouses. The sun was low by now, obscured behind the wattle of leafless branches, and the air had a chilly edge. We took the left-hand cut, which runs into the Thames at an angle. The water was quite deep, and I was having difficulty finding the river-bed with the pole. I twice suggested that we turn back, but Dennis wouldn't hear of it.

When we finally emerged from the mouth of the tributary it was evident that the Thames was in flood. The surface was grooved with the tumult of adversarial currents, the turbid water lapping high at the trunks of willows and alders on the banks. I thrust the pole into the water until my arms were submerged, but in vain. The only hope was to try and paddle to the bank, then work our way back into the safe waters of the Cherwell by pulling on the branches of the shrubs and trees that overhung the river. I accordingly shipped the pole and went forward to get the paddle. Then Dennis got up.

'Why aren't you poling?'

'It's too deep.'

'Let me have a go.'

The current had already sucked us out into the centre of the river, and we were gathering speed downstream. I elbowed Karen unceremoniously aside and grabbed the paddle. Behind me, Dennis had erected the punt-pole and was now drunkenly trying to lower it into the water. As I turned, my shoulder struck the pole, pushing it sharply to one side and knocking him off-balance. Karen instinctively got up to try and help, which made the punt wobble even more wildly. Clasping the pole to his chest, Dennis teetered back and forth, then slowly fell over backwards into the water.

At least, that's our story. If you believe the Thames Valley CID – not the account they gave at the inquest, when the events were still fresh in everyone's minds, but the one they came up with in the months following my return to this country – then having lured Dennis on to the river and dosed him with draughts of spiked bubbly, Karen and I went 'One, two, three' and heaved him overboard. We then hit him over the head with the punt-pole and paddled off out of range of his piteously outstretched hands, cackling demonically as he went down for the third time.

I have made it a point of honour to spare you moral blackmail of the 'Do you honestly suppose for a single moment that I would be capable of stooping to such beastliness?' variety, and I shall not waver even at this supreme moment. Nor shall I again urge the objections cited above to the 'murderous conspiracy' theory. I simply wish to point out that if it is supposed that Karen Parsons and I embarked that afternoon with the intention of drowning her husband, why did we wait till we had reached a point where our criminal acts were overlooked by at least fifteen witnesses? We had already negotiated long stretches of the Cherwell where we were completely hidden from view. Why didn't we do the foul deed there, rather than risk facing a rugby team of accusing fingers at the inquest? Which in turn brings us to the most remarkable fact of all, namely that so far from corroborating the police's recent claims, the witnesses they located and interviewed at the time signally failed to mention any suspicious behaviour whatsoever. Five of them, consisting of a family and friends out for a walk along the towpath, described only a scene of 'noisy confusion' which they ascribed to high-spirited students horsing about. An elderly man bird-watching in Iffley Fields recognized that we were all drunk, and that when Dennis fell overboard Karen and I panicked with tragic results. Despite being equipped with an excellent pair of binoculars, however, he made no reference to any signs of murderous intent on our part.

But the most striking evidence came from an Oriel Eight out

training. As we drifted across the river, their cox first shouted a warning, then ordered the crew to angle their oars to avoid fouling the punt. As a result their practice run had to be aborted, and we thus had their full and indignant attention as we came alongside. This happened to be the very moment when I dropped the punt-pole into the water, the idea being that Dennis could grab hold of it and I would then pull him in. Unfortunately the pole was heavier than I had thought, I misjudged the angle and the thing came down on Dennis's head. This incident has since been described, by the tabloid whose lurid prose I regaled you with earlier, as 'a pitiless and cynical *coup de grâce*'. One hesitates to dispute this judgement, coming as it does from a source with such impeccable credentials in pitiless cynicism, but the fact remains that the young men of Oriel didn't see it quite that way. Not that my character emerged unscathed from their testimony. 'Frenzied and totally ineffective bumbling', 'drunken hysteria' and 'blind panic' were some of the less offensive phrases mentioned in the coroner's court. Out on the river, their language was less guarded, and we were treated to a variety of epithets which no Merton man, I hope, would have allowed past his lips in mixed company. But the vital point is what was *not* said. I may have been called a pillock and a dickhead, but no one asked why I had tried to brain my companion. It is also noteworthy that the Oriel crew – who may be presumed to have known a thing or two about rowing, given their record in recent years – also failed to remark on the fact that I or Karen were allegedly paddling *away* from the drowning man. What they saw, as one put it, were two people who weren't up to boating in the bath, never mind on the Thames in spate.

A more substantial objection is why neither Karen nor I had dived in to try and save Dennis. At the time this criticism was directed at her rather than at me. Karen was not only Dennis's wife but also a physical education instructor who could, as the coroner facetiously remarked, have swum to her husband's rescue using either the crawl, breast-stroke, back-stroke or butterfly. This betrays a complete lack of understanding of the actual circumstances. The very newspapers which subsequently pilloried our 'cowardice – or worse' are constantly bemoaning the deaths of people who rashly attempt to rescue swimmers in distress, only to perish themselves as well. Dennis was thrashing about so vigorously that even a trained lifeguard would have had difficulty in retrieving him. To throw ourselves into those turbulent waters and then be unable to regain the punt would have put paid to any hope of rescuing Dennis. Of course it is easy to argue now, with the benefit of hindsight, that Dennis was doomed anyway, but it didn't appear like that at the time. When he first fell in, I remember shouting at him impatiently to stop fooling about. It seemed inconceivable that a mere punt trip could end in death. Even after the pole struck Dennis on the head and he disappeared from sight, I remember thinking that he would pop up at any moment alongside the boat, like a coot. If either Karen or I had had any idea that it was possible for someone to drown so quickly, we would no doubt have thrown caution to the wind and dived in. Not that this would have made the slightest difference to the outcome. The simple fact of the matter is that we should never have been there in the first place.

The coroner concurred. In his verdict, he called for consideration to be given to regulations restricting punts to the relatively safe waters of the Cherwell and to review the conditions under which they could be hired. 'It is striking,' he concluded, 'that while strict laws govern the use of motor vehicles, anyone may hire a marine craft and then, with no experience whatsoever, without a life-jacket, unable to swim and in a state of advanced inebriation, attempt to navigate a busy and treacherous public waterway. As long as this state of affairs continues, tragedies such as this will necessarily recur.'

No policemen leapt to their feet, protesting at this travesty of justice. Indeed, the police treated us both with the greatest sympathy and consideration from the moment I rang them from a callbox on the Abingdon Road. The river authorities contacted the lock-keeper at Iffley and it was there that Dennis's body was eventually recovered later that evening. Karen was at home by then, under sedation.

The next time I saw her was at the crematorium. Thomas and Lynn were there too, to say nothing of Roger and Marina, if that's her name, and the rest of them. Clive also attended, visibly gleeful that he had spared the school any undesirable publicity by unloading me in the nick of time. The only other person I recognized was Alison Kraemer. She expressed her condolences briefly and tactfully, in marked contrast to some of those present, who couldn't quite bring themselves to approach the grieving widow but were quite prepared to quiz me at length about the details of Dennis's last hours. To keep them at bay, I engaged Alison in close conversation. It turned out that she was a freelance editor for OUP, with a daughter in her early teens and a seven-year-old son for whom she had been caring single-handedly since her husband's untimely death. I found it supremely restful to talk to her, and when we finally parted I told her I hoped we might see each other again some time. A lanky cleric oozing good intentions and bad faith then launched into an address that was squirmingly anxious to avoid giving offence to persons of any or no belief while still suggesting that, who knows, there might after all be, you know, *something* out there. While we all coughed and looked at our shoes in embarrassment, the gleaming casket containing Dennis's mortal remains was spirited away to the nether regions of the crematorium.

Afterwards we trooped outside and stood awkwardly saying our good-byes. I sniffed deeply. There seemed to be a new aroma in the air. A sweaty, gamey, meaty nose, I thought, drying out a touch at the finish, not much body to it.

It was probably my imagination.

The media were later to make much of the discovery that a few weeks after Dennis Parsons's death, Karen and I had spent a weekend at the same hotel in mid-Wales. 'Nights of Passion in Rhayader' remains my favourite headline, although 'Drowning Duo's Dirty Welsh Weekend' runs it close. When journalists resort to this sort of thing you can be sure that the facts are drab in the extreme, and believe me, they don't come much drabber than our Bargain Weekend Break at the Elan Valley Lodge. The only interesting thing about it is that it happened at all.

When I say that I saw Karen at the funeral, I mean that quite literally. I *saw* her. She saw me too, no doubt, but that was it. We didn't exchange a word, or even a glance. With Dennis's demise our intercourse, as they say in the classics, had become problematic. Not that it seriously occurred to either of us that anyone might think we had murdered Dennis. It's difficult to get across to those who didn't know him just how outlandish this idea seemed. Dennis Parsons was so deeply and intrinsically boring that it was almost impossible to imagine anything as exciting as being murdered ever happening to him. Nevertheless, it clearly wouldn't do for Karen and I to be seen together immediately afterwards. If I'd been seen popping in and out of Ramillies Drive, tongues would inevitably have begun to wag. Legally, though, we were in the clear. Even the insurance adjusters, who proved infinitely more assiduous than the police, finally agreed that Dennis's death fell into one of the approved categories listed in the small print.

It never occurred to me that Karen might be grieving for her late husband. I don't want to sound unduly negative, but I simply couldn't see what there was to mourn. There was a photograph of Dennis on one of the wreaths at the funeral, and I didn't even recognize it. I don't think I'd ever really looked at him, to be honest. I didn't need to. I knew he was there, and that if I tried to move in a certain direction I'd bump into him. Now that he was gone I supposed that the crooked would be made straight and the rough places plain. But in death, every wally shall be exalted. Dennis's absence proved much more potent an obstacle than his presence had ever been.

My first inkling of this came when I phoned Karen shortly after the funeral.

'I want to see you.'

Silence.

'When can I come round?'

Silence.

'Karen?'

Blubbery sobbing, followed by a loud sniff.

'Never.'

'What?'

A longer silence, and more damp hankie noises.

'We killed him.'

'For Christ's sake!'

Years abroad had made me wary of what I said on the telephone. While I was in the Gulf, one of our teachers vanished temporarily after a call to a colleague in which he had made disparaging remarks about members of the local royal family.

'We did!' she insisted dully.

'Karen, it was an *accident*.'

'If only we could have had a child. Then at least something of him would be left.'

'I know it's difficult to accept what has happened,' I said in an unctuously compassionate tone. 'In a way it would be easier if someone *had* killed him. At least then there would be a reason. That's why people invent gods, even vicious, vengeful ones, to account for all the awful things that happen.'

'There is a God, and He's punishing me for our sin, punishing me through Denny.'

'Look Karen, no one is sorrier than I am about what happened. It was a horrible tragedy, a cruel waste, absurd and unnecessary. But having said that, what about *us*? It's been nothing but Dennis, Dennis, Dennis for days now. What do I have to do to get some attention, jump in after him?'

She hung up on me. This was all to the good. The more my words hurt, the sooner she would acknowledge their truth. But I wasn't prepared to sit patiently on the sidelines while this process took place. More importantly, I couldn't afford to. As an attractive young heiress Karen might quickly become the target of unscrupulous bounty hunters. It was no use trying to resolve anything over the phone, though. My hold over Karen was physical, not verbal. If the magic was to start working again, I had to get her alone and in person for a few days. The trip to Wales was simply my first idea. I sent her a brochure I had picked up at a travel agent, together with a bouquet of roses and a letter. I was worried about the strain and stress she must be under, I said. What we both needed was to get away for a couple of days, to go somewhere peaceful, relaxing and free of any association with the past, where we could work out where we stood.

Much to my surprise she agreed, on condition that we had separate rooms and made our own travel arrangements. This meant I faced a five-hour train journey, with two changes, and then – having retrieved my bicycle from the guard's van – a fifteen-mile uphill ride. It would no doubt have been quite attractive in fine weather, and the same applied to the countryside around the hotel, an imposing pile by Nightmare Abbey out of a Scotch baronial shooting lodge. As it is, my memories of the weekend are dominated by the image of two diminutive figures crouching in the nether reaches of a vast vaulted interior, their sporadic and tentative remarks amplified by the vacant acoustics into portentous gobbledegook. The other guests are all asleep, or possibly dead and stuffed. The staff are under a spell. Time has come to a standstill. Outside, a soft rain falls ceaselessly.

In my letter I had told Karen that the purpose of the trip was to discuss the future of our relationship. I quickly discovered that in her view it didn't have one, and that the only reason she had agreed to see me was to get this across once and for all. As far as she was concerned, she told me over and over again, we were responsible for Dennis's death. If she hadn't yielded to a guilty passion then she would have been a better wife to Denny. The implication was that with a bit more happening in the sack, hubby wouldn't have felt he was getting past it and tried to prove his virility by punting up the north face of the Thames.

'If I'd been more, you know, responsive and that, then Denny'd still be here today. And the only reason I wasn't is, well, because of us.'

I assaulted this position from every angle, ranging from thoughtful analyses of the male mid-life crisis, its nature and origins, to sweeping *ad absurdum* dismissals in which I demonstrated that by the same token Trish and Brian were equally culpable, because if they'd gone out for the day I would have stayed at home and we would never have met in the first place. But all my wit and wisdom were wasted on Karen's one-track mind. Just as the inhabitants of the *barrios* here defend their pathetic shanties to the last, defying the well-meaning efforts of the authorities to relocate them, so the poor in intellect cling to whatever feeble idea they have been able to fashion out of the odds and ends they have foraged. Be it never so humble, there's no place like home.

'That's the way I see it,' was Karen's doggedly repeated bottom line, 'and nothing you say is going to make me change.'

Fair enough. I'd never set much store by rational argument where Karen was concerned. It was body language I'd been counting on to win her round. Given our record, I'd imagined that it would be impossible for us to spend a night under the same roof without spending it together. Not only didn't this happen, however, but it never seemed remotely likely to happen. To my dismay, the sexual charge between us had disappeared as though a switch had been thrown. When Karen and I used to feast on each other's bodies, Dennis was the unseen guest at the table. Even when he wasn't there, we conjured him up, putting on his rank, night-sweated pyjamas, recounting his doings and sayings. Dennis was our ribbed condom, our french tickler. He made sex safe and savoury at the same time. Now he was dead, it would be too dangerous and too dull.

So far from convincing Karen she was wrong, by the Sunday afternoon I had come round to her point of view. Most couples, however fossilized their relationship, have some interest in common, if it's only cooking or travel or pets. We had nothing. We were like creatures so different that their scales of vision are incompatible. To myopic Karen my world was a featureless, threatening blur, while for me hers was a chaos of microscopic inanity. To seduce Dennis's swinging wife had been a welcome compensation for my social and financial humiliations, but to lay siege to his frigid, guilt-stricken widow was a very different matter. What on earth was I doing pursuing this common gym mistress instead of a woman like, say, Alison Kraemer?

Once this sunk in, my manner changed abruptly. No longer did I bother to appear gracious, sympathetic or understanding. On the contrary, I told Karen that she was quite right. We had no future together. The weekend had been a failure – or rather a success. Having settled our separate bills, we walked out to the car park together. For the first time that weekend the rain had stopped, and although it was still overcast we could make out something of the beauties of the landscape. Suddenly it came home to me with tremendous force that this was my last chance, the very last of all the countless chances I had thrown away just like this, because I had been too lazy or too proud to exploit them properly. If I squandered this one there would be no more. The door to a BMW would never beckon again. I would be on my bike for the rest of my life, stuck on the stopping train to nowhere. This wasn't just another tiff we were having. We wouldn't kiss and make up later. There wouldn't be any later, unless somehow, at the eleventh hour, I freed Karen from her sterile remorse. But how could I achieve in a few minutes what I had failed to accomplish after hours of trying?

'Let's go for a walk,' I said.

She shrugged listlessly.

'What for?'

'I've got something to say to you.'

'You can say it here.'

I felt as though I were seducing her all over again. She wanted to, she really did, but she needed to be made to feel she could, or rather that she couldn't *not*, that it was out of her hands, that she couldn't help herself.

'Come up to the lake with me. It's not far.'

In view of the significance of the Elan Valley in later developments, it would perhaps be as well to sketch the local topography briefly at this point. Set on the fringes of the Cambrian Mountain chain, the valley was flooded to satisfy the thirst of Victorian Birmingham and incidentally create a picturesque 'feature', a series of artificial lakes connected by dramatic waterfalls. A century later, to eyes hardened by exposure to the brutalities of reinforced concrete, the dams and weirs seem part of the landscape from which their stone was taken. Only the water itself, its wildly fluctuating level carving a swathe of devastation along the shore, betrays the deception.

We walked along a path which wound attractively through a pine forest and round a spur of the hillside to a viewpoint overlooking the lower lake, which is spanned by a narrow bridge across which a minor road leads up into the mountains. After we had admired the panorama for some time in silence, I said, 'It's lovely, isn't it?'

'Mmmm,' Karen agreed vaguely.

'Really makes you feel life's worth living.'

She was silent.

'Believe me, Karen, I understand how you feel. This is an appalling tragedy which will haunt us for the rest of our lives. We shall never be again as we were. Dennis is gone, and we are the poorer.'

She looked away, biting her lip.

'But in the midst of death, we are also in life. If it was wrong for us to acknowledge our love while Dennis was alive, it would be even more wrong to deny it now. If we have been indirectly responsible for a death, there is only one way we can make amends.'

She frowned.

'What do you mean?'

'First of all, let me ask you something. On the phone the other day you said that if only you and Dennis had had children then something of him would have survived. Now he told me, that night we got so drunk, that it was because of you that it hadn't happened. Is that true?'

Her head shook minimally.

'We had tests done. They said it was some illness he had when he was young. Denny never accepted that, though. He always claimed it was me.'

'Did you consider using a donor?'

'You mean like they do with cows? Some bloke you never

meet jacks off with a copy of *Penthouse* and then they pump his come up you with a syringe? No thanks, I'm not that desperate. It's not just the baby, you know. It's *whose* baby.'

'So what were you going to do?'

'I tried not to think about it. I suppose I hoped Dennis might, you know, get better. It happens, sometimes. We still had plenty of time, or so I . . .'

She broke off, wiping her eyes.

'That was one reason why I tried to stop us, you know, going all the way,' she went on. 'You thought I was on the pill, of course, that's why you never used a sheath or anything. But I wasn't. There was no need, you see. Not with Dennis. And with you . . .'

Tears started to roll down her cheeks.

'That was the worst thing I did. I mean trying, well not trying, but I wasn't . . . I mean, if I'd got pregnant he might have thought it was his, that he'd got better somehow. He'd have been ever so proud! And I still would have known the real father, known him and loved him. But it was wrong, terribly wrong. That's why I've been punished through his death. And the worse thing is that now there's nothing I can do about it. It's too late!'

I put my arm around her in a chaste, consoling embrace.

'It's never too late, Karen.'

'What do you mean?' she sobbed softly.

'You can still have that child. With me. If it's a boy we'll call him Dennis, and if it's a girl, Denise. Let us return life for death, Karen, good for evil. We have caused enough harm by our thoughtless, irresponsible, selfish behaviour. Now let's strive to live for others. This is a turning-point in my life. It may have come too late to save your husband, but I beg of you, Karen, spare the life of our unborn baby!'

This seems to you exaggerated, melodramatic, in poor taste? I quite agree. But it was a question of horses for courses. My speech was directed at Karen Parsons, and whatever reservations you or I may have about it, I can assure you it went down a treat with its target audience.

'Do you really mean that?'

There were still tears in her eyes, but for the first time that weekend there was colour in her cheeks as well. I'll spare you my reply. If you found the opening pitch a bit over the top, the follow-up would gross you out completely. But Karen lapped it up and came back for more.

'I never thought . . . I mean, it was great in bed and everything, but I thought that was all it was. I thought all I was to you was just a good lay.'

I smiled ruefully.

'You were certainly that. The best I've ever had. But that was never *all* you were, Karen. It wasn't just the sex. There was always something else as well.'

Overcome by emotion, she turned away, gazing out over the black waters of the reservoir. Then a violent shiver convulsed her. At the time I assumed she was thinking of Dennis, but I now wonder if she had a premonition of her own fate. At all events, it only lasted a moment. Then she looked back at me and smiled a brave, convalescent smile, not yet well, but on the mend, cured in spirit.

'Let's go home,' she said.

And home we went, in the BMW, my bike tucked away in the capacious boot. While she drove, Karen talked non-stop about her childhood, her parents, her hopes, her dreams, her problems. In turn I told her a little about my own background, as though we were out on a first date.

I didn't tell her about my vasectomy.

The vasectomy dated from 1980, when a girl I'd been sleeping with told me she was *embarazada*. So was I. The expectant mother was sixteen years old and one of my students at the school in Barcelona where I was five months into my first teaching job. My contract was promptly terminated with extreme prejudice. The girl's family paid for her to fly to London to get an abortion. I went by train.

After that I was blacked by the quality schools, but I soon landed a job for the rest of the year with a cowboy outfit in Italy who needed a replacement teacher in a hurry. Before going, though, I had it out with my dick. This wasn't the first time it had got me into trouble, but I intended to make damn sure it was the last. Let's face it, those who can, have fun. The others, too poor in pocket or spirit, have children. Any parent who says he enjoys it is a liar. You might as well say you enjoy being crippled. Karen saw things very differently, of course. She just couldn't wait to go through with the whole messy, life-destroying business. The absurd excitement she displayed at the prospect of becoming a mother confirmed my worst opinions of her. Feminism has been wasted on women like that.

The most amusing thing about the period of my engagement to Karen was the degree of role reversal involved. Not only were we going through the timid rituals of conventional courtship after a six-month diet of take-away sex, but I was the one who insisted that it stay that way until we were legally united. It's incredible what an aphrodisiac the prospect of motherhood can be for some women. Once the magic word 'baby' had been spoken, Karen was in a permanent state of arousal. Sex with me was no longer a sin but the way to salvation. *Magna Peccatrix* was about to be beatified as *Mater Gloriosa*. All she needed was a touch from my magic wand.

That was all very well, but I had my own position to consider. You know what women are like. They'll promise you the earth to get you to come across, then treat you like dirt once they've satisfied their maternal cravings. I couldn't afford to risk being left on the shelf once Karen had had her way with me. Her desires were my only hold over her, so despite her frantic pleas I refused to go any further than finger-fucking until she had signed on the dotted line.

When the formalities finally took place, it was a very brief ceremony. Our solicitors had prepared the necessary 'instruments', and all Karen and I had to do was 'execute' them, but when we emerged into the mild sunshine of Beaumont Street twenty minutes later, my life had been changed out of all recognition. I entered the premises an unemployed teacher living on charity in a rented two-up, two-down off the Cowley Road. Now I was a man of property, the joint owner of a large house in North Oxford, with investments so extensive I had no detailed idea of their scope and access to current and deposit accounts totalling well into six figures. I felt all weepy and emotional as Karen and I drove home together. Happy endings always make me cry.

Two days later I drove the BMW back to Winston Street and cleared my room. Trish and Brian were out at work. I left a cheque for the amount Trish had loaned me, plus a month's rent in advance and a brief note saying that I was going to stay with an unspecified friend in North Oxford. I didn't mention my marriage. At my suggestion, Karen didn't tell any of her friends either. Although we both knew that we were acting from the best possible motives, I argued, other people were always ready to place a malicious interpretation on their neighbours' doings and it might therefore be better to wait before breaking the news.

Karen welcomed this as further evidence of my tact and seriousness, which she ascribed to a sense of responsibility at the prospect of becoming the pater of a tiny foetus. I was amazed and terrified at the change I had so casually brought about in her. I felt like Frankenstein, quailing before the monster I had created. The Karen I had known a few months earlier, a simple, straightforward creature with healthy appetites, had been metamorphosed by my spells into a raving obsessive who regarded the spawning of offspring not as a lowest-common-denominator activity like excretion but as a moral and creative achievement on a par with, say, painting the Sistine Chapel ceiling. All we had to do was bump our uglies.

No problem, you might think, given our track record in that particular event. And as far as Karen was concerned you'd be right. There were changes of style and technique, of course. Oral sex was definitely not in favour any more. This and all the other alternative orifices fell into disuse. Henceforth all traffic was routed down the main line. Even once we were acceptably coupled, though, the differences were obvious. Before, Karen had made love with hysterical urgency, a compulsive satisfying her greed. Our sex was anarchic, sufficient to itself, without perspectives. But that was in the past. Now the expression on Karen's face as she lay beneath me, knees pulled up to her chin to facilitate maximum penetration, was of a recent convert taking communion. Rapt, ecstatic, she willed me on to ever-greater feats of ardour. It wasn't just impregnation she was after, it was *quality* impregnation. She might have been wearing a sign like those you see in car windows: GIVE MY CHILD A CHANCE – DON'T PULL BACK.

In principle I was quite prepared to oblige. I may have my faults, but ungratefulness is not one of them. Karen had done her bit for me and I would have been more than happy to reciprocate. But though the spirit was willing, the flesh was weak. It wasn't a question of impotence. I just couldn't come.

In the old days this would have been all to the good. There

was nothing Karen had liked better than being taken on a guided tour of three or four climaxes. But the new Karen had become sickeningly selfless in bed. It was no longer *her* orgasms that excited her, but mine. Her own afforded her nothing but a transient thrill, but mine supplied another dose of semen to chuck at the uterine wall where, sooner or later, she reckoned, some of it must stick. Marathon bonking was therefore frowned upon. What the market demanded was frequent and copious ejaculation. And since the supplied response was lacking, I had to fake it.

The simulated male orgasm has attracted very little attention by comparison with its female equivalent, not because it isn't as common, but because it's in no one's interest to publicize the fact. Both sexes like the idea that women pretend, men because it confirms their suspicion that their partners are basically frigid and devious manipulators, women because it gives them a delicious sense of power to think that the delirium which men fondly ascribe to their virile prowess is no more than a hollow civility, like laughing at Grandpa's jokes. By contrast, neither party has any desire to suggest that men might do the same thing. We males naturally reject the idea that we're not at all times ready to cream anything that moves as a monstrous slander on our virility, while women certainly don't want to think that creatures whose sexual urges are so undiscriminating that they have been known to rape grannies and animals and even *corpses*, for God's sake, could possibly find them so unattractive that they need to simulate orgasm.

But it's a funny old business, sex. In order to keep an erection long enough to fake orgasm, I had to imagine that I was making love to Karen. I *was*, of course, but that wasn't enough. I needed the fantasy angle. I needed to call up the heroic days when Dennis was still around, and we were young and carefree, bonking our brains out while he shouted banalities from the foot of the stairs. In Dennis's presence I became an outlaw once again, and Karen my moll. When he was there we were Bonnie and Clyde, now he was gone we were Blondie and Dagwood. Or rather, now he was gone, *I* was Dennis.

If I'd been smarter, or less vain, I might have realized that this meant that my former role was now vacant.

The news that Karen and I were married was made public at a buffet brunch given by Thomas and Lynn Carter to which we had been invited – or rather Karen had been invited, and had asked if it would be all right to bring me along. Thomas and Lynn owned a spread on Boars Hill, an annexe of Oxford closely resembling the WASP's nest suburbs of Tom's native Philadelphia. It spelt money, but in a style which brought the denizens of North Oxford out in flushes of embarrassed superiority. It was a further proof of Thomas Carter's blissful innocence that he evidently had no idea that his swimming-pool, tennis court, fitted kitchen and high-tech appliances were as contemptible to the class whose values he so admired as the Parsons' van Gogh prints and Dacron three-piece suite. He blithely led his guests to the picture-window framing the classic 'dreaming spires' view of the city, pointing out the various features, distinguishing the cathedral from St Mary's, Merton from Magdalen, the fantastic lacework of All Souls from the monastic sobriety of New College. 'He really knows his Oxford!' he thought we thought, while every enthusiastic word and expansive gesture in fact revealed that the poor bugger hadn't a clue about the place.

The gathering was a complex affair, socially. A representative sampling of Osiris Management Services' clientele was there, beefy ballocky blokes who prized the rugby scrum of life as much as an opportunity for putting the boot in as for winning the ball. To them, the occasion was just another hospitality tent, an opportunity to claw back some of Thomas's fees by consuming as much of his food and drink as possible. They ganged together round the buffet, whingeing about business and interest-rate hikes, doing gamesmanship numbers on each other, exchanging racy stories and tall tales and laughing fit to bust their considerable guts. These hearties certainly weren't aware that Thomas was wrong-footing himself. If they had any reservations about the amenities he was so tastelessly flaunting, it was only to ask themselves what his profit margin must be if he could afford this stuff.

After some time one became aware that members of a quite different clan were also to be found scattered in little clusters throughout the open-plan living area. Both sexes were clad in essentially masculine garments which looked as though they had been in the family for generations: waxed jackets, sensible shoes, chunky pullovers, indestructible tweeds and cords. They came complete with miniature versions of themselves, flawlessly self-assured offspring called Ben, Simon, Emma and Kate, who had been breast-fed dry sherry and even drier wit. Their demeanour was one of fastidiously ruffled *pudeur*. Identifying one another like fellow nationals grounded amid alien hordes in a foreign airport, they exchanged glances dense with judgement. Poor Thomas! He had installed the obligatory Aga cooker, but also a microwave, an indoor barbecue, and a 24-inch remote-control colour television. He drove the statutory Volvo estate, but left it parked outside the two-car garage beside his wife's Honda hatchback and his son's Kawasaki motorcycle. Wince! Cringe!

I was busily listening to these subliminal hisses of disapproval when Alison Kraemer appeared at my elbow. Within minutes we were discussing a recent television series adapted from a classic novel and disagreeing about why it had been so unsatisfying. I suggested that the subtlety and depth which characterize good fiction must inevitably be lost in any version acceptable to the *box populi*. Alison signalled her appreciation of this pun, but took a neo-McLuhanite line herself, arguing that since actuality was the essence of the medium, watching a classic novel on television was as odd as reading it in a newspaper. I'm quite sure she didn't believe a word of this, but in Oxford it is considered good manners to take an adversarial position so as to generate an interesting conversation and allow both parties to display their intelligence, knowledge and eloquence. Once this had been achieved, and we had given each other that little nod of recognition with which one acknowledges an intellectual equal, I moved on to the question that really interested me, which was how Alison came to know Thomas Carter in the first place.

'A management consultant? It doesn't seem quite your . . .'

I left the phrase hanging.

'Oh, it's got nothing to do with *business*,' Alison replied with a laugh that ever so gently reprimanded me for my mercantile preoccupations. 'We make music together.'

There was, as they say, no answer to that – or at least none that I was prepared to touch with a barge-pole.

'He's easily the best of us, technically,' Alison went on. 'He can sight-read almost anything we do.'

'And what *do* you do?'

'Sixteenth century, mostly. Byrd, Tomkins, Morley, Wilbye, Weelkes, some Palestrina and Victoria.'

The North Oxford brigade had by now formed a coherent clique at one end of the room, separated by a buffer zone of bare carpet from the jolly tradesmen.

'And these people . . .?'

This time Alison refused the bait, merely gazing at me with her large, bovine eyes. I felt an enormous sense of peace and security in her presence. It was like going for a walk in a Constable painting.

'What brings *them* here?'

'I really can't speak for all of them. Some will be friends they've made through Ralph and Jonathan, I expect. Dragon School mafia, you know. Quite a few are from the madrigal group, or people Tom's got to know through it.'

I nodded.

'And what about you?' she said.

'Sorry?'

'What brings *you* here?'

Before I could answer, a shrill peal of laughter cut through the air like fingernails dragged down a blackboard. I looked round to find Karen standing in the centre of a group of businessmen who were eyeing her up and down in a blatantly sexual way. One leaned forward, his face almost touching hers, and made some comment to which she responded with another shriek of mirth.

Instantly my position became hideously clear. In my analysis of the social and intellectual divisions at the party, it had never occurred to me to question where I stood myself. I had included myself in the North Oxford set as of right, a right seemingly confirmed by the way Alison had approached me and the ease with which we had conversed. Just like Thomas, I could sight-read anything she threw at me. I had completely forgotten Karen until her squeal of laughter reminded me of the answer to Alison's question. Why was I there? I was there because Karen had brought me.

Alison stood waiting for me to reply, but I couldn't. I was completely paralysed by the realization of what I had done. I had delivered myself over, bound head and foot, to the yahoos. Soon Alison would know, the Carters would know, everyone would know, and once they knew they would cut me dead. My clever chat would avail me nothing in the face of the fact that I had chosen to ally myself with a woman who practically peed her pants at some salesman's blue jokes. I just hoped Karen wouldn't go any further, that she wouldn't get so drunk that she tried to mount some leering admirer who happened to step on her toe by mistake.

My speculations were cut short by the appearance of Karen herself at my elbow.

'You've been talking a lot,' she said aggressively.

'And saying very little, I'm afraid,' replied Alison, effortlessly defusing the situation.

Karen glared at her.

'Has he told you we're married?'

She was perceptibly drunk, and for a moment Alison hesitated, as though she might be joking. But the steely 'So fuck you, smarty-pants, 'cos he's mine' look in Karen's eye soon put paid to that idea. Alison stood looking us both up and down, the gold-digger and the whore. Then she stage-coughed and muttered gracelessly, 'Indeed?'

This was the black cap. If even Alison Kraemer's perfect manners could not cope with the news, then our marriage must be an intolerable scandal. Within moments, Alison had found a pretext to excuse herself. All I wanted to do was to get away, but Karen refused point-blank. When I insisted, she flew into a rage, and the newly-weds had a very public row in the course of which I was termed a wet-rag and a killjoy who was too old to have fun any more. One of the businessmen sniggered and whispered a comment to his neighbour, who burst into raucous laughter. 'Are they the hired entertainers, Mummy?' a North Oxford brat inquired in piercing tones. I had achieved the remarkable feat of uniting the two factions at the party in mockery of me. Gown despised me for selling my soul to a shrill shallow shrew, town for being an old fart who couldn't satisfy his frisky young mate. I hadn't a friend in the room. What Karen didn't realize, in her moment of cheap triumph, was that she didn't either.

As the months passed, the fact of our social isolation gradually began to sink in. One by one the Parsons' former friends and acquaintances found reasons not to accept our invitations, and although they claimed to be anxious that we should 'get together some time', that time never came. I ran into Trish in the Covered Market one day, and I felt so lonely I asked her to have a coffee. It was fun hearing all the gossip from the school. Clive's latest wheeze was to have the students – now referred to as 'customers' – grade the teachers on a scale of one to ten. These points were then totalled and posted up in the staff room, and at the end of the year those at the bottom of the list were dismissed.

But the hottest item of news concerned my ex-student Garcia. 'It turns out he's got a human rights record as long as your arm,' Trish told me. 'Torture, murder, kidnapping, you name it. Terry got on to it through Amnesty International. Apparently when the military junta was overthrown Garcia managed to get sent over here through a contact in the embassy. Now the new regime want him back to stand trial, but to get extradition they have to establish a *prima facie* case under British law and their system is so different from ours that their evidence won't stand up over here. His student visa is only valid as long as he's enrolled at a school, so we went to Clive and tried to get him expelled. You can imagine the response.'

' "The Oxford International Language College is a non-ideological, non-denominational, profit-making organization dedicated to bring together people from many different cultures and walks of life. Nation shall speak peace unto nation, and I shall grab a piece of the action. Any member of staff who feels unable to live up to this high ideal is at perfect liberty to hand in his or her resignation. There were over forty applicants for the last post . . ." '

For a moment, Trish's laughter made me regret leaving the chummy, easy-going atmosphere of Winston Street. But only for a moment. Trish might have found my imitation of Clive's cant amusing, but the fact remained that she was still in his power and I wasn't. I had to keep reminding myself of that. All my life I had chosen the soft options: good times, good company, good fun. Now I was finally growing up. It might not be easy, but it was the only way forward.

Karen's line on our ostracism was that everything would be all right once people heard she was pregnant. She may well have been right about this. It's quite possible that people shunned us not so much as a mark of outrage at what we had done, but to avoid the frustration of not being able to satisfy their curiosity about what exactly it was. The questions our friends were dying to ask were those which the tabloids have trumpeted ever since the case came into the public domain. Since they couldn't talk about that, they preferred not to talk at all. Having a baby would have taken us off the front pages, making us safe and dull again. Other people's sexuality is always threatening, a hot dark secret from which we're excluded. Birth brings it out in the open. Look, the proud parents exclaim, here's our sexuality! Come and tickle its tiny toes and admire its baby-blue eyes! And everyone heaves a massive sigh of relief. There they were imagining satyrs and succubae and God knows what manner of obscene delights, and all the time it was just a *baby*!

The only problem with this pleasing scenario was that there wasn't going to be any baby. This wasn't for want of trying. If effort had counted for anything, we would have had a family of Catholic proportions. We were even using the papally approved contraceptive method, only in reverse. Karen carefully calculated the period when she was most fertile, and while that window of opportunity was open I was on standby twenty-four hours a day. Knowing it was all a pointless farce sapped my morale as much as the rigorous regime did my physique. I churned out orgasms to order, squawking and spluttering like Sylvester the Cat on acid. Karen was too desperate to notice. By now the soggy British spring was upon us. Purple and yellow crocuses were popping up all over the lawn, the hard winter outlines of shrubs and trees were blurred by new growth like the fuzz on an adolescent's upper lip, even the rows of savagely pruned rosebushes at the front of the house, separated by concrete walkways like a cemetery of spider crabs buried upside-down, were shoving out shoots and buds. Nature was blooming and burgeoning, but poor Karen couldn't get gravid for love or money. If fecundity continued to evade her, the question of responsibility was bound to come up sooner or later. Who was at fault? Was it Bill or was it Ben? Which of those two flowerpot men, her ovaries or my semen?

Up to now I've avoided mentioning our day-to-day domestic life, for much the same reason that ex-prisoners are reluctant to talk about their time inside. What brought Karen and I together was sex, but sex in Dennis's shadow, agitprop sex, perilous, defiant and liberating. Now the tyrant was dead, sex was no longer a revolutionary gesture but establishment policy, with demanding productivity quotas and output targets. Our spare time was devoted to a vicious, unrelenting guerilla war inspired by Karen's massive inferiority complex. Her tastes merely appalled me, but she felt threatened by mine. She couldn't live and let live. She had to search and destroy, scorch and defoliate, and she made the most of her one point of advantage, namely that I was a kept man.

I had naively imagined that marriage would magically obliterate the origins of the wealth we shared, melting Dennis's laboriously acquired treasures down into a common heap of anonymous gold. But there is notoriously no such thing as a free meal. Karen never let me forget that everything we owned was originally hers and hers alone, and that I had not only contributed nothing to our joint capital but wasn't bringing in any income either. For appearances' sake I maintained the fiction that I was setting up an independent enterprise in the EFL field. Under cross-examination I added a few more details about my supposed activities. The idea, I claimed, was to exploit my extensive network of influential contacts with a view to offering special courses for foreign businessmen involving saturation experience in an authentic English-speaking work environment. At the moment this innovatory scheme was still at the planning stage, but once it got off the ground I couldn't fail to gross a minimum of fifty thou in the first year of operation, after which the sky was the limit. Every morning I climbed into the BMW and swept off, just as Dennis had once done, except that once I reached the Banbury Road I had nowhere to go. I told Karen that I was visiting factories and offices in the Oxford area and sounding out the management with a view to future co-operation, but in fact my mornings were spent driving aimlessly around the highways and byways of rural Oxfordshire. Then one day, just for old times' sake, I paid a visit to Winston Street.

Someone here once told me a story about the most notorious of the dictators who ruled this country at the turn of the century. It was some time after the construction of the capital's tramway system, and it may well be that the true origins of the tale lay in a superstitious dread of this foreign technology. On certain days, it was said, a tramcar of unusual design was seen circulating slowly along the lines which passed through the poorest and most deprived slums in the city. Its windows were silvered and the doors locked, and it never stopped to let passengers on or off. The official explanation was that the car contained instruments for monitoring the condition of the track. Some people, however, claimed that at the end of its run the mysterious tram disappeared on to a private spur line leading into the grounds of the presidential palace. Eventually the story spread that the dictator himself was aboard, observing his subjects through the mirror windows.

At first this was merely the usual paranoid rumour inevitable under a ruthless regime where informers abounded, but after a time a more imaginative version emerged. The dictator was indeed inside the tramcar. The purpose of his trip, however, was not spying but something more extreme, more perverse, more savagely contemptuous. The tyrant was bored. For years he had starved and destroyed, tortured and killed. What more could he inflict on his subjects? They had nothing left but their suffering, the pain and misery of their daily lives. So he determined to take that too. While they fought to draw water from a broken tap, he looked on from the safety of his armoured tram, sipping iced champagne. While they scavenged rotten vegetables from the rubbish tip, he gorged himself on imported delicacies. The poverty of their lives played across the silvered windows like a back-projection in a film, lending perspective and contrast to the satiated self-indulgence of his.

It doesn't matter whether or not this story is true. What is significant is that it was universally believed, because, like a fairy tale, it embodies a profound truth. Only contrast can create value. At first the contrast is between what you have and what you want, but what do you do once you have what you want? That trip back to Winston Street taught me the answer. After a month or two at the wheel, the BMW had become completely transparent to me. It was just a car, a way of getting about. Daily visits to East Oxford soon restored it to its former glory. I would put on a tape of Tudor madrigals – a new interest – and lie back in the contoured leather seats, letting myself melt into the crevices of Morley's sinuous six-part harmony and observing the surrounding misery with mounting satisfaction. To think that not so long ago I had been one of these creatures, peddling off through the drizzle to a dead-end job! From time to time a harassed mother might rap angrily on the window to complain that she couldn't get her push-chair past the car, which I had parked blocking the pavement. I didn't reply. There was no need. The car spoke for me. I simply stared into her eyes through the layer of toughened glass which divided her world from mine. Not only was I indulging a harmless pleasure, I was also doing her kids a favour. It was too late to save the mother, but by flaunting my privileges under her nose, taunting her with the contrast between my power and her weakness, my wealth and her poverty, I was helping to ensure that her children's chances in life would never be blighted by the well-wishing do-goodism which had crippled me. What makes the world go round is not love or kindness, they'd learn, but greed and envy. The more those kids were deprived and maltreated, the more motivated they would be to get aboard the enterprise culture and start creating wealth.

Even with rows of parked vehicles on either side, North Oxford streets are still wide enough for cars to pass abreast, but east of Magdalen Bridge driving becomes a continual game of 'chicken'. Success depends to some extent on your class of motor. Delivery vans are the kings of the jungle, but I didn't do too badly in the BMW. The only people who drive luxury saloons in East Oxford are drug dealers who do karate with their rottweilers to relax. I'd therefore grown used to getting a certain amount of respect from other drivers, so when I found one of the clapped-out Toyotas favoured by Asian families in my path one morning I expected a free passage. In fact the car turned out to be a souped-up grease-wagon piloted by an ageing rocker eager to prove he still had it in the nuts. By the time I realized this we were less than twenty yards apart. I stood on my anchors and the BMW's much-vaunted braking system came good. A moment later there was a loud crash aft as someone rear-ended me. Getting out to inspect the damage, I found myself confronting a shocked Alison Kraemer.

'I'm most dreadfully sorry,' she burbled. 'I was miles away, I'm afraid. I had no idea . . .'

She broke off, staring at me.

'Oh,' she said shortly, 'it's you.'

'I'm afraid so. You should have stayed up your own end of town. You get to run into a better class of person there.'

She coloured.

'I'm sorry if I sounded rude. I'm a bit shocked.'

The damage to the BMW turned out to be negligible, but Alison's elderly Saab had suffered a broken headlight and badly buckled fender.

'Doesn't look too good,' I told her. 'You'd better have a mechanic check it over before you try and drive it.'

'I've got some camera-ready proofs in the back. I can't leave them here.'

'I'll run you home.'

I visualized Alison as living in a classic North Oxford mansion set on a bosky avenue amid the murmuring of innumerable dons, so I was surprised to find myself directed up the hill to Headington. We turned down a flagrantly suburban side-street near the football ground. A few hundred yards further on, though, venerable stone walls sprang up on either side and we were suddenly in a picture-book Cotswold village tucked away out of sight in the ignoble fringes of the city. We passed a rural church, a country pub, and then turned down an unpaved cul-de-sac running through a dense cluster of beeches and pines to a four-square Edwardian villa with overhanging eaves and low-pitched roof.

'Thank you very much for the lift.'

'Why don't we ring a garage and have them meet me at your car with the keys? It'll save them a trip out here, with all the time and expense that'll involve.'

If the location of Alison's house was a surprise, the interior was everything I had expected. Antiphonal choirs of rosewood and mahogany gleamed darkly in rooms dominated by the rich pedal-tones of velvet curtains and hand-printed wallpaper. The furnishings were genially promiscuous, a jetsam of objects of every style eloquently evoking the varied and wide-ranging currents which had washed them up together here. Alison led me through the hall into the kitchen, a sprawling space with a flagstone floor dominated by a huge table, a Welsh dresser and rows of large cupboards. A set of battle-scarred Le Creuset pans nestled on the Aga where a Persian cat was profoundly asleep. On the wall nearby was a notice-board to which were pinned various notes and lists, telephone numbers, business cards and two concert tickets. While I looked around, Alison set about phoning one of the 'little men' who supply her class with everything from free-range pork to spare parts for obsolete typewriters.

'That's all arranged then,' she told me, putting down the phone. 'I said you'd meet him at the car in ten minutes.'

I had fancied myself a connoisseur of contrast, a gourmet savouring the sweet-and-sour clash between my present life-style and the one I had left behind me in East Oxford. But it was quite a different contrast that struck me there in Alison's kitchen: the aching disparity between the woman who stood there, impatient for me to be gone, and the one I was going home to. I had gained much by marrying Karen, but now the thought of all I had lost rose up to overwhelm me. I found myself wondering who that second concert ticket was intended for. For some reason, Thomas 'we make music together' Carter crossed my mind, so after delivering the keys to the mechanic I stopped at the ticket agency. The concert was the following Wednesday. That was Karen's yoga night, so there would be no difficulty there.

That night in bed I had a genuine orgasm. By now this was so unusual that Karen didn't even realize I'd come until I told her. What I didn't say was that I hadn't been making love to her but to Alison, taking her from behind on the kitchen table, her rump high in the air and her toes squirming helplessly an inch or two off the floor. As I've already explained, I felt absolutely no lust whatsoever for Alison Kraemer. I'd made love to her class of Englishwoman before, and had no particular wish to renew the experience. They're all gauche and giggly in bed, by turns prudish and gushing, fidgety and frenetic one minute, in rigor mortis the next. If by some miracle they manage to achieve an orgasm, they don't know whether they're coming or going. Indeed, most of their problems spring from the fact that for them the two functions are deeply connected. 'Have you finished?' they ask as you lie gasping, and when they switch on the light you expect to see a sign over the bed, NOW WASH YOUR HANDS.

Despite this, it was Alison Kraemer I made love to that night and every night thereafter. As engaged couples used to make conversation and play parlour games in lieu of the physical pleasures they were forbidden, so I imagined erotic scenes with Alison to console myself for what was denied me: walks and talks, games and jokes, company, solace, an end to my dreadful, soul-destroying loneliness.

It was for her daughter, of course, the second ticket. I never thought of that. I thought I'd exhausted every possibility, rivals of every pedigree from the Nissan Professor of Modern Japanese Studies to a rough-trade gamekeeper out at Shotover, but I never thought of family. Lovers don't. Family's the other mob. Family's legit, but we're where the action is. They're a safe investment, but in love you can make a killing overnight. Metaphorically speaking, I hasten to add.

Anyway, there she was, a pert little fourteen-year-old following the action in her score and pointing out all the wrong notes, mistaken entries and interpretative lapses to her doting mamma. They cost a hell of a lot, these Oxford prodigies, but it's worth every penny. The effect is even more telling than the BMW, because while anyone with the necessary can buy one of those, these kiddies are not just paid for but born and bred as well. In short, they're advertisements not just for your financial status, but for your impeccable intellectual and social credentials. When Rebecca Kraemer remarked, as the last murmurs of the slow movement died away, that it was such a pity the conductor was still following the now-discredited Haas edition, she was telling everyone within earshot – which included half the audience – everything that Alison could have wanted them to know but naturally wouldn't have dreamt of mentioning herself.

I slipped away before the encores and hung around in the courtyard outside the Sheldonian until the Kraemers emerged. I then plotted a converging course through the crowd and greeted Alison with feigned surprise and genuine pleasure. She appeared disconcerted, even flustered. Hello, I thought, maybe there's something in this for you after all. A woman as socially assured as Alison Kraemer doesn't get her knickers in a twist just because an acquaintance, however unsuitably married, asks her how she enjoyed the concert.

'Are we going soon, Mummy?' demanded young Rebecca, who seemed to have taken an instant dislike to me.

'Past your bedtime?' I joked.

The child glared at me so fiercely that I tried to ingratiate myself by asking who was her favourite composer.

'Fauré,' she replied.

'Mine too.'

She arched her eyebrows.

'I'd have thought Brahms and Liszt would have been more to your taste.'

The two names she had mentioned are of course rhyming slang for 'pissed', but nothing in Rebecca Kraemer's innocent little face betrayed whether or not she was aware of this. I turned to her mother.

'Alison, there's something I want to say to you.'

'Is your wife here?'

This threw me, but only for a moment.

'That's what I wanted to talk to you about.'

'To *me*?'

Rebecca was looking pointedly from one of us to the other like a parody of a spectator watching a tennis rally.

'Look darling, there are Rupert and Fiona Barrington,' Alison said. 'Do just pop over and ask them whether Squish and Trouncy can make it under their own steam on Saturday or whether they'll need a lift.'

With a mutinous glance, Rebecca sped off. Her mother looked at me, her face as still and hard as a life mask.

'I can't bear you to think ill of me,' I said.

'I don't.'

'You do! You must. You couldn't be all that you are without despising me. But it's not what you think, you see. It's not what you think at all.'

Rebecca bounded back like a retriever with a stick.

'Squish broke his ankle in Klosters and is being invalided home and Trouncy wants to know if she can bring Jean-Pierre, their French exchange. She says he has amazing hands, whatever that might mean.'

'All right, but what about transport?'

Rebecca hared away again.

'Anyway, I really can't see that it matters one way or the other what I think,' Alison said.

'It matters very much to me.'

'Well I'm not sure it should.'

'I'd just like you to know what really happened, that's all. The situation is very different from what you suppose, from what *anyone* supposes.'

Rebecca was already on her way back.

'Will you meet me for tea one day this week?' I said urgently. 'How about that place in Holywell Street?'

Tea has always seemed to me a childish and pointless affair, but it has the advantage of being morally blameless and socially safe. Nothing naughty has ever happened over tea.

'Fiona says we can all fit in the Volvo,' Rebecca announced, 'but Rupert says he doesn't see why they should act as bloody chauffeurs for their friends all the bloody time.'

'Reb*ecca*!'

'I'm just quoting, Mummy. Anyway, Fiona told him not to be so bolshie, they'll come about twoish and don't forget you promised to give her your recipe for *clafoutis*.'

Alison waved largely at the Barringtons, who semaphored back.

'I'm particularly fond of the slow movement of his second piano sonata,' Rebecca confided to me.

The kid was coming round, I thought. My charm wins them all over in the end. Conscious that it would be very much to my advantage to have an ally within Alison's gates, I replied warmly, 'Me too.'

Rebecca gave a squeal of delight.

'Really? It's an unfashionable point of view.'

'Is it?'

'Definitely. A downright *faux pas* in fact.'

Alison regarded me as though I were a dosser who'd just importuned her for some spare change.

'Will Friday do?' she said.

'What, Mummy?' asked Rebecca, suddenly anxious.

'Nothing, darling.'

Oh but it was, I thought. It was really quite a lot.

When I got home I looked up Fauré in the Oxford Companion. He didn't write any piano sonatas, of course.

'First of all, let me just say that everything I am going to tell you is the complete and absolute truth.'

The little tea-shop was pleasantly uncrowded. Full Term had ended a fortnight earlier. The Easter tourists hadn't yet arrived. For a few weeks Oxford seemed like a normal city instead of a theme park.

'You sound so serious.'

'It's no joking matter, at least to me. But I suppose I also intend a warning.'

Alison raised her eyebrows.

'As in "this programme contains scenes which some viewers may find distressing or objectionable".'

She nodded.

'Go on.'

'When Karen broke the news of our marriage so crudely at Thomas's party, and I saw the look on your face, I understood for the first time the force of that old cliché about wishing the floor would open up and swallow one. I could tell what you were thinking. You were thinking that I had married her for her money, and that she'd married me for . . . all the wrong reasons. You were wondering how long we'd been lovers. Perhaps you were even wondering about Dennis's death. Did he fall or was he pushed?'

'No!'

Alison's denial was so forceful it attracted the attention of a couple at a neighbouring table. Like a batsman rehearsing a shot after playing and missing, she repeated quietly, 'No. That's not true.'

'I don't mean to impute mean or vulgar opinions to you, Alison. But I saw judgement in your face, and it shattered me, precisely because I knew I must seem to deserve the very worst that anyone could imagine. And it wasn't just anyone, it was you. That made it almost unbearable. Right from that very first day in France you made the most tremendous impression on me, Alison. When we met again at the funeral, I knew that I had to see you again soon. I said so at the time, if you remember. I looked up your number in the phone book. I was going to call you and . . .'

I broke off. Alison refilled our cups and for a moment we took refuge in the polite rituals of milk and sugar.

'A few days after the funeral,' I said, 'Karen phoned to ask if I'd come over and help her dispose of some of Dennis's effects. She said she couldn't face tackling the job on her own. The Parsons had been good to me. It was the least I could do to help Karen out now. We spent two or three hours bagging up clothes to take to the charity shops. Then Karen went downstairs to make some tea. When she came back . . . she didn't have any clothes on.'

Alison herself was wearing a rather shapeless dress made of some fabric suitable for curtains, which covered her body like a dustsheet draped over furniture. Her fingers twitched nervously at the buttons of the high collar.

'The ridiculous thing is that I wasn't remotely attracted to Karen. Those scrawny, neurotic women are not my type.'

I allowed myself a brief glance at Alison's ample contours.

'That's no excuse, of course. I knew perfectly well when I allowed Karen Parsons to seduce me that I was not acting rightly. I was simply too stunned to protest. I thought she must be unhinged by grief. It never occurred to me for a moment that she had planned it all in cold blood.'

'I don't find it particularly surprising that you allowed yourself to be seduced by her. What I *do* find surprising . . .'

'Is that I married her.'

She sketched a shrug.

'It's no earthly business of mine, of course . . .'

I leant forward.

'After what had happened I couldn't face trying to contact you. I felt polluted, tainted, defiled, unworthy of anyone except Karen, who repelled me. I told her I didn't want to see her again. She pleaded and begged me to change my mind, but I was adamant. Finally she dropped the bombshell. She was pregnant, she said, and I was the father.'

Alison looked away out of the window at the facade of New College opposite. I sighed deeply.

'I couldn't see any other honourable way out. Perhaps I'm old-fashioned. Perhaps I should have been frank with her, admitted honestly that I didn't love her and that if she insisted on marrying me she would be condemning both of us to a joyless union. But I just couldn't bring myself to do it. I honestly thought she loved me so much that she'd been prepared to get herself pregnant to trick me into marriage. However badly she'd behaved, it was my duty to stand by her and the child. Telling her the truth about my feelings, or rather the lack of them, would just have made our life together even more intolerable.'

To harmonize my body language with Alison's, I turned to look out of the window. As our eyes met in the glass, I realized that she was not admiring the flaking stone blocks opposite but using the window as a mirror. It was me she had been looking at all that time, but secretively, like a girl.

'It was Karen's idea to keep the wedding quiet,' I went on. 'She claimed people might be shocked at her remarrying so soon after Dennis's death. The real reason was that she was afraid of what I might find out. She couldn't know who Dennis might have told, man to man, after a few drinks. If I had learned her secret before the marriage was legal, all her devious schemes would have come to nothing.'

'What secret?'

'You don't know?'

'Know what?'

'In my worst moments I thought *everyone* knew, except me.'

'Knew what, for heaven's sake?'

I fixed her eyes.

'That Karen has had a hysterectomy.'

Alison looked suitably appalled.

'Two weeks after we were married, I asked how her pregnancy was going. She turned red and started stammering. Then she burst into tears. I tried to comfort her. She said she'd lost the foetus. It sounded as though she'd left it on a bus or something. Then she started laughing at the top of her voice. I thought it was just hysteria. Living with her, day in day out, I was beginning to realize how unstable she is. Her mood swings quite frighten me sometimes. Anyway, to calm her I said not to take it so hard, we could always try again. It was then that she told me about the hysterectomy.'

'What did you say?'

'Like a fool, I told her that the only reason I'd married her was because she'd told me she was pregnant. You can imagine the reaction that got.'

'But she had deliberately deceived you!'

'Exactly! She tricked me, Alison. That little bitch tricked me! Forgive my language, but I think I have every right to feel bitter. Not only am I forced to share bed and board with a woman for whom I feel nothing but disgust, but for my pains I have been branded a disreputable opportunist by all and sundry. And worst of all, I have lost the respect of the person I hold most dear in all the world.'

I fell silent, my head bowed in exhaustion and despair.

'I'll divorce her, of course. But it will take time. She'll fight every inch of the way. She's crazy about me, for some reason. And what will everyone think? They'll say I took advantage of a widow's grief to marry her for her money, then cold-bloodedly ditched her as soon as I had a chance. It's all so hopeless! Why on earth did this have to happen to me? What have I done to deserve it?'

This sort of feeble whining goes down a treat with women like Alison. They like their men to be useless. It gives them a purpose in life.

'Well it's not for me to advise you, of course . . .'

'On the contrary! If I thought that I might be able to count on your friendship, despite all that's happened, then . . . Well, that would make an enormous difference. It would make *all* the difference.

'Then I think you should separate as soon as possible. The sooner the situation is clarified, the better for everyone concerned.'

She gathered her shopping together.

'And now I must be going. I have to collect my youngest from Phil and Jim.'

Outside in the street I took her hand for the first time.

'It's been such a comfort talking to you, Alison. You don't know how it's helped. Will you . . .?'

'I'll do everything I *can*,' she said, freeing herself.

I nodded meekly.

'Don't look so glum!' she added. 'It's not the end of the world.'

And off she went to collect her son from St Philip and James Primary School.

Strange the tricks that life plays, I mused as I drove home, popping the tape of madrigals into the player. A few days earlier I had been thinking of calling my doctor to assess the chances of having my vasectomy reversed in order to save my marriage to Karen. Now I would be calling a solicitor to see how I could get it dissolved on the best possible terms. The last thing I wanted was to make some hasty move which might invalidate my claims to a large share of our joint estate. But these were mere details. The main thing was that my intuitions about Alison had been confirmed. She was far from indifferent to me, I felt sure of that, but neither would she contemplate carrying on an affair with a married man. That was fine. I didn't want to have an affair with Alison. My intentions were entirely honourable. Whoever would have guessed it, though? What a tease life was, to be sure! What a little caution. With a fol-rol-rol and a hey-nonny-no.

Much to my surprise, Karen greeted me at the front door with a glass of champagne in her hand and, still more unusual, a smile on her face.

'Guess what?' she said archly.

Not best pleased at being awakened from my reveries, I shrugged impatiently. Karen threw her arms round my neck, spilling champagne everywhere.

'I'm pregnant!' she shrieked.

III

A dense mental fog, known locally as a Kidlington Particular, grips the city, casting its Lethean spell over Members and non-Members of the University alike. Stupefying vapours shroud the environs of that ubiquitous old hostelry 'The Temporary Sign'. Within, a throng of potential witnesses studiously ignore the two men huddled in furtive confabulation. One is short, swarthy and stout. He wears a filthy poncho, a wide-brimmed hat and spurred boots. Cartridge belts criss-cross his chest and he picks his teeth with a razor-sharp dagger. The other man is tall and saturnine, with brilliantined hair and a cruel smile. He is dressed in a white double-breasted suit and slip-on patent leather shoes and is smoking a Turkish cigarette in an ivory holder.

I – you have of course penetrated my feeble disguise – drawl languidly, 'I want you to kill my wife.'

'Sí, señor!' grins Garcia (for it is he).

Bundles of greasy banknotes change hands and both conspirators disappear into the night. The next moment the pub itself has vanished, together with its faceless regulars and anonymous landlord. Only the fog remains, an impenetrable wall of obscurity and confusion, dense, dim and very, very *thick*.

What do you mean, you don't believe this? Are you aware that no lesser an authority than Her Majesty's Home Secretary has given this scenario his seal of approval, and that it forms the basis of the extradition proceedings currently before this court? What's that? You find no mention of a poncho? Very well, I'll waive the poncho. Strike the poncho from the record. The fact remains that I am accused of conspiring with a person or persons unknown to murder my wife.

There is one point which needs to be made right away, which is that instead of providing me with a motive for murder, the discovery that Karen was pregnant removed any interest I might otherwise have had in her death. So far from the jealous fury wished on me by the press, my feelings were of quiet satisfaction. Had I not been wondering how to rid myself of Karen without prejudicing my financial position? Now all my problems were resolved: I had Karen exactly where I wanted her. She was no longer the woman who had been taken advantage of, but a common adulteress. I was no longer a ruthless and cynical adventurer, but the deceived husband. Since I was demonstrably not responsible for inseminating Karen, all I needed to do was find out who was. Once the identity of the lucky donor was revealed, I could start divorce proceedings. The proof of my wife's treachery was alive and kicking in her belly, and a paternity test would prove beyond a shadow of doubt that Mr X was indeed the proud father. After that, the hearing would be a mere formality. Karen would be packed off to make the bed she had lain in while I wept all the way to the bank.

It should thus be clear to the meanest intelligence that even if I could have disappeared Karen without the slightest risk to myself, it would not have been in my interests to do so. As always, I stress my interests, because in them you can trust. I make no claims about what I might have done in other circumstances, I simply assert that those circumstances did not in fact arise. And legally, gentlemen, as I need hardly remind you, that is all I *need* to do. This court is not required to decide whether I am a nice person, but whether there is reasonable evidence that I committed the crime named in the extradition request. But it was simply not in my interests to commit such a crime. It was a fact *against* my interests.

What were those interests, by this time? When I first met the Parsons they had been very simple. I wanted the lifestyle which other people of my age and education enjoyed but which I had forfeited because of the wayward direction given my life by the humanistic propaganda I was exposed to in my youth. I didn't crave fabulous riches or meaningless wealth, I simply wanted my due. Now I had achieved that, and I had also met Alison. She was my equal, my complement, my destined mate. The time and effort I had spent cultivating Mrs Parsons had not been wasted, however. While I had had no qualms about courting Karen without a penny to my name – she was bloody lucky to have *me*, never mind money as well! – I couldn't have approached Alison on those terms.

But if personal insolvency would have created awkwardnesses *du côté de chez Alison*, the violent death of my wife would have been still less desirable. 'We have already missed three trains,' Wilde's Lady Bracknell observes. 'To miss any more might expose us to comment on the platform.' As always, Oscar is right on the money when it comes to the English gentry. To be exposed to comment was still the nightmare of Alison and her kind, and whatever the other disadvantages of murdering one's wife, it does inevitably tend to make one an object of some general interest. If the previous husband of the wife in question has also died in mysterious circumstances not long before, with the result that one has inherited the couple's entire estate, then one may expect to attract a very lively class of comment indeed.

Quite apart from the not-inconsiderable risks of plotting to kill Karen, I thus had two excellent reasons not to do so. Dead, she would have proved a considerable social embarrassment. Alive, and carrying another man's child, she guaranteed both my financial future and a smooth transition to life with Alison, who would welcome me with the sympathy due someone who had tried in vain to make an honest woman of a deceitful slut. True, I would have to reconcile what I had told Alison about Karen's hysterectomy with the news that she was pregnant, but that could easily be made to seem like one more strand of the wool which had been pulled over my innocent eyes. As long as Karen was alive, I had nothing to fear and everything to hope for. So far from hiring someone to kill her, I would, if I'd known how, have striven officiously to keep her alive.

What I *did* need to do was find out the identity of my stand-in. I lacked both the patience and the experience to do this myself. I needed an outsider, a professional. Money was a problem, however. Our bank accounts were in both our names, but since love's sweet song had ceased to work its magic, Karen had taken to scrutinizing the statements with an eagle eye and demanding explanations for every penny I withdrew. In common with all middle-class householders, we received a large amount of junk mail practically begging us to borrow money from them for any purpose whatsoever. I now replied to one of these offers, from a financial institution with which we had no previous connections, and had no difficulty in securing a loan of £5,000. I planned to use the capital to meet the monthly repayments until the divorce settlement came through, then repay the principal in full.

I still hesitated to call a private detective agency, though. To make my situation a matter of record with a third party who was subject to various legal constraints wasn't necessarily in my interests. Suppose Karen's paramour turned out to be married, with cash on tap and a reputation to lose. In that case it might well be advantageous to make a settlement out of court, the terms to be arranged after mutual consultation between the interested parties. I didn't want any officially accredited ex-policeman limiting the options available to me, eg blackmail. Ideally I needed someone who was himself compromised, someone marginal and transient, with no leverage on the mechanisms of power. It was just a matter of time before I thought of Garcia.

Trish had given me a brief account of the allegations against him, but just to be on the safe side I phoned Amnesty International, posing as a researcher for a TV current affairs programme. Their response was unequivocal, a detailed catalogue of union leaders, students, newspaper editors, civil rights workers, Jews, feminists, priests and intellectuals tortured and murdered, a whole politico-socio-economic subgroup targeted and taken out. I was dismayed. With a record like that, Garcia might well regard the menial task I had to offer him as beneath his dignity.

I needn't have worried. In the event Garcia proved only too eager to co-operate in any way, as long as there was money in it. The mysterious rendezvous where we hatched our devilish scheme, incidentally, was a roadside cafeteria near Eynsham called The Happy Eater. I bought Garcia a hamburger and chips and listened to him bewail his situation. It did sound rather bleak. His student visa ran out in a month and he couldn't renew it without proof of re-enrolment at the school. Clive had stoutly resisted the teachers' attempts to have Garcia blacked, but his idealism did not extend to forgoing the fees. Garcia's funds were almost exhausted, and he couldn't replenish them without putting his student status in jeopardy and risking instant deportation. Nor was his *persona* particularly *grata* outside the United Kingdom. No other country in Europe would take him, and, much to Garcia's disgust, neither would the United States.

'We do their dirty work for them and they won't even help out when things get tough. Look what they did to Noriega! Makes you sick.'

'What do you expect, Garcia, unemployment insurance? That sounds like Commie talk to me.'

'A man should stand by his friends,' the unhappy eater complained.

His own friends, it turned out, were now lying low in a certain Central American republic, and Garcia's only wish was to join them. The problem was that he needed the best part of a thousand pounds to obtain a false passport and a plane ticket. I told him that I would be prepared to make a substantial contribution and then explained what I wanted. Garcia flicked his hand as though brushing away a fly.

'No problem,' he said in his evil English.

Back at Ramillies Drive, I bugged the telephones. The law covering electronic surveillance is a koan on which those who seek enlightenment about the British way of doing things would be well-advised to meditate. Under UK law it is legal to buy and sell bugging equipment, but a criminal act to use it. Thus the purchase of a sophisticated radio tap transmitter and actuator switch like the one I bought in the Tottenham Court Road, solely and specifically designed for the clandestine interception of other people's telephone calls, is no more problematic than that of a clock-radio. Parents who use an intercom to monitor their baby's sleep, on the other hand, are guilty of criminally violating the infant's privacy.

The hardware set me back a couple of hundred pounds, but the salacious details I hoped to pick up would certainly be worth a bob or two when it came to the divorce. I knew from personal experience that Karen's sexual behaviour was fairly unfettered, so depending on the proclivities of her partner there seemed a good chance that they might drop the odd reference to one of those practices which can so alienate the sympathies of a jury. I imagined my counsel fixing Karen with a beady eye. 'In the course of a telephone conversation with the co-respondent, you referred amongst other things to a bottle-brush, a set of rubber bands and a jar of mayonnaise. Would you explain for the benefit of the court the precise use to which these items were subsequently put?'

The first few recordings yielded nothing more interesting than a long conversation between Karen and her mother about the trials and tribulations of early pregnancy, but on the Thursday afternoon I struck gold. Karen had made two calls that morning. The first was to a hotel in Wales, reserving two single rooms for Saturday night and quoting her Barclaycard details in lieu of a deposit. The second was answered impatiently by a man whose tone promptly went all smarmy the moment Karen identified herself. But I wasn't listening to her. I was listening to the background noise, the cacophonous Eurobabble, the sudden eruptions of pidginshit English. In my mind's eye I stood surrounded by the polyglot bratpack, fielding questions about the difference between 'they are' and 'there are' from a neurotic Basque girl while waiting for Clive to finish on the phone so that I could go in, cap in hand, and ask for an advance on next month's salary.

But Clive was in no hurry to finish. He was gazing out of his window at the traffic on the Banbury Road, the receiver clutched tightly in his sweaty paw, his voice caressing his caller like a cat licking its fur. He was discussing their forthcoming weekend in the Elan Valley. He was discussing it with my wife. She told him that the surroundings were lovely and she could recommend the hotel. She had been there, she said, before.

If it had been anyone else, I wouldn't be here, Karen wouldn't be dead, none of this would have happened. Karen was no longer of any concern to me. I'd got what I wanted out of her. All I wanted now was rid. If it had been anyone else, I'd have wished them both the best of British and turned the matter over to my solicitors.

But it wasn't anyone. It was Clive, and that changed everything. Karen didn't matter to me, but Clive did. Clive and I went way back. We had scores to settle. I don't just mean his shabby treatment of me at the school. That particular Clive Phillips was merely the latest model in a continuing series which had haunted my life. Back in the sixties, when I was demonstrating against the Vietnam War, having meaningful relationships, pondering the purpose of life and seeing God in a grain of sand, the Clives were out there wheeling and dealing, cheating and hustling, packaging my dreams and hopes and selling them back to me at a profit. It didn't bother me, not then. From the lofty parapets of my ivory tower, I looked down on them going about their mean, grubby business in the mire far below and reminded myself that they hadn't enjoyed my advantages in life and were thus to be pitied rather than despised, difficult though this was.

Most of my peers came down to earth during the seventies, but I kept floating. OK, the acid dream was dead, flower power a flop, but hey, it'd been a learning experience, right? And the alternative still stank. I got into booze and books, travelled widely, did a bit of casual work to make ends meet, and had less and less meaningful affairs. The Clives were a lot closer now. I had dealings with them as employee and tenant. I felt their contempt for me, and it shook me. So I went abroad, insulating myself in the cocoon of expatriation. On my return to this country ten years later, I found the Clives in charge. They'd been there all along, of course, but keeping their heads down, disguising their true nature. Now the wind had changed and they'd come out of the woodwork, big and hungry and confident. I was tossed to them like a badger to dogs. When Clive Phillips condescended to use me, I was grateful, and when he turned me out I went quietly, because by then I had finally accepted the rules of the game. Instead of making vain protests to the referee or sulking on the sidelines, I set out to win. As we have seen, I succeeded.

Now I found myself humiliated and despoiled once more. Clive wasn't to know that he was doing me a favour by giving me a motive to divorce Karen. Clive didn't do anyone any favours. Like all free enterprise propagandists, he hated competition in any form, and took a particularly dim view of any of his employees trying to emulate his success. When three of his teachers left to open a school of their own, Clive told everyone that giving the consumer a choice kept everyone honest and he wished the lads well. Then he got his Italian agents to make block bookings at the new school for the next six months in the name of a fictitious company. The owners of the new school were ecstatic at this stroke of luck, and having spent a lot of money on advertising they were forced to turn down all requests for places as the school was full until Christmas. At the last moment the Italian company mysteriously cancelled its bookings, and that summer the school had more teachers than students. In October the bank foreclosed on the loan, and in November the teachers asked Clive for their jobs back. He said he would put their names on the list, but it was first come first served, fair was fair.

In short, Clive was not only a prick, he was a vindictive prick. Since he could no longer reach me in any other way, he'd reached me through my wife. It wasn't Karen that Clive was fucking, it was me. A terrible fury swept over me, a rage so intense it was physically painful. But anger would avail me nothing, I knew. The teachers who had taken Clive's on-your-bike homilies at face value got angry when they discovered how they'd been bought and sold, but their anger didn't repay their bank loan or give them their jobs back. It merely confirmed what losers they were. While they got mad, Clive got even. That's what I would do, I decided. I wasn't an ineffective dreamer any more. If Clive wanted to play dirty, that was fine with me. With Garcia on my side, I could play dirty in ways that Clive had never even imagined.

Over dinner that evening, Karen announced that her mother had to go into hospital for observation as her chronic back complaint had taken a turn for the worse. She felt she should go up to Liverpool for the weekend to be with her. I generously offered to drive her, but she said she preferred to go by train. I would only be in the way, she went on, becoming rather flustered, there was really no point in it. I conceded the point, but insisted on at least driving her to the station. This she accepted. She would be getting the 10.14, she said. I already knew this, having overheard her and Clive arranging to meet at Banbury, where the train stopped twenty minutes later. I thought it was quite a wheeze getting your husband to drive you to the train and your lover to meet you off it, but Karen did not seem unduly impressed. Ever the pragmatic scrubber at heart, she saw no more in this arrangement than its convenience.

Next morning I was up betimes. First stop was the railway station, where I consulted timetables. Then it was back in the BMW and up the road to Banbury, a pleasant market town some twenty miles north of Oxford. Its railway station proved to be a charmless sixties structure with a large car park tarmacked over uprooted sidings. Once the morning rush hour had subsided it appeared little-used, and between trains was almost completely deserted. It only remained to locate the facility which I thought of abstractly as 'the site'. After driving around the countryside for several hours, I eventually settled on a disused quarry a few miles outside Banbury. A lorry-load of broken concrete fence-posts and other construction waste had been tipped near the entrance, but there was no other sign that anyone had been there recently. There were no houses in the vicinity, and once inside one was completely hidden from the road.

When Garcia appeared at our rendezvous that lunchtime, he was almost beside himself with furtive cockiness and suppressed self-satisfaction. The manifest reason for this was that he had filled the order and was about to deliver the goods, but the real cause was malicious glee. Not only wasn't he the cuckold, but he knew who had made me one. I swiftly pulled the rug from under his feet by revealing that I did too.

Garcia's first thought was that I was trying to get out of paying him. He was therefore pleasantly surprised when I handed over the agreed sum without a murmur. I then asked how much he still needed. His face fell. It was quite a lot. When I asked how he'd like to have it on Monday he looked at me like the pooch in the Pedigree Chum commercials.

'You want me to keep watching? Take some photographs maybe?'

By now we were driving around the ring road, Garcia munching his way through a pack of sandwiches I'd bought at a garage. With what I had in mind, we couldn't risk being seen together, even at a roadside eatery with a high turnover.

'There's no need for that. I know enough. It's time to act, to punish those responsible.'

'Your wife?'

I shook my head.

'I'll deal with her. No, I'd like to put your professional skills to use.'

He looked suitably flattered.

'Clive has hurt me. He's hurt my pride, my honour. All I can do in return is hurt his body. It's not much, but it'll have to do for now. I would handle it myself, but I'm afraid I'd get carried away. He'd call the police and I'd be charged with assault.'

Garcia shook his head in disgust. The discovery that British justice offered no protection to husbands who took revenge on the man who had dishonoured them confirmed his worst suspicions about his country of exile.

'But for me it's an even bigger risk,' he pointed out.

'I'll make it worth your while. Everything you need to leave, plus a hundred pounds fun money.'

'Two hundred.'

We haggled amicably for some time.

'Clive is planning to go away with my wife this weekend,' I explained, once Garcia's scruples had been overcome. 'She's taking the train to a town called Banbury, where Clive is meeting her. I'll drive her to the station and put her on an earlier train. She won't dare refuse for fear of making me suspicious. What she won't know is that this train doesn't stop at Banbury. My wife will thus have been sent to Coventry, a phrase which you may recall from our work on idioms but which in the present case is to be interpreted literally.

'As soon as I've seen her off, I'll come and collect you. The train Clive is meeting doesn't arrive till ten forty, which will give us plenty of time. When we reach Banbury, you lie down in the back of the car with a blanket over you. I'll go and find Clive and tell him that I know all about him and Karen, and I think we should have a little talk. In broad daylight, in a public place, he'll have no reason to be suspicious. I'll get him to come and sit in the car so that we can discuss the situation without being overheard. Then, when the coast's clear, I'll turn on the radio. That's your signal to come out of hiding and disable him.'

'Forget the radio. Just punch him in the balls, like this.'

He made a fist and brought it down like a hammer between my thighs, pulling up at the last moment. I stifled a premature gasp of pain.

'While he's busy counting his nuts,' Garcia continued unperturbed, 'I give him a little tap on the head.'

By way of illustration, he skimmed my scalp with the open palm of his right hand.

'I knew you were the man for the job.'

'Then what?'

'Well, once Clive's feeling no pain, to use an idiom which I don't think we studied but which seems particularly appropriate in this context, we hood him and proceed to a secluded spot I have in mind where the two of you can conduct your business in complete privacy. When you've finished, we leave him there and drive back to Oxford, where you pop into a travel agent and book a seat to the destination of your choice.'

This vision glowed in Garcia's face for a moment. Then he frowned.

'But he'll know it was you.'

'Exactly. I *want* him to know it was me. What I don't want is for him to be able to prove it. And he won't, as long as you do your job right. The important thing is that you leave no marks. Can you do that?'

Garcia pursed his lips.

'We need electricity.'

'Electricity? You must be joking.'

'Believe me, it's the best! Clean, convenient, effective. No fuss, no mess.'

I tapped the steering-wheel impatiently.

'You're wasted as a torturer, Garcia. You should be writing ads for Powergen.'

As our eyes met, I had a chilling glimpse of how he must have looked to his victims, bent over them, electrode in hand, ready to place it on nipple or penis, or insert it in vagina or anus. But why should I worry? Garcia's skills were no threat to me. On the contrary, they were at my service.

'Anyway that's out of the question. We're talking about a disused quarry miles from anywhere. Strictly no mod cons.'

'No problem. Hire a generator, one of those petrol-driven ones. We'll need a resistor, too, to vary the current, and some leads and a couple of spoons.'

We were now stuck in a traffic jam at the roundabout by the Austin–Rover works. The rear window of the car in front informed us that the owner loved Airedale terriers, that blood donors did it twice a year and that if we could read this, we should thank a teacher. Since he couldn't, Garcia didn't thank me.

'And it really hurts?' I asked.

'Worse than anything you ever imagined. It's like your body's coming apart at the seams. And afterwards there's nothing to show, as long as you use the spoons properly. It's like cooking meat. You've got to keep them moving, otherwise it burns. We had an instructor from the CIA give us a demo when they delivered the equipment, but later on some of the guys got a little sloppy. You know how it is.'

'There's no risk of him dying, though?'

'I'll keep the current down.'

'Not *too* low.'

Garcia laughed briefly.

'Don't worry, he won't think it's too low.'

We drove on past Sainsbury's and over the soft-running Thames.

'What about noise?' I asked. 'Perhaps we should gag him?'

'If you like. But they don't really sound human. Anyone who hears us will think we're castrating pigs.'

It was perhaps this bucolic image that caused me to start whistling a tune which I later identified as the traditional folk song, *As I Was Going to Banbury*.

'Well that all sounds jolly satisfactory,' I said.

If my arrangement with Garcia had included the usual 'cooling-off period' designed to protect consumers from rash decisions, I'd probably have invoked it that evening. Once I'd had a chance to think the whole thing over I realized that it had all got a bit out of hand. What I'd envisaged was basically an up-market beating, tastefully applied, but essentially a good, old-fashioned, hands-on job. Somehow Garcia had made this scenario seem crude and unsatisfactory. It was like talking to a builder. You say, 'I'd like this and that done,' and he gives you this withering look and replies, 'Well if you're sure that's what you want, squire, we can certainly do that for you toot sweet, no problem at all, it's entirely up to you.' Which is how people end up with knocked-through en-suite kitchen conservatories when all they wanted was a cure for that damp patch on the loo wall.

It was the weekend, so of course every rental generator in Oxford and environs was already booked. In the end I had to drive to High Wycombe. In case Clive attempted to press charges I was using Dennis's driving licence as identification. Another incredible thing I am going to have to ask you to accept is that in Britain driving licences are accepted as valid identification despite the fact that they carry no photograph and do not expire until well into the next millennium. Since I was posing as Dennis Parsons, though, I couldn't use my own cheques or credit cards, so on top of everything else I had to make time-consuming side trips to cashpoint machines to finance the rental. Add a three-mile tailback on the A40 coming into Oxford, and there was another day gone.

Karen was in the shower when I got home. I took advantage of her acoustic isolation to phone Alison Kraemer. I hadn't as yet told Alison about Karen's pregnancy. Since that tea-time conversation in Holywell Street our relations had been friendly but correct. Now I felt the time had come to take her further into my confidence, and I therefore proposed meeting for lunch the next day. Quite apart from anything else, this would do me no harm at all in the event of Clive invoking the law. 'Now let me just get this straight, officer. Your contention is that prior to meeting Ms Kraemer for lunch at Fifteen North Parade – I can really recommend their venison in madeira and celeriac sauce, and the Château Musar '82 is drinking very nicely – I had spent the morning torturing someone in a quarry near Banbury. Is that correct?'

After some humming and hawing Alison agreed to see me, although she said she'd have to be home by four.

'I've got the Barringtons and the Rissingtons to dinner and I'm making a rice timbale. It's very good, but God, the preparation!'

The splashing and banging noises from the bathroom were still in full swing when I put the receiver down, so when Karen turned on me that evening and accused me of carrying on an affair with Alison behind her back, I was taken completely by surprise.

Karen and I shared the chores like the thoroughly modern couple we were. One night I loaded the microwave and Karen the dishwasher, the next we reversed roles. That day it was her turn to be creative. She'd selected something which looked like a slab of concrete wrapped in plastic foil when it went into the oven, and like a miniature hot-mud geyser when the timer pinged three minutes later. At no point did it resemble the illustration on the packet, but we ate it anyway, although as so often I felt that it would have made more sense to eat the packet and throw away the contents. We washed it down with one of the last surviving bottles from Dennis's cache of wine, a ballsy Australian red weighing in at about fourteen degrees. This was of course on top of our two official G and Ts each, plus whatever Karen had been tippling on the side.

Dessert consisted of some slug-like tinned fruit in a slimy liquor, topped with a non-dairy aerosol mousse whose main selling point appeared to be the fact that the propellant was environmentally friendly. Once we'd scoffed this off, Karen launched her assault. On returning home, it seemed, she had phoned British Rail information to check the time of her train the next morning. The line was engaged, so she went to have a shower and tried again later, using the automatic re-dial facility. Since I had called Alison in the interim, her call was answered not by BR's timetable touts but by a female voice which she identified as belonging to 'that Crammer woman'.

Everything that happened subsequently was really down to my inability to react fast enough to this freak occurence. What I should have done, of course, is concoct a specious excuse for having phoned Alison. This would not have been so hard. I could have claimed to be returning a call from her I'd found recorded on the answering machine, for example. This would have given me time to work out a suitable cover-story, and also to brief Alison in case Karen phoned her to check.

Instead, I stupidly denied that I had ever made such a call. Alison was one of those people who recite their number when answering the telephone, so Karen had been able to confirm her suspicions by checking with the directory. Not only wasn't I believed, but by lying about the call I had made it impossible to claim that it had been insignificant or innocent. There was no help for it, I realized reluctantly. I was going to have to go nuclear.

'So did you manage to get through to station information in the end?'

'Don't try and change the subject!'

'Oh I'm not, Karen. It's very much the same subject, isn't it?'

She looked hesitant, unsure as yet whether there was anything to be worried about.

'What exactly did you want to know?' I inquired archly.

'About the trains, of course.'

'The trains to Liverpool, or to Banbury?'

Something flared briefly in her eyes, like a dud firework.

'How did you find out?'

In other circumstances I would have stood up and cheered. Her response had not only put mine to shame, she had also returned my volley with awkward bounce and heavy top-spin. If I admitted bugging the phone, she would want to know what had made me suspicious. The answer, of course, was her pregnancy, but I couldn't tell her that without revealing the truth about my vasectomy, which was far more than I was prepared to admit at this stage of the game. So I said the first thing that came into my head.

'Clive told me.'

He eyes opened wide in shock.

'No!'

I held my tongue.

'He wouldn't do that!' she cried.

'I can't help wondering just how well you know him, Karen. Other than in the biblical sense, of course.'

She scrabbled in her handbag and popped a couple of 4 mg slaps of nicotine-rich gum.

'I dropped by the school this morning to sound Clive out about the EFL business idea. We chatted for a while about how much he'd want in return for letting me access his network of overseas contacts and so on. Then he suddenly turned to me and said, "Look here, I think you'd better know that I've been stuffing your wife." '

Karen flinched as though the child she was carrying had suddenly kicked her.

'I told him I didn't believe him. "You don't need to take my word for it," he said. "You see she's carrying my child." '

'But he doesn't even know! I never told him.'

'You don't need to *tell* him, Karen. There are lots of little signs which a man as sexually active as our Clive has doubtless seen before. Anyway, that's all a bit beside the point, which is that while you've supposedly been working on your yoga every Wednesday night, you've actually been practising positions of a rather different kind.'

'That's not true! I only saw him once or twice, when things were going so badly between us two. We had a thing together before, when I was with Dennis. The only reason anything happened this time was because you were being so horrible to me. I wanted to reassure myself that I was still desirable.'

I laughed savagely.

'Oh I see, it was all *my* fault!'

'It was both our faults. But it wasn't important. It was just a bit of fun as far as I was concerned. It meant more than that to him, though. That's why I agreed to go away with him this weekend, to tell him that it's all over.'

'Seems rather a long way to go for that.'

Karen adroitly brought the waterworks on stream.

'I was afraid! Afraid for *us*. Clive can't accept that I don't love him. I quite fancy him, but I don't love him. I was terrified about what he might do when I told him I was pregnant by you. He'd been asking me to go away with him for ages, so I finally agreed, just so as to have time to explain things properly, to make him understand that if he cared for me he had to let me go.'

'Sure, Karen.'

'I wasn't going to sleep with him! Do you think I could do that, knowing that I'm carrying your child inside me?'

'Speaking of which . . .'

'Look, let's forget Clive. Let's forget this woman you've been seeing. This is between you and me. Nothing else matters but this life we've created together. The rest is just play, but this is real. I know it won't be easy. We're too different for that. But we've got to try and make it work. We owe it to our child!'

I recognized this tune. I'd sung it myself once, back in the days when I was a penniless suitor and Karen a wealthy widow. But times had changed, *nos et*, it goes without saying, *mutamur in illis*. Karen was the suitor now, and I was not in the giving vein.

'I'm afraid the prospect of surrogate fatherhood doesn't attract me, Karen.'

As usual, she skipped the word which did not compute.

'But you said you *were*! You said you wanted us to get married and have a child . . .'

'Yes, but I was rather taking it for granted that it would be *my* child.'

She stared at me aghast.

'It *is*!'

'That's not what Clive says.'

'What does he know?'

'What do *you* know? You can't have been on the pill because you were trying to get pregnant with me.'

'We used something else.'

'What?'

She hesitated. Close-ups of Clive unrolling a sheath over his engorged member were definitely unsuitable for the family audience to which she was hoping to appeal.

'An old balloon?' I suggested. 'Cavity wall insulation foam? Herbal pessaries? Whatever it was, it didn't work. Be honest, Karen, you didn't even *want* it to work. You were so desperate to get pregnant you were beyond caring who the father was. You'd probably have preferred it to be me, all other things being equal. But you weren't really unduly worried about that aspect of it, were you?'

'That's not true! It's your child! I know it is. Women know these things.'

'OK, let's get a paternity test done.'

'No!'

She glared furiously at me. I shrugged.

'I rest my case.'

'Those tests can be dangerous! I'm not letting some doctor mess around with the foetus just because you're a heartless shit who won't believe what I say.'

'If you think *I'm* a heartless shit, just wait till you tell Clive that he's going to have to assume his responsibilities because we're getting divorced.'

She stood up, her hands over her ears, rocking back and forth on her heels, muttering something I couldn't make out. Then she sighed deeply and stroked her midriff, as though to reassure the foetus.

'You can't wriggle out of it that easily, you bastard! I'll bring a paternity suit. I'll get those tests done all right, once the child is born.'

'As many as you like, Karen. All they'll prove is that the only bastard round here is the one in your womb.'

That did it. She threw herself at me, shrieking and spitting, battering me with her fists and shoes. Women get a good press these days. It's become intellectually respectable, even among those who otherwise reject gender-based distinctions, to suggest that they're somehow intrinsically nicer than men and that the problems of the world would magically resolve themselves if we all became more womanly. In my view this is sexist bullshit. Given the chance, woman can be every bit as unpleasant as men. Karen's expression as she attacked reminded me of photographs of Ilsa Koch and Myra Hindley. She looked quite literally devilish.

'You cunt!' she screamed.

The inappropriacy of this term of abuse was lost on both of us, I fear. Irony was never Karen's strong suit, and I was too busy staving off her frenzied assault to appreciate it. Karen was smaller and lighter than me, but fitter and much more highly-motivated. She kneed me in the groin, savaged my face with her nails and battered my shins and ankles with her sharply pointed shoes. Her energy was demonic, the sudden release of months of pent-up hatred and frustration. I tried to contain her, but my defences were swiftly overwhelmed.

She wanted me to hit her, of course. That would prove her right, prove me to be the heartless bastard she said I was. What worried me was that it would prove it not just to her but to everyone. She could have her bruises examined and described and then produce photographs and medical witnesses in court to discomfort me. Those marital stigmata would transfigure Karen from promiscuous bitch into battered wife, while I would appear a sadistic adventurer who was not content with taking her money but had to beat her up as well. I would be lucky to get off with a suspended sentence, and I could certainly kiss goodbye to any hope of favourable settlement. And to Alison, needless to say.

I *did* hit out, but not physically. Garcia would have been proud of me. I chose a blow that hurt her worse than any punch, but left no marks at all.

'Do you know what a vasectomy is, Karen?'

She kicked me viciously on the ankle. I gritted my teeth, wrenched her arm painfully and repeated my question.

'Of course I bloody well know!'

'Well here's something else you should know. I've had one.'

It took a moment for this to sink in. Then her body went limp in my arms.

'What you mean?'

'I mean that I'm incapable of fatherhood. I've been surgically sterilized. Cut, snipped, gelded.'

Her eyes were wide open, but she was looking inward now, assessing the damage. Reports were still coming in, but already she could tell that it was very bad, a major disaster.

'Then it was all lies.'

I said nothing. I'd made my point, and I wasn't in the mood to chat. She turned away, mumbling the same phrase I'd heard earlier, but louder now, more urgently.

'No love, no love, no love, no love, no love.'

Yes, well, it was all very sad. It would be nice if there was more love around. We thought we could make it happen, back in the sixties. We were wrong. Love's gone the way of Father Christmas, the tooth fairy and the man in the moon. It's for the kiddies, that stuff. We've grown up now. We don't believe in love any more.

I left Karen to her maudlin reveries and went upstairs to lie down for a bit before she came back for the next round. It didn't seem likely that either of us would get much sleep that night.

When I awoke the room was dark. Through the uncurtained window the upper branches of a tree outside the house were backlit by the streetlamp opposite. I was lying fully dressed on top of the covers. Karen's side of the bed had not been disturbed at all. In addition to a totally irrelevant erection, I was suffering from a splitting headache and a nasty case of heartburn. The clock was in one of those positions – ten past two, in this case – where it seems to have only one hand.

I got up and went to the bathroom, where I took some paracetamol and Alka Seltzer. The upper landing was illuminated by the glow of the hallway light. Karen, I assumed, was drowning her sorrows in the dusk-to-dawn movies accessible via the satellite dish which Dennis had installed. She might even have fallen asleep in front of the set. It wouldn't have been the first time. I leant over the banister and peered down the stairs.

For the past week, a magazine wrapped in a plastic cover had been resting on the third step from the bottom, a professional journal which Dennis had subscribed to and which kept arriving despite our attempts to convince the publisher's computer that the intended recipient was beyond caring about such topics as '1992: The Implications for Your Clients'. Now, however, the glossy package was no longer on the step but lying on the floor in the middle of the hallway.

It was the very triviality of this fact which drew me downstairs to investigate. The displacement of the magazine seemed such a meaningless gesture that my curiosity was aroused. I was about half-way down the stairs – almost exactly where Dennis must have been standing the morning he almost caught us in bed together, in fact – when I spotted one of Karen's shoes lying in the doorway to the living room. Even more interesting, her foot was still in it.

A few steps more and I could make out the rest of the body sprawled on the parquet flooring a few inches away from the hideous neo-Spanish cabinet which the Parsons had chosen to 'add a bit of character' to their hallway, an over-elaborate mock-antique affair with metal strengthenings at the corners, cast-iron handles with sharp edges and a massive key protruding from the cupboard doors. Dennis had remarked jocularly that someone would do themselves an injury on it sooner or later. At the time this had seemed just like one of those things you say.

I knelt down beside Karen and shook her about a bit. She looked pale, but not any more than was to be expected after the amount she had drunk. There was a nasty-looking bruise, all puffy and yellow, high up on her right temple, just below the hairline. It was clear what had happened. After a further bout of solitary boozing in the living room she had headed for the stairs, intent either on sleep or another confrontation with me. In her maudlin stupor she had failed to notice the plastic-wrapped magazine, which had performed the same function as the banana skin in the traditional joke. Karen had toppled backwards and fallen head-first against the Spanish chest, knocking herself out.

I felt a heavy sinking of the stomach, as when the washing machine backs up and floods the kitchen, or the car breaks down in a contraflow on the M25. It never occurred to me that her injuries might be serious. All I could think of was the fuss and bother involved, the fact that I wouldn't be able to go straight back to bed. What a bore!

I grabbed her under the armpits and dragged her into the living room. An open bottle stood on the side-table next to a fallen tumbler and a puddle of spilt whisky. I dumped Karen on the sofa. She flopped sideways, totally limp. I slapped her face a few times. I called her name loudly. There was no response.

After a while I became aware of another sound in the room, a mechanical whine I had hitherto associated with the fridge or central heating. After a brief search I traced it to the telephone, which was lying underneath the sofa. Had Karen just knocked it over, or had she phoned someone? And if so, who? I was half-way through making some coffee when I remembered that every conversation on that line was being monitored on the tape-recorder I kept in the spare bedroom. I raced upstairs and rewound the tape to the beginning of the last call.

'This is Oxford 46933. I'm afraid I can't make it to the phone just now, but if you want to leave a message I'll get back to you as soon as I can. Please speak after the tone.'

'Clive? Clive? You know who this is, Clive? It's me, Clive. Me, Karen.'

A long silence.

'Why d'you tell him, Clive? You shouldn't've told him. Now he hates me.'

Silence.

'I don't want to stay here, Clive. I'm frightened. Please come and take me away.'

Silence.

'Please, Clive! There's no love here. No love. It's cold and dark, and things could happen.'

Silence.

'Just for a few days, darling. Until things have settled down again. I don't want to stay here. I'm frightened.'

This was followed by a dull thump, then a groan, and finally a click as Clive's answering machine broke the connection.

I sat there in a daze for some time, replaying the tape again and again. Each time it sounded worse.

Back in the living room, Karen lay where I had left her. She looked utterly lifeless. I couldn't feel any pulse in her wrist, she didn't seem to be breathing, her skin was cold. For the first time I began to worry that she might have injured herself seriously. I recalled an article in the local paper about a child who had fallen off his bike. He seemed perfectly all right at the time, but the next morning had complained of a persistent headache. A few hours later he was rushed into hospital in an irreversible coma and they'd unplugged his life support machine a few weeks later.

Under normal circumstances I would have called an ambulance, but these were not normal circumstances. The message on Clive's answering machine constituted apparently damning evidence against me. *I* knew that the thump on the tape must have been caused by Karen drunkenly knocking over the phone, but to the police it would sound like the blow inflicted with the traditional 'blunt instrument' by the jealous husband who had come into the living room to find his wife secretly phoning her lover. When it was revealed that Karen was pregnant with Clive's child, and that they had been planning to go away together the following day, inverted commas would close in around the word 'accident' like a pair of handcuffs.

I gave Karen another brisk dose of the 'Now stop all this nonsense and snap out of it' treatment, but without the slightest effect. Suddenly I knew she was dead. What else did the word mean if not this maddening indifference, this infinite capacity for sullen withdrawal? The dead are so selfish, so irresponsible! They just piss off, leaving the rest of us to clear up after them. All the arrangements I had so carefully made would now have to be cancelled. Not only was there no hope of getting even with Clive, but I stood a very good chance of being accused of killing Karen into the bargain. A monstrous miscarriage of justice was in the making. It was so unfair, so totally unfair!

The alternative version which eventually began to take shape in my mind seemed at first nothing but a daydream, a childish fantasy of punishment fitting the crime. In an ideal world, if anyone had to take the rap for Karen's death then it would be *Clive*. Quite apart from his unsavoury intervention in my marriage, he was a thoroughly unpleasant character who richly deserved whatever was coming to him. The day he was convicted, a resounding cheer would be heard throughout the EFL world as the victims of his dirty tricks celebrated their vicarious revenge.

At first, as I say, this vision remained purely abstract, but as time passed I began to speculate idly about how it might be put into practice. I fetched a pen and paper and started making notes, more and more excitedly as the scheme came together in my mind. Gradually the plan took on a life of its own, and by the time I had finished working out all the details I couldn't have backed out if I'd tried. The thing demanded to be done, and there simply wasn't anyone else to do it.

I had arranged to meet Garcia near his lodgings in Botley, a suburb of Oxford which sounds like a form of food poisoning and looks like its effects, gobs of half-digested architectural matter sprayed across the countryside with desperate abandon. I reached the rendezvous shortly after 8 o'clock, having stopped at the station to show off the BMW and buy a single ticket to Banbury. I'd only had a few hours sleep, and felt exhausted and depressed.

When there was no sign of Garcia at the grim thirties estate pub where we were to meet, a feeling of panic overwhelmed me. All my plans depended on his help, and by now it was too late to abort them. I drove past the pub and circled the area for a few minutes. When I returned he was there, squeezed into his jeans and leather jacket like one of the apes which spinsters proverbially lead in hell.

'Everything all right?' he asked.

'Fine.'

'Your wife . . . ?'

'All taken care of.'

I passed him one of the pairs of rubber gloves I'd brought and told him to put them on before getting into the car. The beauty of the plan I had worked out was that every one of its numerous and minute details were generated by a simple set of exclusion zones. I existed in the BMW but not in Clive's Lotus. Karen and Clive existed in the Lotus but not in the BMW. As for Garcia, he didn't exist at all.

On the back seat stood Karen's suitcase, coat and handbag as well as a couple of Sainsbury's shopping bags containing a roll of bin-liners, an assortment of nails, scissors, a pair of wellington boots, a navy-blue blanket, plastic food bags, a torch, a large sponge-bag, packing tape and a selection of food and drink to see us both through the day.

'And the generator?' asked Garcia.

'There's been a change of plan. We're going to kidnap him instead. That's almost as good, and far less risky. Twelve hours is a long time to spend bound and gagged in a car boot, particularly when you don't know what's going to happen when the car stops.'

'And what *is* going to happen?'

'Nothing. We just turn him loose in the middle of nowhere. By the time he gets to the police we'll be home. There's no evidence of any kidnap, no generator to trace.'

Garcia clearly thought that this was a pretty wimpy sort of vengeance, but as long I was paying he wasn't going to argue.

Traffic was light and we made good time. A few miles south of Banbury I turned off the main road and let Garcia take the wheel. He had assured me that he could drive, which was true, in the sense that chickens can fly and horses swim. When it came to piloting military vehicles in a country where they enjoy absolute priority over all other traffic, Garcia's roadcraft was no doubt perfectly adequate, but for the purposes of my plan he had not merely to get the BMW from A to B while avoiding collisions with other vehicles and the surrounding landscape, but also without attracting the attention of the police. It was too late to worry about this now, however.

After Garcia's brief test drive we pulled over to review the practical arrangements. He pointed out that Clive wouldn't be able to breathe through the waterproof lining of the sponge-bag I'd brought to use as a hood, so I stabbed a few holes in it with the scissors. Then we slid the front seats of the car forward, making room for Garcia to lie down in the back. I covered him with the blanket and we set off.

The station car park was full of rows of commuter cars, but apart from a few taxis there were only two vehicles outside the station building. One was a florist's van, the other Clive's yellow Lotus sports car. I gave a sigh of relief. My greatest anxiety had been that Clive might have replayed the messages on his answering machine, suspected that something was wrong and stayed away. I parked on the other side of the florist's van. The train from Oxford arrived six minutes late. The passengers dispersed rapidly on foot and in the taxis. The van driver emerged with three flat cardboard boxes of flowers. He gave the BMW an incurious glance before roaring off.

Inside the station building, Clive was just hanging up the receiver of one of the public telephones when he caught sight of me. He glanced away again, as though it might be one of those embarrassing cases of mistaken identity. I walked over to him. He looked again. This time there was no mistake. It was me all right. Oh dear. Oh dear, oh dear.

'I think we'd better have a little talk,' I said, gesturing towards the BMW.

Clive followed without demur. He knew there was no point in trying to bullshit his way out of it. If I was there, it could only be because Karen had confessed.

We got into the car. Clive adjusted his nifty blouson and chinos and sat there like the player he was, waiting for me to pitch. Already he was looking calmer, more his old smarmy self.

'I know what's been going on,' I said.

'Do you?'

His tone was aloof, almost scornful.

'You've been stuffing my wife.'

Clive regarded me with distaste.

'Yes, I suppose that *is* how you'd see it.'

I would have hit him there and then, but an ageing Morris Marina had just pulled into the slot vacated by the florist's van. A bald man wearing a baggy cardigan and trousers with perpetual creases emerged from the Marina. He looked around with a vaguely benevolent smile and then toddled off into the station.

'Where is Karen?' Clive asked.

I was terribly tempted to tell him!

'She changed her mind about this weekend. There's a message on your answering machine. Didn't you check it?'

He shook his head.

'I was out pretty late last night.'

'Quite right too. Make the most of your freedom while it lasts.'

He looked at me and frowned.

'Pardon?'

'Oh, didn't she tell you? You're going to be a daddy, Clive.'

In the rear-view mirror I could see the bald man returning with an elderly woman who was walking with the aid of an aluminium frame. I just had to keep the conversation going for a few more minutes. Then they would be gone, and Clive's brief reprieve would be over.

'She's . . . pregnant?' he breathed.

'That's right. And I opted out of parenthood several years ago. I don't affect the tie, but I'm a fully-fledged member of the cut-and-run club. Which leaves you holding the baby.'

He sat staring straight ahead through the windscreen.

'Did Kay know that?' he said eventually.

His use of the past tense startled me, until I realized that it referred to the implied continuation 'when she married you'. It's little things like that which can be so tricky to explain to a class.

'About my vasectomy? Of course. You don't think I'd keep a thing like that from my wife, do you?'

His face lit up.

'Then she did it on purpose!'

He sounded disgustingly moved.

'Of course she did!' I retorted. 'To trap you into marrying her.'

'*Trap* me? I've been begging her to marry me for years, but all she's ever done is go out with me a few times when the marriage wasn't going well. But this proves she's changed her mind!'

'All it proves, Clive, is what everyone already knew, namely that you're a first-rate prick.'

I had raised my voice, which unfortunately attracted the attention of the Marina owner, who was still loading Granny into his wallymobile.

'I'm sorry,' Clive replied in a soothing tone. 'I forgot how painful all this must be for you. How did you find out about us? Did Karen tell you?'

'Not in so many words. I overheard her talking to you on the telephone the other day. Do you know how that felt?'

'I can imagine,' he murmured sympathetically as the Marina drove away.

'No, you can't. But you don't need to. It felt like this.'

And I hammered my fist into his groin.

From behind the wheel of the Lotus, the entrance to the quarry looked bumpier than I had remembered. The possibility of the low-slung sports car grounding out occurred to me for the first time. I revved up and took a run at it. There were one or two loud metallic sounds like waves slapping the bottom of a dinghy, then I was inside the quarry. A few moments later the BMW appeared, cruising with ease over the uneven ground. Everything was going my way. A patina of the Lotus's underbody paint would remain like lichen on the rocks at the entrance to the quarry for the forensic experts to find, while the high-riding BMW would leave no trace of its presence.

The quarry had not been in use for a long time, and owing to the friability of the local stone and the thick covering of weeds and undergrowth it might have been mistaken for a natural feature except for the perfectly level floor of reddish earth. That brick-red soil interested me, because I knew it would interest the police. It was distinctive, characteristic and definable. It could be weighed, measured, subjected to chemical and spectroscopic analysis and then produced in court in a neat little plastic bag marked 'Exhibit A'. In short, it was a *clue*.

That's why I'd brought the wellies for Garcia. He was going to drive the BMW, and since the BMW had never been to the quarry, we couldn't have any of the distinctive red soil ending up inside it. He parked alongside the Lotus, as I'd instructed him, revving up the engine in the best macho fashion before switching off. I opened the front door of the BMW. Clive was lying in a foetal crouch forward of the front passenger seat, the sponge-bag tightly laced around his neck. The bag was a sporty model for jocks on the trot, sheeny acrylic with a go-faster stripe. It complemented Clive's outfit so well he might have chosen it himself.

Our departure from Banbury had gone very smoothly.

While Clive was still writhing, a blanket-draped form had risen from the back of the car like the awakened kraken to apply the *coup de grâce*. Garcia's idea of 'a little tap on the head' consisted of a vicious blow from what looked like a salami wrapped in a sock. It certainly did the trick. Clive collapsed like a marionette whose strings have been cut. Garcia explained the construction of the weapon – a sand-filled hemp bag covered with cotton and a plastic sheath – and assured me there would be nothing to show. It was all his own work, he added proudly, right down to the motto inked into the cotton underlay: TRADICION, FAMILIA Y PROPIEDAD.

While Garcia struggled into the green wellies I carefully wiped the door handle, fascia and leather-work of the BMW to remove any prints which Clive might have left. Then we lifted his inert body back into a sitting position in the front seat, taped his ankles and knees together, twisted his arms behind his back and taped them just above the wrist. It was strong packing-tape, easy to cut but impossible to tear, and less likely to leave marks than wire or rope. By the time we had finished, Clive was trussed like a chicken. I got out his key-holder and inspected the contents. There were big keys, small keys, short keys and tall keys, each marked with a different coloured blob of paint to tell Clive which compartment of his life it opened. Only one, a battered Yale tethered next to the Lotus's ignition key, bore no marking. I removed it from the case and placed it carefully in my wallet.

The boot of the Lotus contained Clive's overnight bag and a slurry of EFL promotional material. We transferred this to the back seat and pulled the spare wheel out of its housing. I told Garcia to dump it among the rocks on the far side of the quarry. As he rolled the tyre away I opened the boot of the BMW. The lid slid smoothly up on its hydraulic supports. I almost screamed aloud at the sight that met my eyes.

Seven hours earlier, back at the house on Ramillies Drive, I had carefully packaged Karen's body for the journey. I had taped her arms and ankles together, then fetched the roll of plastic dustbin-liners from under the sink and worked one bag over the head, shoulders and chest and another over the legs, hips and stomach. I then wrapped a third bag around the overlap between the other two and taped the whole issue together in the manner approved by the Post Office for large and bulky objects of irregular shape. I was amazed at how easy it was to think of Karen as a large and bulky object of irregular shape. Her death didn't mean anything to me. In my heart, I believed she was upstairs in our bedroom, snoring in the way which Dennis had so graphically described on another occasion. In the morning we would greet each other grumpily over breakfast as usual. Meanwhile I had this body to dispose of.

I picked up the bundle, lifting carefully from the knees so as not to do myself an injury, and carried it through to the back hallway. The BMW was still on the gravel sweep at the side of the house where I'd parked it when I came home that afternoon. The same streetlight that illuminated the tree in the bedroom window fell on the car, and I didn't want any insomniac neighbour noticing that Karen was leaving home horizontally, so I let off the handbrake and pushed the car round the corner into the shadows at the back of the house. The boot was filled with all the miscellaneous junk I had rented or bought for my now-aborted project with Garcia. I transferred the portable generator to the garage and the rest to the back seat, then returned to the house, picked up my home-made body-bag and loaded it into the boot. This amorphous, impersonal package was what I'd been expecting to see when I lifted the lid again at the quarry. Instead, I was confronted by a dishevelled mass of torn plastic through which Karen's feet, elbows and horribly distorted face projected like a butterfly emerging from the chrysalis.

I touched her cheek. It was almost cold. She was dead now all right, but apparently she hadn't been when I put her there. At some point she must have regained consciousness, only to find herself entombed in a cold steel vault. Perhaps she had called out. She had certainly struggled hard to free herself, but all she had been able to do was muss up her plastic shroud a little and prepare a nasty surprise for me, a surprise which had used up the precious seconds I needed to do what had to be done. Already Garcia was on his way back.

'Not there!' I called to him. 'Further away! In the bushes!'

Once his back was turned again, I picked up the corpse and carried it over to the Lotus, dumped it in the boot and ripped the remains of the plastic sheathing off. I then snipped through the tape bindings with the scissors and let the limbs fall freely and naturally into place. I soon realized that Karen's delayed death had actually worked to my benefit, since rigor mortis had not set in before I could remove the tape. I then carried over one of the broken concrete fence-posts I had noted among the construction waste on my first visit to the quarry and laid it out next to Karen. I hurriedly added her suitcase, coat and handbag. By the time Garcia returned, the Lotus was closed and locked and I was lining the boot of the BMW with plastic bin-liners split and taped together.

The next shock was that Clive was no longer on the front seat where we had left him. A moment later I saw him grovelling helplessly about among the driving pedals, his back bent at a painful angle over the gear housing, calling for help in a voice muffled by the sponge-bag. I bent down and struck the garishly swaddled head hard with my fist.

'There's no one here to help you, Clive. There's no one here but me, and I'm not going to help you. Do you know what I'm going to do? I've got a pair of garden shears here, Clive. I'm going to use them on you. I'm going to prune you. You've been getting a bit *rampant* lately, Clive, a bit rank and luxuriant. I'm going to have to cut you back, I'm afraid. I'm going to have to *dock* you.'

I paused.

'Or there again I may not. It all depends. It depends on so many things. On my mood, on the weather, on the number of magpies, black cats and squashed hedgehogs we pass, on whether I can pick up anything worth listening to on the radio and whether my piles are giving me gyp after a day in your shoddy little bucket seats. It depends on all that and more, far more than I could ever express in words. But one thing all those ineffable factors have in common is that there isn't a single solitary effing thing you can do about them. You would therefore be well-advised to make the most of the one way in which you can attempt to influence the eventual outcome, Clive, which is by SHUTTING THE FUCK UP!'

The hooded figure was silent and still. I took Garcia to one side – it wouldn't do for us to be heard conversing in Spanish – and told him to put Clive in the boot. I'd had enough of humping bodies about for one morning.

When I had planned out the day's activities earlier that morning, the drive to Wales had appeared as a sort of *entr'acte* between the strenuous and demanding dramatics before and after. To them I had devoted intensive care and detailed scrutiny, but I'd hardly given a thought to the journey itself. Time was not a factor. We could do nothing until darkness fell anyway. Since the Lotus and the BMW were too distinctive to risk them being seen together on the little-used cross-country roads, I had planned a roundabout route using motorways as much as possible. Garcia's instructions were very simple. He was to maintain a constant speed of 60 mph. I would remain some distance behind, keeping the BMW always in view. As we approached each junction, I would accelerate past and lead him to the correct exit.

Foolproof, eh? I certainly thought so. But I hadn't done any motorway driving since returning to Britain, so I was unaware that in practice the 70 mph limit now indicates a *minimum* speed, barely acceptable even in the slow lane. Poor Garcia did his best to obey my instructions, but what with the queue of irate and contemptuous drivers building up behind him, and the exciting responsiveness of the BMW to the slightest pressure of his foot on the accelerator, he was very soon out of sight. And there wasn't a damn thing I could about it, because Clive's fancy little roadster turned out to be underpowered, badly tuned and apt to ramble all over the road if you took your mind off the driving for a second. It was while I was staring gloomily at the speedometer that I noticed the needle of the fuel gauge leaning over like a drunk against a bar, deep inside a red zone marked EMPTY.

Objectively speaking, the fifteen minutes which followed could hardly have been more banal, but they were in fact the most stressful part of the entire day. As I said, my plan was constructed on a series of strict exclusion zones. I was in one of these and Clive's Lotus in another, and never the twain should meet. I had been extremely careful to avoid leaving any traces of my presence in the car, but all that would count for nothing if I broke down on the motorway and had to be rescued by the police. Even if they didn't happen to open the boot and find the remains of a Caucasian female, the incident would be logged, and the link between me and the Lotus thus become a matter of official record. By keeping speeds low and coasting down any hills I managed to keep the Lotus going through a seemingly endless tract of motorway without turn-offs or signs of any sort, but when an exit finally appeared I knew I was going to have to take it. Apart from anything else, there was far less chance of attracting the attention of the police once I was off the motorway. As for Garcia, I tried not to think about what he might be getting up to all on his own.

I found petrol almost right away, on one of the roads leading away from the junction roundabout. I hastily filled up and returned to the motorway. A few miles further on I had to slam on the brakes when I caught sight of the BMW parked on the hard shoulder with the hazard flashers going, the doors wide open and Garcia standing there in his bouncer's outfit and rapist's gloves having a smoke and admiring the scenery. The only thing missing was a large sign saying BOOT SALE HERE TODAY.

After that things went relatively smoothly. I kept Garcia in sight to the end of the motorway, just beyond Telford, and then overtook to lead him along the country roads to our destination. Dusk was just falling as we left Llangurig along a verdant valley in which one of those squeaky-clean Welsh streams was fleetingly visible. After about ten miles we turned right up a narrow mountain road which climbed steeply to a pass and then dropped into the high valley of the Elan river, at this point little more than a shallow stream artificially widened by the dammed waters of the upper reservoir. I parked the Lotus by the roadside and walked back to join Garcia in the BMW. I was no longer worried about the cars being seen together. Apart from a few neurotic-looking sheep, there was no one to see them. We ate the rest of the food I had brought while the darkness gathered. From time to time there was an occasional thump from the back of the car. I mentally drafted a letter of complaint to BMW. 'Dear Sir: On long trips my wife and I are frequently disturbed by the weeping and wailing of our Filipino maids, who travel in the boot. It is quite intolerable that a car of this supposed quality . . .' Sign it with an Arab name and an address in Knightsbridge.

When we had finished our snack I gave Garcia further instructions. They were brief and simple. He was to wait one hour exactly, then drive on along the road until he saw me. I left him there with a pack of chocolate digestives, a can of Coke and a rather faint and crackly German pop station he had managed to find, and drove off in the Lotus.

The road ran for several miles along the hillside overlooking the upper two lakes, before dipping down into a wood and zigzagging across the overflow stream to hug the eastern bank of the lowest and largest of the three reservoirs. It was dark by now, but I remembered the scene clearly from the walk Karen and I had taken on the last day of our stay in the Elan Valley. I particularly recalled Karen's shiver as she looked at the black waters far below.

I continued along the bank of the reservoir and across the narrow viaduct of roughly finished stone carrying a forestry trail off into the mountains on the other bank. When I reached the far side I turned the car around, then drove part of the way back. It was pitch-dark and had started to rain, a steady hushing which merely seemed to intensify the silence. I opened the boot of the Lotus and propped the torch on the support strut. Karen showed no further signs of undead activity. There was no doubt now that I was dealing with a corpse, pale, cold and stiff, the back of the legs and neck a nasty greyish-blue colour, as though posthumously bruised by bumping around in the Lotus's boot. I'd always assumed that there was a big difference between the living and the dead, some glaring and obvious distinction, but apart from the cosmetic details I've mentioned, a sort of accelerated ageing, Karen seemed much the same person I'd known and loved all along. If there was something missing then it certainly wasn't anything I'd cared much about in the first place. For most men, I suppose, sex rarely amounts to much more than necrophilia with the living.

Rigor mortis was fairly advanced by this stage, so instead of trying to wrap Karen's arms around the concrete post I laid it along her spine. I had originally intended to tie the body to the post with the lengths of electric wire I'd bought for the torture session, but among the miscellaneous items in Clive's boot was a tow-rope, so I naturally used that instead. I wound it round and round the two rigidities and tied the ends together in a no doubt excessive number of knots.

The next step was to hoist the corpse on to the broad parapet which ran along the bridge to either side at about chest height. As soon as I tried to do this I realized that I had made a mistake in roping it to the post first. I simply couldn't lift Karen *and* the length of reinforced concrete. But I simply had to. At the first attempt we both ended up lying in the roadway, me on my knees and Karen flat out in the gutter. By leaving one end of the post there, I was able to hoist the other on to the edge of the parapet, with Karen roped to it like Joan of Arc at the stake. It was at this point that a pair of headlights appeared on the other side of the reservoir.

The vehicle circled round in the parking area at the far end of the bridge and drew up facing the water. It had to be the local Water and Sewage Authority officials, I reckoned. I couldn't see what anyone else would be doing up there at that time of night. They would no doubt feel the same, and drive over to investigate. It was too late to heave the body over the side without being seen and apprehended, if only for contributing to the state of the nation's water supplies which has led to an understandable confusion in many people's minds between the two activities for which the Authorities are responsible. No, I was just going to have to bluff my way through it. 'Good evening. Just admiring the view. This is my wife. Yes, she's rather poorly, I'm afraid. Well in fact she's dead, but we don't like to mention it in front of her.'

Fear lent me new strength. I heaved the other end of the post up on to the parapet, slid it across, and shoved the whole issue over the edge. A moment later there was a satisfyingly loud splash. I opened Karen's handbag and added the single ticket to Banbury I had bought that morning, then threw that in along with her suitcase and coat. I slammed the boot shut, got back into the Lotus and drove it hard into the parapet, denting the wing and scraping a bright patch of yellow paint off on the stonework. Another clue. The cops were going to love this one.

As I slowed to turn off the bridge I caught sight of two pale faces peering out at me through the misted glass of the parked car. Just a courting couple out for a Saturday night snog. I drove fast along the bank of the reservoir, over the stream and up the winding road through the forest to the bare moors above. There were only ten minutes left of the hour I had allowed before Garcia came looking for me. I must have been feeling a bit light-headed. It had been a day of uncommon stress and responsibility, following an almost sleepless and extremely fraught night. At any rate, I totally misjudged one particularly sharp and inclined hairpin, and the Lotus spun off the road, hit a tree and bounced off into a large patch of mud.

Advertising executives dream about people like me. Such was my slavish adherence to the 'clunk, click, every trip' slogan that even when driving away from a mountain reservoir after dumping my wife's body, I had not neglected to fasten my seat-belt, so I was shocked rather than crippled for life by the collision. When I tried to reverse out of the mud, though, I discovered that the car was hopelessly stuck. All the better. My original idea had been to disable the Lotus by driving a nail into one of its tyres – the spare wheel had been removed at the quarry, supposedly to make room for Karen's body – but my accident had achieved exactly the same purpose, and even more convincingly.

Garcia rolled up in the BMW a few minutes later. We drove back up the valley and across the bleak mountain pastures to a spot I had selected earlier, just beyond a cattle grid. I parked the car so that the headlights illuminated the field of operations and gave Garcia careful advance instructions. When we opened the boot, Clive looked a very Sorry Rabbit indeed, lying there on the plastic sheeting, his co-ordinated leisurewear steeped in his own urine. I cut through the tape binding his ankles, knees and arms. I replaced his key-holder in his pocket, minus the Yale front-door key I'd retained, and motioned to Garcia to help me lift him out of the car. When we laid him down in the road he showed the first sign of life so far, moving his limbs feebly like a clockwork soldier in need of rewinding.

We picked him up and frog-marched him off the unfenced road and across the adjacent wilderness to the top of a steep slope overlooking a marshy depression at the end of the upper reservoir. There we stopped, holding him by one arm each. He made no attempt to struggle. I loosened the sponge-bag from around his throat and looked expectantly at Garcia. Then I plucked off Clive's hood, and in the same moment we heaved him forward over the edge of the slope. He fell without a cry, rolling head over heels, arms and legs flailing uselessly until the darkness below swallowed him up.

The return journey passed uneventfully. It was shortly after midnight when we reached the pub where I had picked Garcia up that morning. I handed him a sealed envelope containing the sum we had agreed on. He counted it carefully. I then outlined the true nature of the events in which he had just participated, and explained that in the eyes of the law he was an accessory to murder. This resulted in a prolonged outburst of unpleasantness in the course of which aspersions were cast upon the legitimacy of my birth, the virility of my anonymous father was openly derided, and it was further alleged that my mother habitually engaged in unnatural practices involving donkeys, goats and – I found this a bit far-fetched – vultures. For his final sally Garcia switched to English.

'You drop me into it, you bloody heel!'

'You were already in it, *amigo*. But if you shut up and move fast, this will get you out.'

He stuffed the cash into his pocket and climbed out of the car, slamming the door behind him. I never saw him again, but I eventually learned from Trish that he had disappeared from the school the following week. This had aroused no particular comment. Garcia's precarious situation was by now notorious, and everyone assumed that he had fled without warning in an attempt to throw the human rights hounds off the scent. In any case, no one at the Oxford International Language College cared much what had happened to Garcia by then. They were too absorbed in the latest twists and turns of the real-life soap opera starring their very own principal, Mr Clive Phillips.

I had one more chore to attend to before going home. This involved driving across town to the up-market Victorian property on the side of Headington Hill where Clive lived. The lower floor was dark, but a light showed in one of the bedrooms and another from a small window in the roof. I parked the BMW some distance away, slipped on my rubber gloves and made my way back on foot. The gate had been stolen or vandalized. I walked up the tiled path to the front door. From the nearby Cowley Road came whoops of drunken revelry. I got out the Yale key I had removed from Clive's holder and tried it in the lock. It went in all right, but it wouldn't turn.

I almost wept. After all I'd been through, I just couldn't handle this. Then a light suddenly came on in the hallway. The front door consisted of a semi-transparent sheet of ornamented glass through which I could now make out a flight of stairs. I followed the path round the corner of the house and hid in the shadows. A moment later the door opened. It didn't immediately close again, however. Instead, there ensued a leave-taking whose ardour and duration made the balcony scene in *Romeo and Juliet* look like a skinhead kiss-off. About a quarter of an hour passed before Romeo reluctantly dug his bike out of the bushes and took off. Juliet bolted the front door and ran upstairs to weep in her pillow.

It was the sound of the bolt that did it. Surely Clive wouldn't be best pleased if he returned home unexpectedly to find the door bolted against him? So maybe that wasn't the door he used. Maybe the front door was for the lodgers, while Clive retained a separate entrance to which he alone possessed the key. I followed the path along the side of the house. Sure enough, it ended at a door near the rear of the premises. This too was fitted with a Yale lock, and the key turned in it.

I switched on the lights and started to search the flat. The front hallway of the original house had been narrowed into a mere passageway leading from the front door to the stairs and the rented rooms upstairs, while the original sitting and dining rooms together with an extension containing a modern kitchen and bathroom had been retained for Clive's personal use. I'd been expecting fake-fur rugs and see-through cocktail cabinets, recessed strobe lights and a sunken Jacuzzi. The stud's stable, in short. Clive Phillips will be standing tonight. Service while you wait. Instead, it looked like a student's crash-pad. Clive was the next best thing to a millionaire, yet he'd been living in virtual squalor.

Then I saw the photo. It was a framed enlargement, sitting on a table which Clive had used as a desk. It was not a recent shot. Karen was sitting on a wooden bench, squinting slightly in the bright sunlight. She looked prettier than I had ever seen her, younger too, almost a different person. I had been obliged on several occasions to look through the Parsons' photographic archive, all sixteen volumes of it, but I had never seen this picture before.

'Clive?'

The door of the living room opened as though of its own accord.

'No,' I said. 'Not Clive.'

On the threshold stood Juliet, poised for flight.

'I'm a friend of Clive's,' I told her, smiling nicely. 'He knows I'm here. Look, he gave me the key.'

She was in her early twenties, the ideal clarity of her teenage beauty already slightly compromised by the gravity of the adult she would become.

'I see lights on. I will telephone to the police, but then I think maybe he is come back before.'

'Good for you. The thing is, Clive's in a spot of trouble. There are one or two things he has here, documents and so on, which he doesn't want falling into the wrong hands. So he asked me to come round and pick them up for him.'

'Why he doesn't come himself?'

'He can't, darling. He just hasn't got a window free for anybody.'

I picked up a pile of papers from the table as though these might be the incriminating documents I had come to remove. I noticed Juliet staring suspiciously at my rubber gloves. I held them out to her, strangler fashion.

'I'm not supposed to be here. Understand? I've never been here. No one has ever been here. Above all, no one has taken anything away. This is very important. Otherwise Clive will be sent to prison for a very long time. I'm sure your family wouldn't want you involved in anything like that, now would they?'

Her solemn face swung from side to side in fervent negation.

'Now then, do you happen to know where the phone is? I need to make a quick call, let Clive know everything's all right.'

She led me into the next room and pointed out the combined phone and answering machine. While I pretended to dial, I extracted the tape cassette from the machine and slipped it into my pocket. I put the phone down.

'No answer. He must have gone to bed. Which is where you should be, young lady.'

I left Clive's key on the hall table and walked Juliet back to the front of the house.

'Remember,' I told her, 'not a word to *anybody*!'

She nodded seriously. I was pretty sure I could depend on her not to talk. The trusting child thought that poor Clive's fate was in her hands. As it was, indeed, although not in quite the way she believed.

IV

One of the many false starts in my life was when I tried to take up golf. My father considered golf, like the *Daily Telegraph* and Bell's whisky, to be one of the essential elements of civilized male society. As in the palaeolithic era, learning to swing a club was a rite of passage. To me it was just a game, and a singularly boring one, just the sort of thing a bunch of old buffers like my dad would go in for. The last straw was the way the coach kept on about 'working on your follow-through'. Once the ball's gone it's gone, I thought. How you swing your club through the air afterwards can't make a damn bit of difference to where it ends up.

So I thought at fifteen. Now, at forty-something, I finally understood what my old golf coach meant, and as a result the following Sunday was very far from a day of rest for me. I didn't get home until almost 2 o'clock that morning, by which time I was too exhausted to do more than verify that the tape I had taken from Clive's house was indeed the one containing Karen's incriminating call, and then erase it. There was a message for me on my own machine, but I felt unable to cope with any more news, either good or bad, and went straight to bed. It took true grit to set the alarm clock for 7 o'clock, but I didn't want to botch my follow-through.

The first thing I did on awakening was return the various household items I had used to their place, having first carefully cleaned them. I devoted especial care to removing all traces of the red mud from the wellingtons Garcia had worn at the quarry. Then it was time to take out the rubbish. I packed all the plastic sheeting, the gloves, the sponge-bag and the used packing tape into a large dustbin-liner, put it in the BMW and drove around until I found a house where building work was being done, and dumped the sack in the skip outside. Then I proceeded to the car-wash at Wolvercote roundabout, where the BMW was mechanically sluiced, mopped, hosed, scrubbed, waxed, rubbed and blown dry. Thanks to Clive's incontinence the boot stank like a public lavatory, so I bought a litre of motor oil from the garage and poured most of the contents over the carpeting. Then I cross-threaded the cap so that it wouldn't close properly, and tossed the container in.

Back home I phoned Karen's mum in Liverpool. Old Elsie and I had never got on. She disapproved of her daughter's hasty remarriage, and still more of her choice of partner. Oddly enough, Elsie was the only one with the courage to come out and speak the truth, which was that Karen should have 'stuck to someone of her own sort'. This was a remarkable intuition. Dennis Parsons and I were not born that far apart on the social ladder, and by the time he had gone up in the world and I had gone down, the difference was as subtle, if as definitive, as that between Bordeaux and Côtes de Bordeaux. But such distinctions are second nature to women of Elsie Braithwaite's generation. She spotted immediately that Dennis, for all his glam, was 'Karen's sort', while for all my grot, I was not. Our Elsie was also a member of a fundamentalist sect which believes that making a phone call on the Sabbath constitutes an infringement of the Fourth Commandment, so I got doubly short shrift. No, I certainly couldn't speak to Karen. Karen wasn't there, and Elsie didn't know what on earth had possessed me to think that she was. I made my apologies and hung up.

The action of replacing the phone triggered one of those abdominal depth-charges which are nature's way of telling you that you've cocked up. Phones, the fatal row with Karen, my call to Alison, our luncheon date! While I was cavorting up the motorway in hot pursuit of Garcia, Alison would have been sitting in the restaurant where I'd arranged to meet her, glancing repeatedly at her watch while the waitresses and other customers tittered amongst themselves and whispered

'She's been stood up!' No woman would easily forget or forgive such a slight, least of all Alison Kraemer. Once the facts of the case came to light, my whereabouts on the Saturday in question were bound to be a critical issue. If Alison were to inform the police that I had not only unaccountably failed to show up, but hadn't even phoned to explain or apologize, my position would become awkward in the extreme.

I took a deep breath and called her number. The phone was answered by young Rebecca.

'Can I speak to your mother, please?'

'Who's speaking?'

I hesitated.

'Thomas Carter. It's about the madrigal group.'

'Hi, Tom! You sound a bit strange.'

'I've got a cold. Is your mom there?'

'She's gone to Dorset. Grandfather's been taken poorly.'

'Oh I'm sorry to hear that. Is there anything I can do? She hasn't left you there alone, has she?'

'No, Alex and I are staying with friends. I just came over to practise. Mum will be ringing tonight. Can I give her a message?'

'No, no, don't bother her. It's not urgent.'

As I hung up, I recalled the winking light on the answering machine the night before and spent five frantic minutes searching for the tape, which I had removed in order to erase the one I had taken from Clive's.

'I'm sorry not to reach you in person,' said Alison's voice, 'but I'm forced to concede that these machines do have their uses after all, and I suppose in the circumstances it's safe enough to leave a message.'

It took me a moment to realize that the circumstances she was referring to were Karen's supposed trip to her mother's. Already I was having a hard time remembering who knew which part of what story.

'I won't be able to make lunch today after all. My father has had a stroke, so I have to go down there and organize things. I'll be in touch as soon as possible.'

I capered round the living room like a manic morris dancer. With luck like this, how could I lose? I snatched up the phone again and called the police. Not 999, just the number in the book. After all, this wasn't an emergency, I told the woman who answered, at least I didn't think so. It was probably nothing at all, in fact, there was most likely some perfectly obvious and innocent explanation, only I was just a bit worried because, well, the fact of the matter was that my wife seemed to have disappeared.

On Monday I took the portable generator back to the hire shop in High Wycombe. When I got home, the police were waiting for me in an unmarked Ford Sierra. There were two of them, a tall sturdy bearded fellow and a shorter, slighter man with the studiously glum expression of a school prefect. I've forgotten their names. Let's call them Tom and Dick. Tom, the bearded one, approached me as I parked the BMW, introduced himself and his colleague, and asked if they could come in for a moment.

'Perhaps it would be better if you sat down, sir,' he suggested once we were inside. 'I'm afraid we've got some rather bad news.'

I lowered myself into a chair. Dick appeared to engross himself in a study of the Parsons' record collection while Tom recited his piece as though reading it from an autocue.

'Powys police have recovered a body which they believe to be that of your wife, sir. We would like you to accompany us to Wales with a view to identifying the remains.'

'Dead? How?'

'The body was recovered from a reservoir, we understand.'

'But that's ridiculous! Kay's an excellent swimmer. She *teaches* it! She's got certificates, cups . . .'

Tom looked at Dick, who stuck his tongue between his upper lip and teeth and sucked hard. He was clearly longing to make some crack about it being hard to swim with a concrete post tied to your back.

We reached Llandrindod Wells, the county town, early that evening. Tom and Dick maintained a discreet silence throughout the drive, like undertaker's assistants. Left to my own devices in the back seat, I reviewed the story I had prepared, searching for loopholes and finding none. After some backchat on the two-way radio we were met by a local police car which escorted us to the hospital where the body had been taken. I was then conducted to the mortuary chapel, where a small group of men were standing around a plinth supporting a polythene-wrapped package. One of them introduced himself as the Home Office pathologist and explained that in order to preserve continuity of evidence it was necessary for me to identify the body before they could proceed.

Two of the others undid the tape binding the package together and carefully parted the flaps so as to allow me a glimpse of the face. It was not a pretty sight. They say that in the first week of a diet you're just shedding water, and spending thirty-six hours in a reservoir obviously has the opposite effect. Karen looked all puffy and pouchy and wrinkled, as though she'd been on a steroid treatment that had gone terribly wrong. They'd positioned me on the left side, so that the injury to the temple was invisible. Nor could I see the concrete post, though its bulk was evident, or the tow-rope binding her to it. It was all very discreet.

I nodded numbly.

'It's my wife.'

The two men immediately set about sealing up the package again. Poor Karen! For the past three days she'd been out of one plastic bag and into another like a bit of left-over food at the bottom of the fridge.

Tom and Dick escorted me back to the Sierra, where we were joined by a Welsh detective I shall call Harry. He was a soft, secretive man with mottled skin, and reminded me irresistibly of a toad.

'First left at the lights, lads,' he told the others. 'There's Sal's cafe burned out since she left the deep-fryer on all night and now it's going to be a Wimpy. Just up here on the right, past the antique shop. Couple from London bought it last year, ever so nice but I can't see how they'll make a go of it with the prices they charge.'

At local police headquarters Tom and Dick went off to the canteen while Harry led me into a bare room rather like an old-fashioned doctor's surgery. I sat in the patient's chair and Harry went off in search of someone called Dai. He offered to fetch me something to eat, but I declined, feeling that a man who had just viewed his wife's corpse shouldn't have an appetite. Dai turned out to be a bluff, cheery man with a red face, like a reporter for the local farmers' gazette. He sat down beside Harry on the other side of the desk, opened a large notebook and licked his pencil as though it were a lollipop.

'We just want to get your side of the story,' Harry explained, 'for the record.'

I repeated the account of events I had given the police the day before. Karen had told me that she was going to spend the weekend in Liverpool with her mother. On Saturday morning I had driven her to Oxford station and seen her off on the train. I then returned home and spent the day alone. When I phoned Liverpool the next morning, my mother-in-law told me that Karen was not there, and that she had not been expecting her.

'Why did you phone then?' asked Harry casually.

'I noticed an announcement in the Sunday paper about a concert I particularly wanted to go to. It would have meant I wouldn't be home when Kay got back, so I wanted to check that she had her keys and so on.'

Harry nodded while his colleague busily scribbled away in shorthand.

'So you took your wife to the station on Saturday morning at about nine thirty, and phoned her mother at about the same time on Sunday. And in between?'

'I didn't see her.'

'What about other people?'

'I was at home all day, apart from going for a walk in the late afternoon.'

'You were on your own the whole time, then?'

'Well there were other people out on Port Meadow, of course, but no one I recognized.'

'No one came to the house or spoke to you on the phone?'

'No.'

Harry nodded.

'Only we've got to ask, see, because of this alleged kidnapping.'

'You think someone kidnapped Karen?'

'No, no. We've got a man here, see, Phillips is the name, claims to have been locked in the boot of a car and turned loose in the mountains round this way on Saturday night.'

'What's that got to do with me?'

'Well, you see, he says you did it.'

I pshawed. You don't often get a chance to pshaw these days, and I made the most of it.

'That's preposterous! I don't even know any Mr . . . Just a minute. What did you say his name was?'

'Phillips.'

'Not *Clive* Phillips?'

Harry's face lit up, as though all our problems were now solved.

'Ah, you know him!'

'Clive? Of course we do! Karen's first husband was his accountant. They were quite close. Actually we haven't seen much of him since our marriage. I particularly didn't care for his manner with Karen.'

'How was that, then?'

'Well, it's hard to describe. He had a way of treating her as though she were still single.'

Harry took out a packet of Silk Cut.

'Smoke?'

'I don't, thanks. Perhaps it would have been different if we'd had children. Without them it's all a bit theoretical, isn't it? Not that Karen seemed to mind, about Clive I mean. But I found it all in rather poor taste.'

'Kiddies are a blessing in disguise all right,' Harry agreed.

'Karen said she didn't want them. It was out of the question of course, with my vasectomy.'

The beauty of the dead, I was beginning to realize, is that you cannot just speak ill of them, you can say what the hell you like without the slightest fear of contradiction.

'If only we could have had a family,' I went on. 'At least there would be something of her left behind . . .'

I broke down. Mugs of tea and packets of biscuits were produced. I gradually pulled myself together.

'Where exactly was she found?' I asked Harry.

'Up Rhayader way.'

'Rhayader? That's odd.'

He looked at me expectantly.

'Oh, it's just a coincidence, but we stayed there once, you see. At the Elan Valley Lodge. Last September, it was, just before we got engaged. Lovely spot. I'll always remember the walks we took together . . .'

Out came the hankie again. While my head was lowered, I tried to think if there was anything else I wanted the police to know. They could surely be trusted to discover that Karen and Clive had been booked into the same hotel the previous weekend, and that the deposit had been secured on one of her credit cards. I couldn't think of any way to communicate the fact of Karen's interesting condition, but that would presumably come to light during the post-mortem that was currently in progress. I had mentioned my vasectomy, so once they found out that Karen had been pregnant, it was going to be a clear case of *cherchez l'homme*. They wouldn't have far to look.

'Right, that'll do for now,' Harry told me. 'I wonder where those two lads from Kidlington have got to. You're not planning on leaving the Oxford area, I take it? Only we may need to get in touch again, see. It's a pity no one saw you that Saturday. Someone you know, I mean. Someone who could . . .'

The words '. . . provide you with a much-needed alibi, failing which you are liable to find yourself in dead lumber with regard to this one, John' hung almost visibly in the air.

I once lived in a flat whose previous tenant kept an incontinent dog. The Parsonage stank of its former owners in much the same way as that flat did of dog piss, and eventually I could stand it no longer. I knew that clearing out my late wife's possessions so soon after her death wasn't the coolest possible thing to do, but I hadn't gone to all that effort just to end up entombed in a perpetual monument to the Parsons' trashy lifestyle. I needed open vistas and unfettered horizons. So the following Monday, a week after my return trip to Wales, I gathered some of the most offensive items together and took them to a charity shop in Summertown.

There was still no clear indication of the line the police were taking with regard to Karen's death. I had heard nothing from either Kidlington or Llandrindod Wells, and the newspaper reports were sketchy in the extreme. An inquest was opened on the Thursday following my trip to Wales, and promptly adjourned to allow the police to pursue their investigations. But beyond the fact that they were treating the case as one of murder and that a senior officer had been brought in to 'head up' the inquiry, little detail emerged.

I had phoned Alison several times during this period, but luckily she was still away tending her aged relative. Until I knew which way the police were going to jump I wanted to keep my options open. The less I told Alison about what had happened, the easier it would be to change my story later if the need arose.

I was in the shower, scouring away the smell of the charity shop with a Badedas body rub, when the doorbell chimed. It's just like the ads say, I thought, things happen. But when I went to the door in a terrytowel bathrobe, I found not a blonde astride a white steed, but Harry.

'All right?' he said.

I assumed this meant 'Are you coming quietly or do I have to use the cuffs?'

'I'll just get dressed,' I said.

'Fair enough. Only it won't take a moment.'

His tone seemed to suggest that he wasn't there to arrest me. 'All right?' I belatedly remembered, was simply the Welsh for 'How are you?'

'I'm just down this way to tie up a few of the loose ends,' he went on, 'so I thought I'd drop by and put you in the picture. We haven't given it to the media yet, but now we've got the confession it's all over bar the shouting.'

'Come in,' I said.

Still feeling shocked, I poured myself a whisky. Harry accepted a bottle of beer.

'It was finding the spare tyre in that quarry that did it,' he explained. 'Up until then he'd denied everything, but when we showed him the telex from Kidlington he broke down. "I suppose I must have done it," he said. Near to tears he was. It's a great relief, you know, getting it off your chest.'

'Yes, it must be.'

For a moment I found myself wondering if Clive really *had* murdered Karen. Not only did the police think so, but so did Clive himself, apparently. Well, he should know, shouldn't he? It was difficult to say what had really happened. My own memories remained clear enough but they were no longer attached to that invisible but solid backing by which we distinguish fact from fancy. They were floating free, just another version of events, perfectly possible, although not quite as plausible as the official account.

Harry now claimed that Clive's kidnapping story had never been taken seriously. That wasn't the impression I had received when he questioned me in Llandrindod Wells, but I didn't say anything. At some point in that last week, a policy shift had taken place which effectively ruled me out of contention as a suspect. At the time, of course, I had no way of knowing what had caused this. Nor did I care. If Harry wanted to rewrite history in the light of this new approach, I certainly wasn't going to embarrass him by pointing out the inconsistencies.

There was one more role I had to play, however, namely the distraught widower who having barely recovered from the shock of his wife's tragic death now learns that she was murdered by a family friend with whom she had been carrying on a clandestine love affair and by whom she was pregnant at the time of her death. I think we can dispense with a blow-by-blow account of this, the predictable emotions (disbelief turning to indignation and disgust), the predictable lines ('Do you mean to tell me, Inspector . . .'). It was a lousy part and I did it justice with a lousy performance. It didn't matter. Now Clive had confessed his guilt, my act of innocence could be as amateurish as I liked. The critics had gone home, the reviews were in. I was a smash. Clive had bombed.

It was very satisfying to learn that all the clues I'd left had been painstakingly uncovered. Karen's suitcase and handbag had been recovered from the reservoir, revealing both the victim's identity and the fact that she had a single ticket to Banbury rather than a return to Liverpool. Forensic analysis revealed traces of fibres from her clothing in the boot of Clive's car. Paint scrapings from the Lotus confirmed that it had been on the bridge from which the body had been dumped and also at the quarry from which the concrete post had been taken, and where the spare wheel had been abandoned in order to make room for the body of Clive's murdered mistress.

'But why did he kill her, Inspector? In God's name, why?'

'Apparently they'd planned to go away together for the weekend. That much he admitted right from the start. He didn't know about her being in the family way, he says. She was only a couple of months pregnant, so most likely she'd been saving the news up till they were alone together. But somehow she blurted it out right away, and he took it badly. Words turned to blows, and . . .'

I shook my head.

'I suppose I should hate him, but I just can't. All I feel is this tremendous pity for both of them. Do you think that very wrong of me?'

Harry smiled a long, wan, lingering smile, expressive of his familiarity with every freak and foible of human nature. He waggled his glass from side to side.

'You wouldn't ever have another of these, would you?'

The mills of British justice grind so slowly that the trial did not take place until almost a year later, but since it represented the conclusion to the events I have just described it seems appropriate to include it here. The digression will be a brief one. When Regina v. Clive Phillips finally reached the courts, it was no contest. Regina cleaned up in straight sets. She hardly dropped a point. Clive was totally outclassed.

Considered as a spectator sport, the trial actually had more in common with cricket than with tennis: long stretches of appalling tedium which so numb the mind that you miss the occasional rare moments of interest. The proceedings invariably started late and were continually being adjourned on some pretext or other. I spent much of my time with Karen's brother Jim, a car salesman from Southampton, who was representing the family. Jim's line on his sister's death was that it was 'a shocking thing, quite shocking'. He reiterated this with the forceful delivery of a public bar philosopher delivering his considered opinion on the topic of the day. I gradually gathered that the most shocking thing about it from Jim's point of view was all the commission he was losing. The reason I cultivated him was that he turned out to be very handy at seeing off the various journalists who pestered me.

Following the news of Clive's arrest, I had been approached by several tabloids offering considerable sums of money for my 'story'. To be honest, I was tempted. I mean if we're talking enterprise culture then dumping Karen, framing Clive and selling the rights for £50,000 is definitely the way to go. Unfortunately I had to decline, as this would have put paid for ever to my chances with Alison. During the trial the reporters took their revenge by continually yapping at my heels, trying to provoke me to some riposte they could quote for free. My strategy was to repeat dully that I had no statement to make, but this was very taxing, and I was grateful for Jim's intervention. He took a more direct line. 'Look, piss off! All right? Just piss off!' This may not sound very clever, but it worked. If I'd said it, they wouldn't have taken a blind bit of notice, but Jim's manner carried conviction. The hacks worked for the house journal of British vulgarity; Jim was a majority shareholder. When he told them to piss off, they pissed.

The reason the trial dragged on so long was that at the last minute Clive decided to repudiate his confession and plead not guilty. I had expected the proceedings to be a mere formality in which Clive's confession would be rubber-stamped and converted into a life sentence, but I now faced the prospect of a Perry Mason courtroom drama in which my appearance in the witness box would be exploited by the defence to highlight my own ambiguous position. A succession of surprise witnesses would then be produced, while clever cross-examination left me impaled on my own contradictions. Clive's counsel would deftly and authoritatively demonstrate the reversability of every shred of evidence against his client, revealing that warp was in fact woof and vice versa. I would end up breaking down in tears, confessing to everything and begging to be locked up for my own good, while Clive walked free without a stain on his character.

It wasn't anything like that, of course. True, when I was cross-examined after giving evidence for the prosecution, counsel did touch on the question of what I had done that Saturday after seeing Karen off on the train, but this was the merest professional habit, the result of a lifetime spent sowing doubt in jurors' minds, for which he was peremptorily called to order after an objection by the prosecution.

Judging by the looks of coherent hatred he lasered across the courtroom at me, Clive must have worked out the truth by now, but it didn't do him any good. Rather the opposite, in fact. You could tell that prison life didn't really suit Clive. He looked not just older but also weaker, internally damaged, structurally unsound, as though some vital load-bearing element had collapsed. Not the least part of his torment must have been the discovery that the truth was not a marketable commodity in his current situation. His legal representatives were prepared to reverse the plea, if he insisted, but not on the basis of his having been kidnapped by myself and A. N. Other. The jury would never buy anything as far-fetched as that.

Instead, his counsel opted for damage limitation. He accepted that his client had met Karen off the train at Banbury, that they had set off together in his car, and that Clive had subsequently attempted to dispose of her body in the reservoir. Where he begged to differ from the prosecution was over the question of how she had met her death. To bring in a verdict of murder, he reminded the jury, they would have to be convinced that the evidence proved beyond all reasonable doubt that Clive had assaulted his victim with deadly intent. A pathologist for the defence would testify that the injury from which she died was consistent with those which might be sustained in the course of a road accident, while evidence before the court would show that the near-side wing of the Lotus had been badly damaged, indicating that it had been involved in a serious collision.

In his summing-up, prosecuting counsel treated this argument with the contempt it deserved.

'It would no doubt be possible to construct an almost infinite number of ingenious scenarios which more or less fit the facts. But if you look at the situation not in the abstract but in the flesh, not as a theoretical problem but as a human reality, taking into account the cold-blooded and methodical manner in which the defendant acted after the victim's death, then you may well conclude that his original account of the circumstances surrounding that event, as contained in the signed confession which he made to the police, is considerably more plausible than this belated and ignoble attempt to evade responsibility for his loathesome crime.'

They did. Clive got fifteen years and a stern rebuke from the judge for wasting everyone's time. The police were complimented on their speedy and efficient handling of the case.

Life is polyphonic, narrative monodic, as I had occasion to remark one evening at Alison's. There were eight of us to dinner, including a local purveyor of up-market crime fiction who monopolized both the wine and the conversation, to say nothing of ogling our hostess in a way I found extremely distasteful. My response was the donnish strategy of rubbishing by implication. To suggest that he was a second-rate writer, although true, would have been unacceptable. To argue that writing fiction is a trivial pursuit of interest only to second-rate minds, precisely because this is evident nonsense, was perfectly legitimate.

To confound the fellow further I illustrated my argument with a musical analogy, asserting that a horizontal medium such as narrative could offer only a faint and passing allusion to, or rather illusion of (appreciative laughter), life's vertical complexities, like the implied harmonies in Bach's works for solo violin. Human experience, however, was not a matter of one or two voices but a veritable *Spem in alium* (ripple of recognition, real or feigned) of whose contrapuntal complexities fiction could never be more than a hollow travesty.

It never occurred to me that the boot would so soon be on the other foot and that I myself would be struggling with the intractable limitations of narrative. For in my attempt to describe fully and clearly the events which followed my discovery of Karen's body that Friday night I have necessarily omitted everything which did not directly bear on these developments, in particular their effect on my relationship with Alison. Each new detail which emerged – Karen's violent death, her illicit pregnancy, Clive's involvement in both – amounted to another brick in the wall which the affair was erecting between us. When such a garish light was being cast on the activities of people close to me, I myself was inevitably lit up in an undesirable way. PLOs ('persons like ourselves', known as 'people like us' to those who aren't, quite) instinctively shun anything and anyone which attracts general attention, from star tenors to vogue foods, let alone the subject of lurid articles appearing in the popular press under such headlines as SEX KILLING HUSBAND STERILE, POLICE TOLD.

But once both Karen and Clive had, in their different ways, been buried, the situation changed dramatically. The very factors which had made Alison take her distance from me earlier became a source of allurement once the whole affair was safely relegated to the past. Old scandals are as much a credit to a good family as new ones are an embarrassment. To the public, the dramatic termination of my marriage was a nine days' wonder, soon forgotten for fresh sensations, but for Alison and me it was a secret we shared, an ordeal we had come through and which brought us closer together, while making it proper for us to be close.

Even so, we were circumspect about it. The public might have forgotten, but our friends hadn't, and it was their judgement which would ultimately make or break us as a couple. This was not some reckless and torrid romance in which we would live for and through each other, letting the world go wag. We were both too old and wise to have any wish to run off to a desert island together. On the contrary, the basis of our mutual attraction was a feeling that the other was a suitable partner to share the lives we already led. I didn't want Alison in the abstract, divorced from the rich and varied habitat which sustained her. Nor would she have wished to be wanted in that way. She would have found such adoration meaningless, and slightly disturbing. Our relationship not only had to be blameless, it had to be pronounced such by a jury of our peers. We had to be seen to have behaved *correctly*.

Our initial encounters were thus fairly furtive affairs, usually taking the form of trips to concerts and plays in London, where we could be reasonably sure of not being seen together by anyone we knew. Occasionally we risked going out to eat locally, and it was in the course of one such evening that our secret was finally revealed when we found ourselves sitting two tables away from a group including Thomas and Lynn Carter.

It was all rather awkward at first, with a good deal of pretending not to pretend not to be looking at each other. Finally Thomas came over and sat down with us. He pointed to Alison's untouched portion of *zuppa inglese*.

'Aren't you going to eat that?'

'Well no, actually.'

He seized a spoon and tucked in.

'Call me Autolycus.'

'I don't get it,' I said.

'I do,' sighed Alison. 'And it's terrible.'

Thomas fixed me with a merry eye.

' "A snapper-up of unconsidered trifles". I didn't know you two were seeing each other.'

'We're not,' said Alison. 'At least, we *are*, but . . .'

'Well we are,' I said. 'Aren't we?'

'Well it depends what you mean.'

Realizing that he'd put his foot into wet cement, Thomas adroitly changed the subject to some problem involving the next meeting of the madrigal group.

A few days later Alison and I received invitations to dinner at the Carters' the following weekend. The invitations were separate, but from the moment we arrived it was clear that we'd been invited as a couple. The other guests were a historian from Balliol whose wife sang with the group, and a senior editor at the University Press whose Dutch husband worked at the European nuclear research project near Abingdon. I was flattered by the quality of the company, and still more by the fact that Thomas had not invited any of the folk I'd met through Dennis and Karen. It was as if he wanted to make clear that that phase of my life was now over.

In return for his thoughtfulness I made a special effort to charm the other guests. The Dutch physicist, though a man of few words, was perfectly pleasant, and his wife was warm and witty, with a fund of anecdotes about a dictionary project she was supervising. The problem was the other couple. The wife was the classic North Oxford matriarch, that formidable combination of nag and nanny, like an intellectual Margaret Thatcher. She was undoubtedly the power behind the Chair her husband held, but he was an even thornier proposition. Eccentric as the comparison may appear, Oxford dons always used to remind me of *gauchos*, proud and touchy, wary and taciturn, their emotions concealed beneath the rigid code of etiquette demanded by a society where everyone carries a knife and is ready to use it at the least provocation. In such company the simplest and most casual remark is apt to draw a challenging glare and a demand to know your sources. It's wiser not to say how nice the weather's been, unless you work for the Meteorological Office. Despite your interlocutor's fame and erudition, you mustn't expect him to say anything remotely interesting. He has nothing to prove, above all to the likes of you. Don't make the mistake of asking about his work, either. There are only four people in the world capable of understanding what he does, and he's no longer speaking to three of them. And don't for Christ's sake mention yours, unless you want to be shown to the tradesmen's entrance.

No, the only safe topic is gardening. Don't ask why but there it is. You don't need to know much about it, though a bluffer's level acquaintance with the local flora won't come amiss. But all that's really required is to show interest and throw in the odd phrase like 'My hydrangeas are very late this year' or 'Do you find tea roses take in this sandy soil?' Not a big effort, then, and one I was quite prepared to make in the interests of cultivating a smooth and personable image. I'm happy to be able to report that it was most effective. One doesn't expect conversation in England to flow, but this one oozed quite satisfactorily. Within a week Alison and I had been invited to sip sherry in North Oxford and drink gin in Abingdon. We were launched.

Everyone agreed that we were a delightful couple, perfectly attuned in some respects, piquantly complementary in others. If I had been less generous or astute I might have begrudged the time I had spent cultivating the likes of Karen and Dennis Parsons. But I was well aware that I was only regarded as a natural partner for Alison because I had money. Cash alone wouldn't have made me acceptable, of course, but no charm, wit or patient attention to tedious monologues and appreciative laughter at stale jokes could ever have made up for the lack of it. As it was, the only obstacle to my complete conquest of Alison Kraemer appeared to be the implacable hostility of her daughter. Rebecca had taken against me with the passionate intensity of her age. I was yuck, I was gross, I was everything that was not awesome, radical, trif, wicked, lush and crucial. Alison in turn felt unable, so she claimed, to proceed further until her daughter's opposition had been overcome. She just couldn't, not while Rebecca felt the way she did, she just wouldn't feel right. It never occurred to me to doubt that Alison would have come across if I'd pressed a bit harder, but that was just what I didn't want to do. I'd done more than my share of pushing and shoving at fortune's wheel recently. Now it was time to sit back patiently and let events take their course.

Karen's death had made me a rich man, and after consultations with a financial expert recommended by Thomas I made a number of investments, the results of which astonished me. I'd had no idea until then that you could make more money doing absolutely nothing than you could in even the best-paid job. There was no point in my looking for work, not with the amount I was earning from the money I already had. Nevertheless I needed a cover. When people ask what you do, it's simply not on, at least in the circles in which Alison and I revolved, to reply, 'I sit at home in front of the TV while my brokers perform obscenely profitable operations with my accumulated capital.' To provide myself with an acceptable occupation, I sank £30,000 in an investment which was, in a sense, to prove the most rewarding of all.

Following Clive's conviction and sentence, the management of his business concerns had passed to his sister, a nurse who had no knowledge of or interest in EFL work. She therefore agreed to a buy-out proposal from a group of teachers at the school, who attempted to run the place as a co-operative. This lasted less than six months. What the teachers hadn't realized was that the secret of the school's success had not been their professional excellence but Clive's unscrupulous and ruthless management, which they were neither willing nor able to emulate. That's where I came in.

Buying a controlling interest in the OILC afforded me the greatest possible satisfaction. Besides giving me a colourable occupation – I appointed myself to the position of Director, while leaving the actual day-to-day running of the place to a salaried subordinate – it completed my revenge for the insults and injuries I had sustained in the past. Clive might have had my wife, but I had his school. I knew this would hurt him far more than Karen's infidelity had hurt me. Everything he had lied and cheated and scrounged and gouged to create had been handed to me on a plate, as one more item in my varied and lucrative portfolio.

I soon turned the fortunes of the school around again by applying the methods I had learned the hard way from Clive himself. I offered the teachers a 25 per cent cut in wages and a one-year contract on the previous terms. Those who objected were dismissed. I then flew to Italy and tracked down Clive's recruitment agent, who had switched to another school when the co-operative refused to pay his cut. In return for a percentage increase and a substantial cash incentive up front he agreed to forsake all others and cleave unto me. After that it was just a matter of finding an anal-obsessive martinet with a sadistic streak to act as administrator, while I swanned in from time to time and played at being busy. I remember my friend Carlos telling me that the difference between North and South Americans is that for the former power means being able to do whatever you want, while for the latter it means being able to prevent others doing what *they* want. At the time I was too much of a gringo to grasp the attractions of this kind of power, but as I lay back in Clive's swivel chair, my feet up on Clive's desk, admiring the view from Clive's window, I finally understood. It is simply the most exquisite and luxurious sensation that life can afford, the ultimate peak experience.

And I had in fact peaked, although of course I didn't see it that way. In the two years following my belated conversion to the doctrine of self-help and free enterprise my life had changed out of all recognition. There seemed no reason to suppose that the changes would stop there. On the contrary, I was full of plans and projects of every kind. Alison and I were ineluctably drawing closer together, and our complete union appeared to be just a matter of time. I dreamed of a large gothic revival mansion overlooking the Parks, where Alison would preside with effortless grace over the elaborate rituals of North Oxford social life. At other times I found myself attracted to the idea of a manor house in a Cotswold village, a gem of classic restraint and rustic charm where we would keep dogs and horses. Then there would be long lazy summers at the cottage in the Dordogne, and, once Rebecca was off our hands, impromptu trips to Venice and Vienna, to Mauritius and Morocco.

Nor were these mere idle fantasies. We had the money, we had the freedom, and even more important we had the taste and the style, the breadth of vision, the experience. But they were to count for nothing, and all because of a man named Hugh Starkey.

If a dramatist were to take the liberty of ascribing what Aristotle calls the catastrophe – an apt enough term in this case – to a totally extraneous character who pops up from nowhere towards the end of the last act, he would rightly be ridiculed. Life does it all the time, though. Forget anything I may have said about the reasons for my present circumstances. The disastrous turn which events were about to take was due not to anything I did or failed to do, but to a man I never even met.

In August 1988 a group of masked men ambushed a Securicor van in Wolverhampton, seriously injuring one of the guards. Following a tip-off from an informant, Hugh Starkey was picked up for questioning and later charged. Starkey was a minor-league villain from the Handsworth area of Birmingham with a long and uninspiring record of rubbishy offences like holding up petrol stations, extorting protection money from Asian and Chinese restaurateurs and breaking into bonded warehouses. While in police custody he signed a remarkably full and copious confession, naming the other members of the gang and citing a string of other unsolved crimes for which they were responsible. So forthcoming had he been, in fact, that it was widely assumed he had done a deal with the authorities in return for a reduced sentence. Much to everyone's surprise, when the case came to court Starkey drew a baker's dozen just like the men he had informed on.

About two years later, while Clive Phillips was awaiting trial for murder, our Hugh got a break. In the course of inquiries into a string of supermarket holdups, Greater Manchester police discovered incontrovertible evidence that on the day the Securicor van had been attacked Starkey had been on their patch, taking part in an abortive attempt to rob a Gateway supermarket in Salford. Security cameras mounted over the entrance had videoed him and two other men as they fled.

This didn't do much to improve Hugh Starkey's image as an upstanding member of the community, but it was extremely embarrassing for the police force which had charged him with the Wolverhampton job. The Home Secretary ordered an inquiry, which discovered among other things that a number of passages had been inserted into Starkey's confession after it had been signed. Disciplinary proceedings were brought against various senior officers, including a certain Chief Inspector Manningtree, who had transferred from the squad six months after Starkey's arrest because his wife was ill and wanted to return to her native Wales. When the police in Rhayader discovered that they had a full-scale murder hunt on their hands, they asked headquarters to send up someone with the necessary experience to handle the case, and who better than a man who had served for five years in a big city Serious Crimes Squad?

When these facts came to light, Clive's solicitor was engaged in the thankless task of preparing to lodge an appeal against his client's conviction. In the absence of any new evidence or witnesses he knew this was a total waste of time. Clive stoutly maintained that he had signed a limited confession under duress, and that this had subsequently been doctored to include statements he had never made. Until now his solicitor had never believed this himself, let alone felt that there was the slightest chance of getting anyone else to do so. The Hugh Starkey scandal changed all that. Within weeks a lively media campaign was underway. The quality papers ran thoughtful, heart-searching articles expressing grave and widespread anxieties concerning the present system of policing, while the tabloids slammed and blasted their readers into a state of outraged moral indignation. From one end of the land to the other, the air was redolent with the stink of bent filth.

The first I knew of all this was during one of my occasional walkabouts at the school. Keep everyone on their toes was the idea. I knew it was no use trying to treat the staff as responsible adults. They wouldn't be working for me if they were. In the teachers' room I noticed an article pinned to the notice-board with three large felt-tipped exclamation marks beside it. It had been cut out of one of the local free papers. The headline read RESERVOIR VICTIM'S FIRST HUSBAND ALSO DIED MYSTERIOUSLY.

With the help of large photographs of Karen, Dennis, the house in Ramillies Drive, the Elan Valley and the Cherwell boathouse, the 'exclusive' article covered a two-page spread. 'Our own reporter' first summarized the events leading up to Clive's conviction and then the 'recent developments which have created demands for the case to be reopened'. But most of the article was devoted to what was termed 'an astonishing oversight' by the police, namely their failure to note the 'disturbing parallels' between the circumstances of Karen's death and that of her first husband, 'local Chartered Accountant and Rotary Club stalwart Dennis Parsons'.

Since these parallels amounted to no more than the banal coincidence that both Karen and Dennis had ended up in the water, one was initially left with the impression that the article was a feeble attempt to fake a sensational breakthrough where none existed. But the facts as printed were *so* scanty in relation to the claims being made that another solution eventually forced itself on this reader at least. The 'disturbing parallel' was not the one which the reporter described, but one which he could not mention for fear of legal action: my involvement in both deaths. My name was mentioned only once – in the caption beneath the photo of the house, where I was identified as the present owner of a property 'marked by death' – but my absence hovered over the whole article like a malign spirit.

I have no doubt whatever that this piece was ghost-written by 'our own reporter' to a scenario supplied by Clive through his solicitor. The rag in which it appeared was after all an advertising medium, for sale by the column, page or spread. Clive's advertisement merely took a rather unusual form, that's all. There was no follow-up in the legitimate press, and I forgot all about the incident until a few weeks later, when my answering machine recorded a call from a Chief Inspector Moss, or some such name.

It was a grey, gloomy day with a bitterly cold easterly wind which had brought the pavement out in grease spots. I had been out for a walk along the canal, and I got home feeling depressed and bewildered, full of disgust for myself and others. In this state of mind the message from the police seemed less alarming than it might otherwise have done. If I had been enjoying the fruits of my crimes more, I might have felt guiltier about them. As it was, I was so miserable that I might as well have been innocent. I called back and made an appointment to see Moss the following morning.

I left the BMW at a cash-and-flash car park and walked to St Aldate's police station, where I was led upstairs to an interview room on the second floor. A paunchy, balding bloke in his mid-fifties sat doing a crossword puzzle. As I entered, he started whistling a phrase which I recognized with some surprise as the Fate motif from Wagner's *Ring* cycle. On the desk in front of him lay a number of folders bulging with typed papers.

Moss stared at me for some time as though considering how best to proceed.

'Several months ago, Clive Reginald Phillips was tried and convicted for the murder of your wife,' he finally said. 'Due to various irregularities in the investigative procedure which have recently come to light, that conviction has been ruled unsafe and is about to be set aside.'

I started gasping, as though I'd just run all the way from North Oxford.

'This will entail various practical consequences,' Moss went on gloomily. 'One, of course, is that Phillips will be released from prison.'

'But he murdered my wife!'

'I wouldn't go around saying things like that if I were you, sir. You could find yourself facing charges for criminal libel.'

'It's enough to make you despair of British justice!' I cried, writhing about tormentedly in my chair.

'Another consequence is that the file on the case will have to be re-examined. Since the Force originally concerned is now the subject of disciplinary action, we in the Thames Valley Police have been asked to take on the task of reviewing the evidence and deciding what further action, if any, to recommend.

He lifted a file from the desk.

'I have to say that one or two items here appear to corroborate the version of events which Mr Phillips gave at the outset. For example there's this florist's assistant who was collecting a Red Star delivery from Banbury station. He remembers seeing two cars parked in the forecourt, one of them a yellow sports car and the other a, quote, red Alfa Romeo, unquote. He was then shown a photograph of a BMW like the one you drive, and he said yes, that was it, he could tell one of those Alfas anywhere.'

I said nothing.

'Another witness, who was meeting his aunt off the Oxford train, not only confirmed the presence of this second car, but also identified Clive Phillips from a photograph as one of the two men sitting in it having what he described as "a loud argument".'

'But none of this was mentioned at the trial!'

'Quite so, sir. Transcripts of these interviews were communicated by us to our colleagues in Wales, but in the light of the overwhelming evidence of Phillips's guilt they apparently didn't consider them relevant to the investigation.'

The door opened to reveal a WPC pushing a trolley laden with styrofoam mugs of tea and coffee.

' "Ye blessed souls, that taste the something something of felicity!" declaimed Moss fruitily. 'Tea for me, please Fliss, since there's nothing stronger. How about you, sir?'

'Coffee,' I croaked.

' "I have measured out my life with coffee spoons . . ." '

'It's a bit early in the morning for Eliot,' I snapped.

'A matter of taste,' Moss replied, patting the woman constable's bottom as she left. 'Personally I have excellent taste in poetry, women, music, beer and crime. And I have to say that this business doesn't do a thing for me. Ah!'

He swooped down on his newspaper.

'The solution was staring me in the face all along. Simple, really.'

I'd had enough of this cat-and-mouse game.

'Excuse me, Inspector, but what exactly was it you wished to speak to me about?'

Moss finished filling in his crossword and sipped his tea noisily.

'Well, sir, the last thing we want to do is waste a lot of time reinvestigating this case when the identity of the murderer has in fact already been established beyond a reasonable doubt.'

He was inviting me to confess! I felt I was going to faint.

'I'd like to call my solicitor,' I muttered.

'What we must remember,' Moss told the ceiling, 'is that just because Phillips is being released, that doesn't mean he's innocent.'

I stared at him open-mouthed.

'It doesn't?'

'Of course not. All the review board has said is that he wasn't given a fair trial. It's entirely a matter of speculation what the outcome might have been if he had.'

'But that's ridiculous! You mean a guilty man could be set free because of some technical detail?'

'Happens all the time. Unfortunately there's nothing we can do about that, but we do try and prevent the innocent being persecuted as a result. Now if the case were to be reopened, it would of course be very distressing for everyone concerned, especially yourself. We fully appreciate that. And that's why I just wanted to check that you're absolutely *sure* there's no one who could verify that you were in Oxford on the Saturday in question. If there was, you see, then I could virtually guarantee the matter would go no further.'

I finally understood. As far as the police were concerned, the significance of Clive's release depended on whether or not the investigation was reopened. If it wasn't, everyone would assume that Clive had been freed on a mere technicality, in which case the slur on the police would also remain purely technical. They'd got the right man, even if they'd used the wrong methods. So the boys in blue were pulling together. All Moss wanted to do was to bury the case discreetly, to write it off as a botched job with no moral opprobrium attached. If he was to do that, he needed me to have an alibi. So why didn't I do us both a favour and go and get one, eh?

Fair enough, I thought. I can take a hint.

'Actually, what I told the police earlier was not strictly true,' I murmured. 'I *did* see someone that day, but I didn't like to mention it because . . . well, it was a woman.'

Moss nodded sympathetically.

'To be perfectly honest, I had taken advantage of my wife's absence to see a dear friend of mine who . . . There was absolutely nothing between us, but, well, you can imagine how it would have looked at the time.'

'And the lady's name, sir?'

'Kraemer. Alison Kraemer.'

Moss noted it down in the margin of one of the papers.

'I'll need to speak to her in the next day or two. It won't take long, just a formality really. Then we shouldn't need to bother you again.'

He turned back to his crossword.

' "The iceman buyeth not his round." Five letters starting with a C. A rather over-elaborate clue, I'd say. The trademark of an amateur.'

'Fine, fine. And you? Really? Good. Super. Listen, I was wondering if we could get together some time soon. There's something I need to ask you. It's a bit urgent, actually.'

I was standing in a glass phone booth amid the roar of traffic in the Westgate one-way system. Alison's voice reached me as though from a great distance. The air was milder there, the vegetation lusher. Somewhere in the background a piano was playing.

'Can you come to lunch?'

The meal was the same as on the day we first met: omelette, salad, cheese and bread. The food wasn't quite as good as it had been in France – the best money could buy, rather than just the best – but the real drawback from my point of view was that we were a threesome. It was half-term, and Rebecca was kicking her heels around the house. To try and break the ice which formed whenever she was around, I asked her if she was interested in crossword puzzles.

'If they're difficult enough,' returned the pert gamine.

'How about this? "The iceman buyeth not his round." Five letters beginning with a C. I just can't get it.'

Rebecca wrinkled her nose.

'The reference to O'Neill is clear enough. Too clear, in fact. Probably a red herring. Oh drat, I shall have to think about it,' she concluded world-wearily, getting up from the table.

'Don't forget your French essay,' Alison called after her.

'J'essaierai!'

'Isn't she amazing?' I said with feigned warmth.

Alison smiled deprecatingly.

'They all are at that age. It's easy to be amazing. What's difficult is to settle down to being ordinary. I fancy Rebecca may find that quite a struggle.'

She rose to make coffee.

'So what was it you wanted to ask me?'

I laughed lightly.

'It's a bit of a bore, I'm afraid. The thing is, the police have been in touch. It's quite incredible. Apparently there was some irregularity in the way the case against Clive Phillips was prepared, and as a result he's being set free. It's a total travesty of justice, of course. No one has the slightest doubt about his guilt, but because the correct procedures weren't observed they have to let him go.'

'How appalling!'

'What's even worse is that the Crown Prosecution Service is considering reopening the case. The police very decently warned me about this in advance, and asked if there was anyone who could vouch for the fact that I was in Oxford on the day Karen disappeared.'

'To give you an alibi, you mean?'

I laughed.

'Well I suppose that's the legal term, but it's just a formality really. I mean no one's accusing me of anything, least of all the police. But they've got to go through the motions, you see, even though they know perfectly well that Phillips was responsible for Karen's death.'

Alison brought two miniature Deruta cups brimming with espresso coffee.

'That's jolly thoughtful of them,' she said. 'But how frightful to think that that man is going to go free. Aren't you scandalized?'

I sighed deeply and shrugged.

'He's not going free. He's just being released into another prison, the prison of his own conscience. For the rest of his life, he's going to have to live with the knowledge of what he did.'

Alison nodded.

'How very true.'

'As far as I'm concerned, the main thing is to avoid the

whole unsavoury business being dredged up yet again. I just want to forgive and forget. That's why it's so vital to do what the police suggest and find someone who will verify that I was here.'

She nodded again.

'Of course. Have you spoken to any of the people you saw that day?'

'That's why it's a bore,' I sighed. 'You see, when you cancelled our lunch date, I was so depressed I just couldn't face doing anything else. I'd really been looking forward to seeing you. In the end I sat at home all day and read, did some cleaning, listened to music, that sort of thing. No one called, no one saw me.'

I marshalled the loose crumbs on the tabletop into a neat line.

'Actually, I was wondering if perhaps you'd do it.'

Alison sipped the last of her coffee and bent over the cup, studying the swirl of grounds on the glazed ceramic.

'Do what?'

'Vouch for me.'

'Me? I wasn't even here myself!'

'What time did you leave?'

'Well, I suppose I left the house about one thirty or two, but . . .'

'That's good enough. Instead of phoning, let's say you drove over to tell me in person that you wouldn't be able to make lunch. We had a brief chat, then you went on to Dorset. It would have been on your way, more or less.'

Alison frowned.

'But I didn't.'

'No, but you might have.'

'But I *didn't*!'

I nodded vigorously, as though we were discussing some abstract issue such as nuclear power or the poll tax.

'I see your point, Alison, but I wonder if you aren't being slightly over-literal about this. Why should we have to go through months of grief and disruption just because fate intervened to break our lunch appointment? All the police want is a token statement. You won't be under oath, no one is going to cross-examine you. You'll just be confirming what they already know, namely that I was in Oxford that day and therefore can't have had any hand in what happened in Wales.'

Alison stared at me for longer than I would have believed possible. Time must have got jammed, I thought, or maybe I was suffering a stroke. Then there was a thunder of feet on the stairs, a thrush gave voice outside the window, and Rebecca burst into the room.

'Crime!' she cried.

Alison's face melted back into an expression of maternal warmth. I realized how unnaturally set and strained it had become.

'What do you mean, dear?'

'The solution to that crossword clue. It's an anagram. The iceman is Mr Ice.'

I forced a congratulatory smile.

'And "buyeth not his round"?'

'Crime doesn't pay.'

As she strode out to the hallway, I felt a shiver of panic, like one who realizes he is the victim of black magic. In the mouth of that unsuspecting child the phrase resounded like the judgement of the Delphic oracle. I knew that nothing would go right for me now.

'I don't know what amazes me more,' Alison said quietly, 'that you should be prepared to perjure yourself or that you imagined that I would. Evidently we don't know each other as well as I thought.'

The Perrier had flowed like water during lunch, but we had

consumed nothing stronger. When I tried to stand up, though, I staggered like a drunk.

'Well thanks, Alison. It's been real. The police will be in touch some time this afternoon or tomorrow, I expect. A Chief Inspector Moss. I'd keep an eye on him if I were you. Just between the two of us, he struck me as a bit of a DOM. Prosing on about female pulchritude with his hands buried deep in his raincoat pockets, that sort of thing. I have a feeling that you're the sort of woman he might go for in a big way, Alison.'

She stared at me in shock. I had never spoken like this to her before. I had never been flippant, ambiguous or disrespectful. Above all, I had never mentioned the Wonderful World of Sex.

'I think you'd better leave,' she said with quiet dignity.

Quiet dignity, like *omelette aux fines herbes*, was very much Alison's forte. She did it superbly well.

I walked along the hallway to the front door. The strains of the piano rang out from the living room, where Rebecca was practising. It was the same piece I had heard over the phone, but the effect was quite different now, like a landscape one is leaving for ever.

On the way home I made a detour through the back-streets of East Oxford, just for old times' sake. I found myself staring out of the window of the BMW with something approaching envy. Yes, there was squalor and despair, but also a range of human contact, a warmth and vivacity quite foreign to the genteel suburbs where I now lived. What violence there was here was only for show, a desperate appeal for help or attention, the uncoordinated flailings of a drunk too far gone to do any damage. But Alison and her kind were kung fu masters, all formal smiles, elaborate politeness and swift, vicious dispatch.

I had thought I was one of them, that was my mistake. I thought my birth and education entitled me to a place among them. I couldn't have been more wrong. My place was here, among the people I despised. Them I could manipulate, as I had Dennis and Karen. From the moment I tried to move up to Alison's level I was lost. I'd wanted her because she was the real thing. It had never occurred to me that I was not. But the real thing is not charm and chat but a clinically precise sense of what you can get away with. And that I lacked. Otherwise I would never have made the fatal blunder of trying to seduce Alison morally. I had mistaken her for a jumped-up shopgirl like Karen, to whom the ties of romantic love were sacred and who would sacrifice anything to stand by her man. Karen would have lied to the police for me without a second thought, but to propose it to Alison was as gauche as asking her to give me a blow-job in the Bod.

Yes, if I had been the cold, calculating killer portrayed by the press, I would have stayed well clear of any further entanglements with Ms Kraemer. Even without her support, I had little to fear from the law. It would have taken more than Clive's word and the lack of an alibi to convict me. If any of the witnesses Moss had mentioned had been able to identify me positively, there could have been no question of keeping the file on the case closed. Even if they had, my chances would have been no worse than even. Not only does the law send innocent men like Clive Phillips and Hugh Starkey to prison, it even more frequently allows the guilty to walk free, particularly if they are white, middle-class, well-heeled and don't speak with an Irish accent.

But if Alison had been dismayed to find that we didn't know each other as well as she had thought, the effect on me was no less traumatic. The woman I had idolized for so long, and for whose sake I had run the most terrible risks, had revealed herself to be a shallow, selfish prig. After all these years, Alison Kraemer still thought right and wrong were as clear and unambiguous as right and left. Even a decade of radical and regenerative government hadn't taught her that her moral code – a ragbag of oddments from religious and philosophical uniforms which no one was prepared to wear entire any more – was as irrelevant to the contemporary world as theories about the great chain of being or the music of the spheres.

Well, the time had come to set her right about this. It was my intellectual duty, as one Oxford man to another, so to speak. It was the least I could do in return for all she had done to me. Mind you, I won't try and pretend that my motives were wholly altruistic. There was undeniably an element of personal satisfaction involved as well. I wanted to scare the living shit out of the stupid bag, to scar her psyche with scenes of horror she would relive every night until she died.

Perhaps if I'd had time to think it over, cooler counsels might have prevailed. But it so happened that the madrigal group met that very evening, so I could count on Alison's absence from the house. The children would be there, of course, but I could take care of them. I rounded up some tools and my trusty rubber gloves, and sat sipping a tumbler of The Macallan until it grew dark.

The lane leading to the house was as quiet as an alley in a cemetery. Most women would have been frightened living there by themselves, but Alison Kraemer's imagination was as well-trained as one of Barbara Woodhouse's dogs. That could change though, I thought as I flitted across the lawn. That docile and obedient pooch was about to go rabid. A light was on in one of the front bedrooms. Rebecca was still up. When she heard me, she would assume at first that Mumsy had returned earlier than usual from her glees and catches. By the time she realized her mistake, it would be too late.

Don't worry, it's not going to get *that* nasty. Murdering children has never appealed to me any more than the other English national pastimes. All I was planning to do to the kiddies was lock them up somewhere while I got on with my business. I was planning to start with the cat, run it through the Magimix and smear the purée liberally about the walls and furniture. After that I'd improvise. It's astonishing how much damage you can do once you put your mind to it. I was quite looking forward to it. Let's face it, there's a bit of the yob in all of us.

I made my way along the side of the house to the kitchen door. This would be locked and bolted, but the window next to it was forceable. Alison had told me she meant to get a security lock fitted, but I knew hadn't got round to it. I slipped on my gloves and got to work jemmying the sash. It took longer than I had anticipated, but in the end the catch snapped in two, sending a fragment of cast iron tinkling loudly about the stone floor. I pushed the window up, hoisted myself on to the ledge and crawled through.

The nocturnal silence was promptly shattered by an astonishing crash as a glass bowl I had failed to notice on the draining-board fell to the floor. My muscles locked up in panic, but no one came running or called out. I lowered myself gingerly to the ground, my shoes crunching on the fragments of broken glass. The light switch was by the open doorway leading to the hall. I made my way across the glass-strewn flagstones towards it, my eyes gradually adjusting to the darkness. I was about three feet away from the door, my hand already raised to the switch, when a disembodied limb reached in out of the darkness of the hallway and clicked it on.

All vision went down in a blinding white-out as the fluorescent tube on the ceiling came to life. I blinked frantically, trying to stop my eyes down to a point where I could see what was going on.

The first thing I took in were the feet. They looked absurd, comic-book clodhoppers, all bumps and lumps and knobbly toes. Above them rose hairy legs, the left one bulging with varicose veins. The rest of the body was clad in a pink silk peignoir secured by a belt of the same material in a contrasting shade. A broad, flat, hirsute chest rose from the *décolletage*, and above it a head I recognized as belonging to Thomas Carter.

'Let's just get one thing straight,' he said. 'I was with Special Forces out in Nam. There are at least fifteen ways I could kill you with one hand.'

I laughed aloud. He looked utterly ridiculous, standing there in a woman's pink silk dressing-gown five sizes too small for him, talking tough.

'Tom? Tom?' a woman's voice called from the stairs.

'I'm OK.'

'What is it?'

'I'll handle it. Go back to bed.'

A series of creaks ascended towards the ceiling.

'Well, well,' I said. 'I've suspected for a long time that you and Alison had something going. What I don't quite see is where I fit into all this. Can't you keep her satisfied, Carter, even with your big all-American Vietnam vet's cock?'

There was a blur of movement, and the next thing I knew I was lying crouched on the floor, a piece of broken glass up one nostril and the taste of recycled malt in my mouth.

'That was what we used to call a SOB,' I heard a voice remark somewhere in yawing spaces above me. 'A euphemism that's also an acronym, we really ate those up. A "soften-up blow". Very popular in the brig.'

'I've never witnessed such a display of unprovoked, cold-blooded brutality,' I gasped indignantly, struggling to my knees.

'Oh but *I* have! I've seen things I couldn't believe were happening even when I was watching them. And the people who were doing these things were kids I'd grown up with, played ball games with, gone to movies with. A month before they'd have peed their pants at the thought of the cops catching them driving out to the lake with an open six-pack on the back seat. Now they were napalming babies, raping moms, torturing grand-dads, never mind what we used to do to any suspected Vietcong we got our hands on. Ordinary everyday atrocities, committed by ordinary everyday guys who would otherwise have been selling cars or pumping gas or serving hamburgers.'

I stood up, leaning on the Welsh dresser. Alison's collection of Sabatier cooking knives protruded invitingly from a wooden block just a few feet away.

'That's what brought me here,' Carter went on. 'When I got back to the States, I found I couldn't pass a car showroom or a gas station or a burger bar without remembering what I'd seen. I didn't believe in natural decency any more. I needed a society with a keel, a tradition of culture and civilization strong enough to balance all that. You want to grab one of those knives? Go right ahead. Stick it up your own ass, it'll save me the trouble.'

I drew my hand back.

'Of course!' I cried. 'I get it! I was the stooge, the decoy! That's why Alison took me to that restaurant that night, knowing that you and Lynn would be there. And that's why you invited us both to dinner right afterwards. It was all designed to divert Lynn's suspicions from you and Alison.'

So potent was Thomas Carter's aura of moral righteousness that I half-expected him to deny the whole thing and claim that he and Alison were just rehearsing a scene from a bedroom farce for a local amateur dramatic society production. I was really quite shocked when he calmly admitted the whole thing. Yes, he and Alison had been in love for several years, but they had kept it secret so as not to upset the children. Once or twice a month Rebecca and Alex were packed off to sleep over with friends the night the madrigal group met, leaving Thomas and Alison free to 'make music together'. Just when Lynn had started to become suspicious, I had conveniently appeared on the scene. Alison had taken advantage of my infatuation as a cover behind which she and Thomas could continue their affair in safety.

'Anyway,' he concluded, 'the real question is what we're going to do about you now, my friend. What the fuck are you doing here anyway?'

'I was beside myself with frustrated desire. I was going to strip naked, put on that dressing-gown and toss myself off to a cracked seventy-eight of Nellie Melba singing "Come into the Garden, Maude". Do you ever get urges like that?'

For a moment I thought he was going to hit me again. Then he grinned, showing his bad teeth.

'Of course I could just call the police and have you charged with breaking and entering.'

'But you won't, because then you'd have to explain what you're doing here at this time of night. Look, why don't we just pretend this never happened?'

Carter shook his head.

'You can expose Ally and me any time you want. I can't risk that.'

'So what are you going to do, kill me?'

He looked at me for a moment as though considering the idea. It was the first time I had ever been regarded as a potential victim by someone who was capable of making me one. I must say it was very uncomfortable.

Carter's face suddenly cleared.

'I know! Alison told me about you asking her to fake an alibi. Well I'll do the opposite. I'll contact the cops and tell them that the Saturday your wife disappeared I went round to your house to keep an appointment we'd made, only you weren't there. I tried several times that afternoon. Your car wasn't in the garage, so I figured you'd gone out. I even rang later that evening, but there was still no reply.'

I stared at him blankly.

'If you do that . . .'

'Yes?' he said with menacing emphasis.

I sighed.

'Then I'm fucked.'

We both burst out laughing.

'Now get the hell out of here,' he said, 'so I can get this goddamn housecoat off.'

I stepped over the broken glass to the back door. As I unbolted the door he added, 'You know the funny thing? We all liked you. We really did.'

I jumped forward like a parachutist, obliterating myself in the night.

The next day I rang my broker and instructed him to liquidate the bulk of my investments and transfer the funds to an off-shore bank account. I had just hung up when the doorbell rang. A police car was parked outside the house. On the front doorstep stood a bulky, balding man in a heavy overcoat, his back turned to me. It looked like Moss. The doorbell rang again, more insistently. I crouched down behind the sofa. The doorbell rang again and again. Finally he gave up and the car drove away.

I ran upstairs and set about packing. It didn't take long. I threw a selection of clothes and some toilet accessories into a suitcase, checked I had all the relevant documents, then showered and changed into a sober business suit, Jermyn Street shirt and old college tie. Before leaving, I indulged a long-standing desire to pee on the Parsons' orange-tawny velveteen sofa. It was extraordinarily satisfying, and I was giggling as I walked out to the BMW.

The last-minute hitch has become such a thriller cliché that I was amazed to reach Heathrow without incident. Traffic on the M25 was even flowing freely, for a wonder. Inside the terminal the information board was fluttering like a flock of nervous pigeons. When it settled I selected a Varig flight to Rio de Janeiro which was leaving in two hours. There was plenty of room in first class, and it was an added luxury to pay with a credit card for which I would never receive a statement.

I put up at a luxury hotel in Copacabana while I made the necessary arrangements to draw on my off-shore bank account, then made my way here. I was pleasantly surprised to discover that the recent currency devaluations had made me even wealthier than I had expected. Less than a month after my departure from Ramillies Drive, I moved into a pleasant furnished apartment in the fashionable Buena Vista district.

What a pleasure it was to be back! It was the small things I noticed most, the details I had forgotten. The constant rain of drips in the street from air-conditioning units, the puddles of condensation that form around your bottle of cold beer in the humid heat, the parked car that seems to move all by itself as someone further along bumps the whole row to get out, the streets studded with crown stoppers embedded in the warm asphalt. Above all it was the people, the men very beautiful, the women very handsome, both sexes pulsating with pride and drive and desire. Each moment of every day was a precious token of a way of life which I only now realized how much I had missed. I spent days at a time simply walking the streets or riding the *collectivos*, immersing myself in the rich and varied scenes on every side. Every night I would seek out the most crowded districts and mingle in the passing throng, exulting in the brutal, explicit, merciless, uncensored scenes I had been reading for too long in the 'improved' and improving versions which the English prefer to the original text.

My only regret was that the friends I had been looking forward to seeing again all seemed to have disappeared. I had been away for some time, of course, but it still seemed surprising that the entire group of which Carlos Ventura was the acknowledged leader had totally dispersed. Even many of the places where we used to meet, bars, restaurants and bookshops, had closed down or changed hands. It was almost as if a deliberate attempt had been made to erase all my memories. This absurd notion was strengthened when I bumped into one of my former students who had been on the fringes of the group I've just referred to. At first he claimed not to recognize me, so to jog his memory I mentioned a mistake in one of his essays which had become a running joke around the school. It was a piece describing the system of government. José had intended to say 'the council of generals are responsible for running the country', but instead of 'running' he had written 'ruining'. To my amazement, he now denied any knowledge of this incident, and when I asked what had become of Carlos and the others he replied angrily that he had no idea who I was talking about, and abruptly took his leave.

I was mystified and saddened at first, but I soon convinced myself that it was all for the best. Any attempt to revive old friendships would have been doomed to failure. My circumstances had changed too much. Then I had been a temporary expatriate, a visiting foreigner with no means, no roots, no responsibilities and no future, here today and gone tomorrow. Now I am a man of substance, a permanent resident with long-term plans and investments. I no longer have anything in common with people whose idea of entertainment was an evening of beer, jazz and politics at some doubtful dive which a respectable citizen such as myself would think twice about entering.

I have reached the end of my narrative. Before you retire to consider your verdict, however, I should like to comment briefly on the spirit in which the application before this court has been presented. This country has a long and complex relationship with the United Kingdom, and one to which Her Majesty's accredited representatives have not scrupled to appeal to in the hopes of influencing your judgement. At the risk of wounding your sensibilities, I would like to dispense with the diplomatic rhetoric for a moment. The fact of the matter is, I'm afraid, that my compatriots think of you, on the rare occasions such as this when they bother to think about you at all, as a bunch of gormless wops hanging about some clearing in the jungle waiting for the man from Del Monte to say yes.

I am not suggesting that the request for extradition should be rejected merely because it is delivered in a spirit of neo-colonialist arrogance rather than as a legal petition from one sovereign state to another. On the contrary, I have every confidence that this court will remain entirely unswayed by such extraneous factors. Its verdict will be delivered after duly weighing the facts, the majority of which are inconclusive and the rest in dispute. The case against me rests not on evidence acceptable to a court of law but on gratuitous moral censure. The British authorities argue that I have showed myself to be a ruthless self-seeker who would stop at nothing to better his social and financial status.

I have no quarrel with this assessment. On the contrary, I am justly proud of the energy and determination I displayed in turning my life around, and I strongly deprecate the attempt to make this the grounds for charging me with two murders which I did not commit. This is a cynical manoeuvre unworthy of the ideals to which the present government is supposedly committed, and to which I endeavoured to dedicate myself. In a free democratic society, law and morality can have nothing whatever to do with each other. The selfish instincts we all harbour in our breasts, and without which a market economy would instantly collapse, are of no concern to the law, which is purely conventional and utilitarian in nature, a highway code designed to minimize the possibility of accidents. It does not ask where you are coming from or where you are going, still less the reason for your journey. Such prying would rightly be regarded as unwarranted ideological interference typical of the now-discredited totalitarian regimes of Eastern Europe. As long as you obey the rules of the road, the law has no claim on you.

Now it may be objected that I have *not* obeyed those rules. This is perfectly true, and I have made no attempt to conceal the fact. On the contrary, I have admitted unlawfully disposing of my wife's body, conspiring to kidnap and inflict grievous bodily harm on Clive Phillips, and lying to the police and the courts about these and other events. I am even prepared to admit that I may be guilty of involuntary manslaughter, since Karen's death apparently occurred while she was locked in the boot of the BMW rather than immediately following the accidental blow to her head. Had any of these charges appeared on the extradition warrant, I should have had no option but to plead guilty and let the law take its course.

But they do not, for the simple reason that none of them fall within the terms of the relevant treaty between this country and the United Kingdom. Unable to request my extradition for the crimes I have committed, the British authorities have therefore resorted to fabricating charges in a category which *is* covered by the treaty, namely murder. The case they have argued before this court is neither more nor less than a blatant piece of expediency designed to obtain my forcible repatriation at any price. The British have no intention of trying me for murder, as they know perfectly well that they would be unable to obtain a conviction. If they get their hands on me, the spurious murder charges will instantly be dropped and replaced by the non-extraditable charges mentioned above. Such a procedure will naturally make a laughing-stock of these proceedings, this court and the republic it represents. It would be impossible to underestimate the extent to which anyone in Britain will care about that. Having served your purpose in this charade, you will be dismissed to go and play in your third-world sandpit until the next time the big boys need you.

I wish to thank the court for having let me make this lengthy statement, and to take this opportunity of acquiescing in advance with its verdict. The deluded humanist I once was would no doubt have drooled and snivelled after the manner of his kind, but I have grown up since then. I know there is no point in sulking because society is unjust, still less in trying to do anything to change it. There is no such thing as society, only individuals engaged in a constant unremitting struggle for personal advantage. There is no such thing as justice, only winners and losers. I have not deserved to lose, but if I do so, it will be without complaint or regret.

10 March

Dear Charles,

Needless to say I understand and share your anger and dismay, but I can assure you that suspicions of slackness this end are completely unjustified. Even H.E., who has taken the dimmest possible view of our hands-on intervention, will confirm that we had been given every reason to suppose that our application would be granted.

As yet I have been unable to ascertain what went wrong. For obvious reasons it would have been injudicious for me to appear in court, but having studied a transcript of the proceedings and assisted at a debriefing of our legal team I can confirm that there were no evidential revelations or technical hitches to justify the judges' verdict. The accused delivered a rambling apologia for his infamies which made the worst possible impression on the court and everyone concerned assumed that the outcome was a foregone conclusion.

I have contacted the Justice Minister and communicated our displeasure to him in no uncertain terms. He was extremely apologetic, but would say only that the decision had been taken 'in the interests of national security'. The Generalissimo himself has been uncontactable, and indeed all our normal lines of communication appear to have gone dead. To make matters worse H.E. is gloating no end over our discomfiture. If he tells me one more time that such delicate matters are best left to professional diplomats such as himself I shall scream. Thank goodness the Corporation has agreed to review its decision to broadcast the offending programme. It really would be too bad if we found ourselves thwarted by internal pressure here and were unable to respond in kind in our own backyard.

Yours,

Tim

16 March

Dear Charles,

Many thanks for your cheering news. Loyalty has always been our great strength, and I am glad to hear that in this instance it has prevailed over the understandable desire to find a scapegoat. The whole affair is of course now stale news, but just for the record you may nevertheless be interested to learn the reason for our discomfiture, the more so in that it fully validates your spirited defence of the way the operation was handled.

I was beginning to despair of discovering the truth before we shut up shop here, when I was quite suddenly summoned yesterday to meet a senior official at the Air Ministry. My anonymous informant revealed that the subject of our extradition order had been detained by a unit of Air Force Intelligence concerned with internal security. The activities of these units, whose existence is officially denied, was of course one of the more embarrassing episodes in the television documentary we managed to suppress. Unofficially, they are estimated to have been responsible for the disappearance of over 5,000 people since the present regime seized power two years ago. An operation this size is bound to leave a few rough edges, of course, and the Amnesty mob have been circulating the usual horror stories, but all in all the Generals seem to have run a pretty clean campaign.

During the long and discursive statement he made to the court, the accused mentioned in passing his friendship with a certain Carlos Ventura, whom he knew during his earlier stay here. It was now explained to me that this Ventura, a labour lawyer with suspected guerrilla sympathies, had been one of the most dangerous opponents of the present regime, and that all his former friends and contacts are regarded as valid targets for the counter-insurgency operation already referred to. Air Force Intelligence therefore moved to block the extradition in order to allow them to pursue their own investigation, which they are no doubt even now doing with their customary vigour and thoroughness.

Despite the embarrassment which this affair has caused us, I feel that the economic reprisals which HMG is reportedly considering would be both inopportune and undeserved. I recall Bernard once remarking apropos of the Charter 88 people that you couldn't make a revolution without smashing a few eggheads. If the Generalissimo and his colleagues have taken him at his word, who are we to criticize them for displaying a degree of realism about which we can only joke?

It will take me a few more days to wrap up things this end so as to leave no loose ends, but I hope to be back in London by the end of next week. I am looking forward eagerly to hearing more about the Dublin assignment. It sounds extremely daring, even by the standards of the house! Do please try and soften up the embassy in advance this time, though. A few discreet hints in advance of my arrival about the possibility of alternative postings in say Baghdad or Beirut might not go amiss.

Yours,

Tim